# DON'T YOU WANT ME, BABY?

RACHEL DOVE

# B

Boldwood

First published in Great Britain in 2024 by Boldwood Books Ltd.

A CIP catalogue record for this book is available from the British Library.

Paperback ISBN 978-1-80483-646-0

Large Print ISBN 978-1-80483-645-3

Hardback ISBN 978-1-80483-647-7

Ebook ISBN 978-1-80483-643-9

Kindle ISBN 978-1-80483-644-6

Audio CD ISBN 978-1-80483-652-1

MP3 CD ISBN 978-1-80483-651-4

Digital audio download ISBN 978-1-80483-648-4

This book is printed on certified sustainable paper. Boldwood Books is dedicated to putting sustainability at the heart of our business. For more information please visit https://www.boldwoodbooks.com/about-us/sustainability/

Boldwood Books Ltd, 23 Bowerdean Street, London, SW6 3TN

www.boldwoodbooks.com

*For all the best friends out there, waiting in the wings.*

# 1

'Seriously Brad, I don't care how many Michelin star restaurants they've backed, we had plans. You keep doing this lately, and it's starting to get right on my—'

Amber sagged against the panelled wall, phone to her chin as she kept one ear out for customers and the other listening to her other half apologise. Again. Lately, the majority of their interactions was her sounding like a nagging partner, and him making excuses and promising things he never delivered on. *When did I become this person? I always said I wouldn't be like this, for anyone. With anyone. Somewhere along the way, I've lost myself.*

'I can't help it, Amber. I said I was sorry. You know I have to jump on these things when they happen. It's all part of the plan.'

*Ah, the plan. Of course. Everything revolved around the plan. His plan.* 'I know, Brad, but it's my only night off this week. It's a bit short notice to make other arrangements. I was looking forward to it, that's all.'

Sharon nudged her out of the storeroom doorway, boxes of crisps and bar snacks stacked in her hands. As she caught Amber's eye she mouthed 'Again?', motioning to the phone. Amber shrugged, Sharon shooting her an apologetic look back.

'I am sorry, baby. I know I've been pretty absent lately, but it won't be forever. Once the new place is up and running, I'll have more time. Sloane's is practically running itself now that the staff are in place. It's the eatery that's taking all my time up.' Another thing Amber was sick of hearing about. Sloane's Eatery was the next jewel in her boyfriend's crown. Tyler said it was a dumb name, and the more she heard it, the harder she agreed with her best friend. 'The investors are making me jump through all kinds of hoops to secure the funding I need. I'm close, Amber. Once that's done, we're golden.'

'I know,' she sighed heavily, feeling drained by the conversation. Déjà vu was tiring, apparently. Maybe he was right, though. She just needed to be patient. A skill she'd perfected of late. 'I get it. It's just been a while since we spent any time together.'

His chuckle made her stomach flip with unease. Was he really not bothered about this? I guess it was easier when you weren't the sad sap waiting for the other to show up. She could imagine him on the other end, driving in his car. Off to the next big meeting, tailored suit as immaculate as the rest of him. 'I slept over the other night. You saw enough of me then, didn't you?'

'Two weeks ago. I mean out, Bradley,' she chided, the irritation ebbing away at his sultry tone. 'You know, in public. With clothes on.'

'Yeah, but that's not as much fun.'

'True.' She smiled. The service bell rang from the kitchen. It was getting to the lunchtime rush. 'I'll give you points for trying to make me horny instead of mad.'

'What can I say,' he breathed, voice low, 'it's a skill.' Brad's call waiting started to beep, cutting through their little moment. 'Sorry babe, I need to take this. Have a good night, okay? I'll call you.'

'Okay, I lo—'

The call had already dropped. *Great.* Her one night off and she'd been stood up. She went back through to the bar, where Sharon was filling one of the wicker baskets on the back wall with crinkly packets of pork scratchings.

'Let me guess. He's made last-minute plans, so you're flying solo again.'

Amber shoved her phone into one of the drawers under the till. 'Yep. Some Michelin starred place in Harrogate is opening tonight; his investors invited him. He needs to keep impressing them 'til they sign off on the eatery.' The kitchen bell went again. 'I'll get that.' Sharon had made no move to answer it anyway; she was too busy winking at the blokes who'd just walked up to the bar from the nearby construction site. 'Shaz?'

Her best mate's head snapped back to her. 'Eh? Oh yeah, cheers. I'll cover the bar.'

Amber pushed her way through the kitchen doors and was greeted by the jingle of pots and pans, Tyler calling out orders in his usual gruff way from behind the stainless-steel counter.

'Ben, that last steak could have walked off the bloody plate. They said medium rare, not raw! Fix it, please.'

'Yes, chef.' Ben scurried to grab the plate Tyler had slid back down the serving counter. 'Sorry, chef.'

Amber checked the dockets. Laid out in precise order, it was easy to spot. 'That bell for table eight?'

Tyler shot her a dogged look. She could see the tufts of his thick, dark hair peeking out under the brim of his chef's hat. A tell-tale sign that her head chef was annoyed. He tended to play with his hat when he was feeling a big jangly in the nerves. Which was usually when he was in the kitchen. The Lazy Slug might be a smallish, country-style pub in the heart of Yorkshire, but Tyler ran it like Ramsay's Hell's Kitchen with marginally less swearing. Inwardly, she pondered to herself why she seemed to be surrounded by competitive, perfectionist men, blokes whose egos seemed to be tied to their chef's aprons. Bradley might not be *in* the kitchen any more, but they were both similar in their passions for the food hospitality industry. That was where the similarities ended. Bradley was a suit and tie man, Mr Life and Soul of the Party. He thrived on schmoozing any room he entered. And Tyler? Well – he was Tyler. Gruff. Sparing with his words until people got to know him. The first couple of months he'd worked there, she wasn't even sure he had teeth, he smiled so seldom.

Their looks were opposites too. Tyler was tattooed. Burly. Broad where Brad was lean. While Bradley was the dapper, lithe gent, her best male friend was more the grunty lumberjack. Bradley bragged about his life; Tyler kept his cards a little closer to his chest. *Mr Mystery.* Still, these days she felt like she knew him a damn sight more than her other half. Which was probably why recently, she couldn't help but compare the two. She watched him, smirking when he tapped his hat top with two fast fingers, causing another lock of hair to spring free. 'It's coming,' he grumbled. 'When Ben manages to stop it mooing.'

'Har-har,' Ben blushed before turning his full attention back to the steak in the pan, spooning the juices over the meat's surface. 'I'll get it right.' Ben's chef whites looked like he'd been bathing in the gravy, compared to Tyler's still white ones. 'Keep your hat on.'

'You'd better,' Tyler muttered. 'I already rang the bell. I need this place in good hands when I go. McDonald's are still hiring, you know.'

'Yeah,' Ben grinned back. 'And I hear you get free milkshakes. By the time you actually take another job, I'll be a pro.'

Tyler laughed. 'Milkshake my arse. You'll be lucky if they let you salt the fries without supervision.' He side-eyed Amber, who was picking at the varnish on her thumbnail and running the phone call over in her head. 'What's up with you?'

'Nothing, why?' She dropped her hands to her sides. Tyler picked up on her tells too. Working together for eighteen months, you noticed a few things. *I wonder if Bradley does that with me. It was harder and harder to work him out of late. Being in the same room might help.* She snapped out of it when she saw Tyler fixing her with a pointed look.

'You look fed up, for one. You pick your nails when you're brooding about something.' His black brows furrowed under the trim of his chef's hat. 'Business plan not working?'

She shrugged him off. 'It's coming along.'

'So not that.' His eyes narrowed in, and she decided that was the moment to check the dockets again. 'Oh, I know. Brad cancelled again, didn't he?'

'No—' Amber started, but there was no point. Shaz would rat her out anyway, and where was she going to go tonight? Tyler was on a double shift; they were bound to cross paths, given that she lived in the flat upstairs. He would find out either way. She had zero back-up plans, so he'd soon suss her out unless she hid upstairs in the dark all night, and that thought was too depressing to consider for more than a panicked moment. Plus, she'd already done that last week when Brad had stood her up for their planned cinema trip. She'd eaten a whole tub of ice-cream in the dark listening to a spicy romance audiobook through her headphones like a teenager hiding from her parents. It was not happening again. She puffed out her cheeks, trying to shake off the bad feeling in the pit of her gut. The one that told her she needed to wise up. 'Yeah. A new place opening in Harrogate, last-minute thing. You know how hard he's being working with trying to get the funding for this new restaurant.'

Ben put the plated steak in front of Tyler, and he inspected it before turning to Ben and holding out a fist. 'We'll make a chef out of you yet.' Ben bumped it and Amber could see he was gleeful when he grabbed the next docket. Tyler spooned his delicious-smelling gravy reduction over the meat, nodding to himself with satisfaction before pushing it closer to Amber. 'Order up.' Amber was halfway out the door when she heard Tyler shout after her.

'You know, these big, flashy restaurant opening nights are never last minute. You are entitled to be mad at him.'

Amber bit her lip. 'I know, and I am, but he's doing what he can to make the life he wants. I can't fault him for that.'

Tyler shrugged. 'I get it. Everyone needs to follow their dreams, Amber.' His eyes locked with hers. 'But life is short, and you have your own dreams too. Remember that.'

The exit doors swished closed behind her. There was no point answering. She wasn't daft; she already knew Tyler was right. Everything he'd said was parallel with the thoughts that had been swirling around her grey matter lately. When she'd first met Bradley last year, it had been one of the things that she found most attractive about him. He was a dream chaser, like her. He hadn't changed. If anything, she had. They had both met knowing where they wanted to be in life, where they wanted to end up. He was just further on. She thought of the five-year plan languishing unticked in her notebook and pushed the familiar feeling of restlessness away. She could use tonight to work on her business plan. She'd been putting it off lately, with Brad so busy. It didn't seem like the right time for loading their plate any higher. If she got her own plans under way for her grandmother's old pub, she'd have no time to spend with him either. With their one-year anniversary coming up, she could wait a little longer. Let him get his second restaurant up and running first. Then maybe they could finally discuss moving in, focus on their other plans together. Everything they'd talked about. Marriage, babies. Running their businesses alongside raising their family. *I still want that: the business, the baby.* Lately, her biological clock had started ticking louder, beating like a tell-tale heart in the same drawer her notebook lay. She would have to live in the new place, her childhood home. Living together in her grandmother's old home would be the dream. Raising her children where she spent her happiest years? If Brad agreed to that, then all of her dreams would finally be complete. She could wait a little longer for her happy ever after, right? After the eatery was opened, maybe they could reconnect. Back to how good they were in the early months of dating, before things changed to guilt and recriminations over the phone. Missed dates and miscommunications. If her grandmother was here to see all this, she'd be getting a dressing down right about now. She'd be agreeing with Tyler. Life was short, and it was past time to get on with it.

Pinning on a smile and reaching table eight, she delivered the order. 'Enjoy your meal.' She grinned, proud of the mouthwatering food she placed on the table. Since Tyler had come to work for her a few weeks after she took the live-in brewery job, the food had been top notch. London trained, Tyler Williams was a damn genius when it came to cuisine. Even with all the rules and stipulations set out by the brewery in regards to the running of the Slug, he had made the menu his own. The old chef was happy with the frozen, reheatable stuff the brewery offered. Tyler soon talked them out of it and, when he took the job, his conditions were met. His kitchen, his menu. When he found a better gig more worthy of his skills, the patrons of the Lazy Slug would really miss out. His dishes had helped her double the takings over the last eighteen months and Sunday lunch was always booked out when he was on shift. Luckily for her, he seemed to be picky about where he landed next. Always talking about when he was gone, but never seeming to follow through on it. He would be sorely missed, and if she could have stolen anything from the Slug to take with her in her new venture,

Tyler would have been her first-choice hands down. *Perhaps we both need a kick up the backside to make the next move.*

'Oh, lovely,' the woman's eyes bulged when she saw the presentation of the food. Tyler took a lot of pride in his work. The vegetables were crunchy; the sauces matched the meat beautifully. Amber's mouth watered at the aroma, and she swallowed behind her grin. 'This looks so fancy.' Amber thought of the whipped foam Brad would be drooling over tonight and watched as the customer tucked into a piece of perfectly cooked meat. Saw the enjoyment on her face. It gave her a lot of pride. Sure, she didn't own the place, but, being live-in manager, she still considered it hers. One day, it would be her plates the customers would be tucking into, her name above a door in more ways than just a brewery licence. Food was part of that. Her grandmother always said the pub game was all about feeding the community spirit, and seeing families share meals always reminded her of that. Hopefully, she would find a chef as good as Tyler. It was a miracle he'd stayed as long as he had, really. His talents were wasted, but he had turned down a few offers now and Amber knew that the day he moved on was coming. She knew Brad kept talking to him about taking on the new eatery, so Bradley could concentrate on Sloane's more, a head chef in each business. He'd never been interested, much to Brad's frustration and her secret relief. Tyler would always mutter something about it not being his thing. Which wasn't entirely true, given that his CV listed some pretty prestigious places. Even turning down Brad's offer, she knew he wouldn't stay at the Slug forever. Much as she would like him to, she knew his talents were made for bigger things. The Slug was his stopgap too. Maybe it was part of the reason she was dragging her feet. She liked things here, how they were. Listening to Tyler train Ben in the kitchen, laughing with Sharon behind the bar as they worked. The customers who frequented the place – it was all like family to her. Knowing that change was coming didn't make it any easier to take. She tried not to dwell on Tyler leaving. It wasn't like they wouldn't stay in touch. She'd gotten used to having the grumpy chef around to talk to. Then again, it's not like she saw much of Brad, and she was supposed to be sharing her life with him. She wouldn't want her friendship with Tyler to go that way. He was a pushy guy in the kitchen, but he was fair too. Made time for life a little more. His passion went into his food, whereas Brad was more a big picture type of guy Always wanting the next thing, whereas Tyler was laid-back. Brad wanted a Sloane empire behind him, and Tyler... well, he just wanted to feed people. Be present. Thrill them with his creations. He could have left for a better-paid job, more prestige. He would be an asset for Brad's restaurant; it suited him better. The timeline fit too, but Tyler never seemed to warm to Brad's flattery or the concept of a brand-new restaurant to make his culinary mark on when he finally closed the Slug kitchen down one last time. Ben would be up to speed and, with another chef under him, her business would be in safe hands. Still, she found herself in no hurry to hand him his P45. He was family, just like Sharon. With all her actual family gone, the two of them and Bradley were it. She didn't relish the thought of losing any more of her people.

She got back to it, straightening menus on tables, chatting with the other diners. Laughing as little Olive, one of the younger regulars, flicked her peas across the table whilst her parents rolled their eyes. She tidied them away, bringing Olive some crayons to distract her while her weary father threw her a grateful grin.

'Don't worry about it,' she told them both, leaning into Olive's grabby handed, sticky hug. 'Just enjoying your food, aren't you Liv?'

'Yeah.' Her mother Lynda laughed. 'You should see the kitchen wall after she enjoyed our bolognaise yesterday.' She helped feed Olive for a while, letting her parents enjoy their own meal. Playing with children was something that had always come easy to Amber, and by the time she left with their dessert order, the whole table was smiling. One thing she was skilled at was making the people around her happy. She didn't need to be in a particular place for that. She might not be running her dream pub, but she was committed to making sure this place was well looked after.

'Good?' she asked her customer as she passed by table eight a short time later.

'Wonderful,' the woman exclaimed, closing her eyes momentarily as she savoured the taste. 'Nothing like a proper bit of home-cooked food, eh?'

Amber smiled. 'Couldn't agree more. I'll pass your compliments onto the chef.' She bussed a couple of tables on her way back to the kitchen. Sharon ambushed her the second she walked past, taking the dishes from her hands.

'Amber, a word.' Abandoning the dishes, she dragged her into the side office between the kitchen and the bar.

'But the bar—'

'Two minutes,' she shut the door behind them.

'Shaz, I know what this is about, and I don't want to hear it.'

'Tough. Sit.' She pointed to the faded, old, grey couch that took up most of the right-hand wall. Huffing, Amber flounced down in one corner. 'You know what I'm going to say.'

'Yeah, so I can go then, eh?' Sharon tutted, and Amber sat back, crossing her legs petulantly. 'Fine. Yes, I know. He cancelled again. Last minute, again. I know you don't like him, but—'

'Amber, I like him. You two were great together but lately, I don't know.' She sighed, a worried frown crossing her features. 'It's just, these days, he's been a bit selfish. He was the one who wanted to make it exclusive; now he's barely here.' She didn't draw breath long enough for Amber to give an answer. 'He's happy to have you draped on his arm when it suits him, but he drops you like a hot spud when something fancy comes along. Where's he been the last couple of months? You work your tail off; you deserve your time away from this place.'

'He doesn't do it all the time, and we're both passionate about our careers. That's why it works. We still have plans. I'm still going to take over my grandmother's pub one day; it just takes time.' Her grandmother's old business, The Bingley Arms, had been closed for a long time. Shuttered up ever since her beloved grandmother passed. Developers had tried to buy the place, but the town council had shut down any proposals for car parks or housing. Her grandmother had been a huge part of Hebblestone and counted the mayor as one of her closest friends. Good thing too, because Amber wanted it for herself. To see the place torn down or made into something else would rip her heart out. If she'd been in a position to buy it at the time, she would be there now. Every moment since the funeral had been about getting back there. Opening it back up and continuing the legacy her grandmother had created. *Well, not so much lately.* She had to admit to herself that, since Bradley, her burning drive had been diluted somewhat, but wasn't that what partnerships were about? Give and take. *Bradley does all the taking, though,* the voice in her head protested. Maybe Shaz had hit the nail on the head. And she was still swinging her hammer.

'Yeah, I know. I want that for you too, but does he *really* care about your life plans? You haven't even mentioned your business plan lately, and I worry you're just waiting around for him to pull his finger out and prioritise you. He did this last month, when we were supposed to do the comedy club thing. Bailing last minute, and he never paid you back for his ticket.'

'It was only thirty quid. And besides, Tyler's date bailed too!' Amber knew she was reaching, but the line of questioning was raising her heckles. *The truth hurts. The memory of eating ice cream in the dark was still as raw as the cookie dough she'd ingested.*

'Tyler's situation was different.' Sharon flicked her blue-streaked hair out of her face with a sigh. 'Date being the operative word, and I set that up anyway. He didn't want to do it in the first place; I just did it because I was bringing that Martin bloke from the Nag's Head and didn't want him third wheeling us all night and taking the mickey.'

It was true. Sharon had set Tyler up with one of her mates and she knew that he wouldn't like it. Stephanie was nice, but hardly his type. Not that he had a type. In all the time she'd known him, he'd never seemed interested in dating anyone. Either way, Stephanie wasn't someone Amber could see Tyler with. In their line of work, you needed someone who understood the unsociable hours. She worked in an estate agent's part time, was home by six every day. She wanted someone who had his evenings and week-ends free, and that just wasn't their world. Sharon hadn't put much thought into it, but that was her all over. Easy going, go with the flow and worry about the blowback later. It was one of the many reasons she loved her. Despite their differences, they were always there for each other. Which was why it was hard to argue with her now. When she was right, it was near impossible. Especially when she remembered Tyler's face when Sharon had told him about the date a couple of hours before they were due to meet. His expression could have split logs. He was often sullen, but that night, his mood had been so stormy that when the four of them got outside the club and a crack of thunder rang out in the night sky, Amber had looked to Tyler for signs he'd caused it. Still, she couldn't blame him. The comedians hadn't been the best, and the pair of them spent most of the evening wincing at the bad jokes and watching Sharon suck face with Martin.

'I told you that wouldn't go well.' She couldn't help the grin that escaped when she looked at her mate's annoyed face. 'He cancelled on Steph the second you told him.' She'd overheard him in the kitchen, letting her down gently on the phone. Even when dumping a date he didn't want, he was still a gentleman. He'd been so nice about it, apologetic. Explaining that he was into someone that Sharon didn't know about, so he couldn't go on a date. Asking her not to let on to Sharon, because it was so fragile. Secret. By the end of the call, Steph had been putty in his hands. She'd even wished him well with the woman he liked. She'd remembered thinking that Bradley could use a few lessons from Ty in letting women down gently.

Sharon gasped in her usual dramatic way, dragging Amber out of the memory. 'I knew it! I thought it was weird she bailed last minute! She said she had to have her cat declawed!' Amber smothered a laugh, watching Shaz as she walked the length of the office and back. 'You should have told me!'

'Tyler asked me not to.' Well, in truth, he'd caught her earwigging and had made her swear not to rat him out in a very red-faced, stammering way. When she'd asked him about the mystery woman he liked, he'd shrugged and muttered something about a little white lie. 'He was nice about it; he might be a loner when it comes to women but he isn't cruel. He just explained he wasn't dating at the moment; it's not his fault Stephanie's bad at excuse making.' Sharon's steps picked up speed. 'Can you sit down? All your pacing is making me ill.'

'Fine,' she huffed. 'I still can't believe you didn't tell me. I'm your best friend!' She sat down in the seat next to her. 'That should trump your other friends. You and Tyler are as thick as thieves sometimes.' Amber laughed, which made Sharon scowl all the more. 'God, he's so stubborn! He's just like you. Refusing to see something for what it is. I'm amazed either of you have ever had a love life.'

'Er, it's nearly a year for me and Brad. I'm hardly some dusty spinster.'

Sharon's eye roll made her eyeshadow sparkle. 'I know, but it irks me, I can't help it. You deserve better, and Brad's not being fair on you. Is it really a year?'

'Nearly.' She'd met him out drinking on her birthday night out the year before. 'My birthday is our anniversary, remember?' She'd spent most of that evening huddled in a corner with him. They'd talked the whole night, and he'd come to work the very next day and asked her for a proper date. Flowers, chocolates. She remembered how bowled over by him she was. How sure he was from the off about his future plans, them together. Like he'd walked into her life at the right time. It was refreshing, intoxicating to feel so wanted. He wanted everything she did: the business of their dreams, the relationship, the family. Nearing thirty, she'd made no secret of the fact she'd wanted children, and soon. Aside from The Bingley Arms, the one thing Amber wanted was a child of her own. A yearning that had increased in volume with each passing year. The fact that Brad wanted that too only made her feel more secure about them, even when he was absent now. It was a blip, that was all. What was a few months to wait when you had forever? If she bailed now, that dream would be further away. A year of her life wasted. One thing Amber wasn't, was a quitter. 'I actually can't believe it's been that long. It's gone so fast.'

'Exactly. A year.' Sharon was a woman decidedly not in the rose-tinted glasses gang. 'In Austen times, you'd be married off by now. You guys were hot and heavy from the start. He was always here; now he's like a ghost. The guy has been saying things would slow down at work, but you know he's just going to keep chasing the next best thing. What's the point of him saying he wants a life with you when he can't prioritise you for a night? Weren't you supposed to be getting engaged? Start making those babies you always wanted?'

*That stung.* Amber could feel her cheeks redden. Sharon was right, but Amber was too embarrassed to admit it. He'd brought up the idea of getting engaged on their six-month anniversary, but he hadn't mentioned it for a while. Not since he'd formed the plan for a second business, the upscale eatery that would complement the fine dining experience of his restaurant Sloane's, without the slightly pricier tag. She hadn't mentioned it either. How could she, when he had been the one to even mention the E word in the first place. She didn't want to be *that* girl. She wasn't the type to be clingy, but rejection was starting to make her want to figure him out a little better. With his second business and an engagement in the mix, it had made her pause on certain things. Like her own aspirations. The damn clock that kept ticking in her ovaries and made her cry at adverts for baby wipes. She kept telling herself it made more sense to save more but, in reality, she realised she was trying to keep her plate just that little bit less full. None of which she was about to admit to the woman calling her out on her bullshit. Sharon, and Tyler for that matter, would be mad. They wanted her to go for her dreams. Tyler was always mentioning her business plan, and it was still languishing in her cloud. Literally, and metaphorically.

'I'm not in some mad rush, Shaz,' she and her reproductive system lied. 'Even if we lived in Austen world, a year is not that long in the grand scheme of things. I've still got time to have a family; and do me a favour. Remind me not to invite you the next time I fancy a Colin Firth fix.'

'Not a chance,' Sharon tittered. 'It's the only reason I endure that romantic drivel. Don't you dare watch the lake scene without me.'

Amber snickered. 'Fine, and it's not drivel. Brad and I are fine. It's a few missed dates, that's all. Besides, we had a laugh without him. I enjoyed that comedy night.' Another lie. *I'm getting too good at this. Lying to my friends. Myself. Things are not good with Brad and deep down, I know it.* She'd stopped thinking of him as the future father of her children. Hardly a good sign. 'It was nice just us, and Martin was lovely.'

Sharon rolled her eyes. 'It was rubbish, and Martin was a drip. He laughed like a hyena in all the wrong places and gave his number to the waitress right in front of me as we left. One date was more than enough.' They sat in silence for a moment, and she could feel Sharon take a deep breath. 'I don't like how he treats you sometimes, that's all. I don't mean to be all heavy about it. I just worry about you getting hurt. Missing your chances just to prop up his ego. If a bloke says he wants to be with you, he'll be there. He'll show up. No matter what. A relationship should be a partnership, where both people can have the room to follow their dreams, but still put the other first.' *Wow. Sharon really was on one today.* Her cheeks felt like they were on fire. She had a point, but it didn't mean that it didn't hurt a little to hear it.

'Shaz, you don't even believe in relationships, and it's not like I'm sat waiting for my boyfriend and knitting booties. And, yeah, I have plans but I don't exactly have them in motion, do I?' *None of them. In fact, lately they seemed further off than ever. Especially the booties part.* 'Brad has his restaurant already; he's just trying to capitalise on his success. Sloane's is the hot new thing at the moment, and you know what the North's like. It's hard to break out against the bigger chain restaurants. Pubs and restaurants are shutting down all the time. My time will come soon enough; my grandmother's place isn't going anywhere. I can afford to save up for a little longer. Plus, if Tyler leaves, I'll have to get a new chef in place before I go.' Sharon was shooting her a pitying look, but she knew her heart was in the right place. The two women were so different; Sharon never wanted anything long term, choosing to live stress free – in the moment – but she always championed Amber to follow her dreams. 'I'm okay, Sharon. I love you for worrying about me.' She patted her hand affectionately. 'But I'm good, honestly. A night in won't kill me.'

'Yeah, well, I still don't like it.' Sharon squeezed her hand back, the worry lines easing on her pretty face. 'He needs to make the effort.'

'Yeah,' Amber sighed. 'I know. I pretty much told him the same thing if that's any consolation. I don't let him off easy you know, but he's working hard.'

'So do you and Tyler; it doesn't automatically make Brad good husband material.' Amber rolled her eyes, knowing Sharon wouldn't let this drop, and she was way off the mark with the Tyler comparison. He and Bradley were very different people. Both competitive – being chefs brought it out in them. Brad was clean cut, a pretty-boy type, petite even, whereas Tyler was a little rougher. Thick muscles, absurdly tall, flannel and jeans, tats everywhere. Brad said tattoos were the artwork of the commoner. She'd told him to never say that to Tyler if he valued keeping his head *on* his shoulders. 'What are you going to do tonight?' Sharon pulled her from her daydream about the two men in her life, reminding her she had another evening off with nothing to do with it.

She had no idea, and that made her mood dip yet again. 'Oh, you know, pine for Bradley. Write some bad poetry. Watch *Bridget Jones's Diary* in my sweatpants.'

'Really?'

'No! I've got plenty to do.'

Sharon's raised brow dripped with scepticism. 'Don't even think about coming down to work.'

'How did you know I was going to—'

Sharon's returning look was all knowing.

'Of course. You always know what I'm going to do.'

'You're not working tonight. You should go out! Dance, let your hair down.'

'Just what I want to do,' she got to her feet, aware that the bar was unmanned. 'Spend the night in a bar, when I live and work in one.'

'Better than crying over Daniel Cleaver in your trackies,' she quipped as they headed out of the office.

'I don't think you understood that movie,' she scoffed. 'No-one cries over Daniel. Not for long, anyway. He's the guy that's the guy before the guy.'

'The guy before the guy?' Sharon drawled. 'Right. That's why women everywhere fawn all over him, is it?'

Amber scoffed. 'Bad boys are all well and good, 'til the bad stuff spills into life.'

As they stood outside the kitchen doors, Sharon paused.

'Yeah, well, I think perhaps you need to rewatch it too.'

They headed back to work, her last cryptic comment hanging in the air between them like a dust mote. Everyone was tucking into their food, the regular lunch crowd nursing their pints, playing cards, laughing and chatting. The usual mix of workers, locals, retirees. 'Everyone good here?' she called out to a couple of the regulars.

'Yup.' George grinned back at them. 'Bill just took Eddie for twenty quid on the darts. He's demanding a rematch. I think we might have to referee at some point.'

'I am not taking any of them to the emergency room again.' She kept her voice low, so only Sharon would hear. 'The nurses laughed for a full ten minutes the last time.'

Sharon giggled. 'Yeah, well, a dart stuck in a forehead is pretty funny.'

'Not for the brewery it wasn't!' Amber protested, but her chiding held no heat as she addressed her regulars. 'I am not losing my licence for you two chuckleheads. They still owe me for the pool table incident. The finance department did not quite buy that

the leg "just fell off". Next time, it's coming out of my paycheck.'
She leaned against the counter, resting her tired calves for a
second. The long shifts had been taking a toll on her lately. Bradley
rubbed them for her usually, running his soft hands along her
knotted muscles. He hadn't done it for a while, she realised. Aside
from the odd quickie, it was a while since they'd been intimate at
all like that. 'Shaz, do you think Brad's a Daniel Cleaver?'

'What?'

'You know, a Daniel Cleaver type. Good on paper, slippery in
real life.'

She watched her friend bite at her lip, a sure-fire sign that she
was trying to be kind with her answer. Sharon always shot from the
hip. Even when it hit like buck shot, she was honest when she fired
off her opinions.

'Well.' Diplomacy won. 'Like you said, he won't always be so
tied up with work.'

'Right.' She nodded sadly, lifting the glasswasher handle and
feeling the steam hit her face. The pair of them started with the
pint pots, polishing them one at a time. Three glasses in, she was
still turning over the conversation in her head. The doubts were
starting to gnaw at her positive attitude. Sharon's wariness was
chipping away, along with her own strong glimmers that something
was off. 'But it has only been a year. You had a point. It's still new,
right? Shouldn't we be ripping each other's clothes off or
something?'

'Well, you've had sex. It's not like you don't.'

'Yeah, but I mean the honeymoon stage, you know? The one
where you can't live without sending the other a text or a daft
message. Wanting to hear how their day went. Telling them you're
missing them. We don't have that, not any more. The last one
Bradley sent me was to remind him about booking his car in for a
service. It should be all sexting and miss you baby's, shouldn't it?

You know. You talk about them all the time, think about them, the usual.'

'Yeah, in books and movies.' Sharon scoffed. 'The last text I got from a date had a dirty picture attached to it.'

'Gross. Martin?'

Sharon tittered. 'Nope. That would have required a microscope and some pretty damn good lighting.' The women cracked out laughing when their eyes met. 'Not everyone's like that, anyway. No-one would get anything done, for a start. If everyone was just screwing each other, fuelled by lust, civilisations would crumble in months. No-one's living like that, ruled by their loins.'

'Of course they are!' Amber countered, lining the clean glasses up just so. 'Where do you think the inspiration comes from for the movies and books? All that stuff people love comes from real life. Every love story comes from something in real life, experiences people live!'

Sharon laughed. 'Yeah, cos the world is full of sparkly vampires, bat boys and spank-loving billionaires who love literature-obsessed virgins.'

'Who's spank-loving?' Bill asked, walking up to the bar at the wrong moment with his empty bitter glass. Sharon took it from him and refilled it, pulling the wooden handle to pump the creamy brown bitter.

'It's from a book, love.'

Bill nodded knowingly. 'Ah right. The missus reads those. All lip biting, innit?'

Sharon smirked, taking his money. 'Something like that, Bill.'

'Cheers duck. She loves those books. Always puts her in a good mood too. Every lass likes a good fairy tale.'

He went back to his mates, and Sharon mouthed, 'Told you so' at her.

Amber bristled. She wasn't going to give up that easily.

'How did you meet your wife, Bill?'

He looked up from his pint, a wistful look on his face.

'Ah well, that was a story.' Amber waggled her eyebrows at Sharon, who stuck her tongue out in reply. Bill's gaze had turned all wistful, and Amber held her breath. 'We met in the dance hall. I was out with my muckers from the gas board; she was out with the lasses from the factory. She fancied my mate Ronnie, but I wasn't having that. Flash git he was, always one for the ladies that one. I put on my best bib and tucker, shined up my shoes and, the minute the music started, I went over to her.' He laughed softly, seemingly lost in the memory. Amber leaned over the bar, propping her chin on her elbow. Sharon made a vomit noise under her breath. Amber shushed her with a bar towel to the face. 'I said, "You might not have been looking for me, my love, but I sure have waited a long time for you. Dance with me and put a poor man out of his misery."'

'Wow,' Amber breathed. 'And that did it?'

Bill huffed, the wistful look disappearing like a light going out. 'Did it buggery. Ronnie, the smooth-talking blaggard, walked in right in the middle of my speech and she ended up seeing him for a couple of months. She cried on my shoulder for a full week when he ran off with another bit of skirt.'

'Ha! In your face!' Sharon crowed. 'Sorry.' She winced in Bill's direction.

Bill mockingly shook his fist in her direction.

'But you're together now, though, aren't you?' Amber tried to rescue the love story that popped like a balloon in her head, along with her hope. 'That was worth all the heartache, surely?'

Bill's smile returned. 'Aye, it all came good in the end.'

He went back to chatting with his pals, and Amber stuck her chin out at Sharon. 'Case closed.'

'Case closed,' she scoffed. 'Hardly love at first sight, was it.

People don't always get that big, epic romance you know. Some people just pick someone and make the best of it.'

'Wow.' Amber sighed. 'Don't try writing for greeting cards any time soon, mate.'

Sharon threw the towel back. 'Listen, life is short, my friend. You have to get on with what makes you happy and bugger the rest. That stuff's for the Hallmark channel. You don't have to give everything you have to a bloke. It never ends well. The best way to be is to sort yourself out, and then find someone who will let you do that and like you for it.' The service bell rang, and Sharon gave her a pat on the shoulder as she passed. 'But what do I know, eh? It's not like I have this relationship thing sorted out. None of us do. We're a public house full of lonely hearts.'

## 2

The conversation stayed with Amber long after the end of her shift. *Full of lonely hearts.* Her grandmother used to spout things along similar lines, especially after grandad had passed too soon. And it wasn't like Amber's own parents had anything to report in the true love stakes. Their story was more horror than romantic comedy. Was she really an idiot, believing that she could have a career and a love worth having? Would she have her own romantic story to relate to her own grandchildren, when she was battle scarred and grey haired? Right now, the only relationship she really had was with time, and wasting it. The night ahead was a prime example.

She'd had a few ideas of how to spend her evening in. She could watch that period drama box set everyone was talking about online, so she'd finally understand all the memes people were sharing. She could clean the flat, except that she'd not really been in the place so there wasn't much to do. It took all of an hour until she was back twiddling her thumbs again. All she wore lately were sweatpants, PJs and her uniform, so her washing was done in two loads. Sharon had come up on her break to grab a coffee with her, but, other than that, the night dragged. At half nine, when Sharon had gone back downstairs, Amber had taken one look at her laptop and decided that the TV would win for tonight. She wasn't in the mood to focus on her business plan and, when she'd texted Bradley to see how his night was going, he'd left her on read. *Nice.* She flumped down on the couch, trying to get into the show playing on the screen. She'd woken up some time later, still wearing her work clothes and feeling groggy from the nap. She could hear people leaving downstairs, the usual comforting sounds of customers she'd known for years saying goodnight and heading home for the evening.

'Well,' she sighed to herself. 'Great night off, Amber. You need to get a life, girl.' It had started to feel off, hearing everyone leave at night. Living alone had never bothered her before. Sharon and Tyler lived close by, they both had their own places in Hebblestone, but she had gotten used to having Bradley here. He'd used to sleep over a lot, and now... now he didn't. Brad had a flat of his own, the typical steel and glass bachelor pad, in a block of up-market apartments just outside Hebblestone and nearer the big city life in Leeds. She'd only slept over once, but it wasn't a home like her place was. Brad called her place cluttered, which, after seeing his bare space, she took as a compliment. Seeing her things in place, the photos, the furniture her grandmother had left her, soothed Amber as she took in the silence around her. It was so quiet, the stillness of the night only punctuated by the odd car passing by.

Looking at her phone on the coffee table, she told herself she wouldn't check her messages. But her phone sat there on the tabletop, begging her for attention. When it beeped, she pounced on it. *Tyler.*

> All locked up, I left the key in the lock box. Sleep tight

> Ty

She tapped out a reply of thanks before looking for notifications. Bradley hadn't replied. *Knew it.* Huffing, she dropped her phone on the couch. *Time to get ready for bed.* She'd get showered and get some sleep. Deal with everything tomorrow. It had been a cool day for late July, but she still felt icky from the long day.

She lingered under the hot spray of the shower for far longer than necessary, conditioning her hair twice just for something to do with her hands other than beat at the wall. Why had Bradley not messaging her irked her so much? He was busy; he was working. He wouldn't be sitting on his phone. He might even be home by now, asleep for all she knew. Still, Tyler always took the time to text her when he left. To tell her he'd locked up, even though she knew he would never forget. He did it to make her feel safe, to say goodnight. If her friends showed they cared, why the hell didn't Bradley? Why was she even bothering if things were this hard twelve months in? She thought back to Tyler's words earlier. He'd noticed the change. They both had. Sharon had definitely said her piece tonight too. Whether she'd wanted them to or not, they were both trying to help.

At the comedy night, she'd had fun, but it had stung to be stood up in front of them. Now it had happened yet again, and she felt... stupid. Rejected. She'd told her regulars she had the night off, that she was spending it with Bradley. Instead, she'd been upstairs all on her lonesome, drooling into the sofa cushions instead of enjoying the time off in a better way. Her friends were going to be full of it tomorrow when she told them she hadn't heard from him. She wouldn't lie to them, but justifying Bradley's actions was starting to feel a little wearing. The three of them were the best of buds, but lately she'd felt a shift in the trio dynamic she loved. Like she was a wonky corner of the triangle somehow. Over the last few weeks, she'd caught the odd look pass between them when they thought she wasn't looking. It made her feel... uneasy. Stupid, like they were talking about things without her. Possibly forming an I Hate Sloane fan club. A few things bothered her of late. With the silence, it was hard not to notice all of the loud doubts in her head. This wasn't just a rough patch in their relationship. This *was* the relationship. She'd been playing dumb even to herself, but she couldn't deny it any more. This wasn't the life she wanted. She'd never have a family with Bradley. Not really, even if they did sort things out and took the next steps they'd planned together. She'd be a single parent, waiting for him to show them attention. The thought of that was the decider. She wanted The Bingley Arms back, she wanted to raise a family in that place, her family of regulars and friends around her. She wanted that for her. Not Bradley, not to reclaim the legacy her grandmother had left before she got sick and had to sell up. They were her dreams, her life. A life she had checked out of in recent months, waiting for a man who didn't deserve her in the first place. She didn't want to wake up in ten years' time with regret and resentment. Her parents had never put her first. There was no way in hell she was going to have a child and watch the poor thing long for a parent who just wasn't there.

She was going to have to lay it out for Bradley. He either shaped up or shipped out. She didn't care if she sounded like some baby-crazy control freak. She knew what she wanted, and the woman she used to be would never have floundered like this, and there was nothing like another trip around the sun to wake a person up. Her impending birthday was going to be the marker for the next chapter in her life. *Life begins at thirty, Amber. Time to get on with living it.*

'Oww!' She winced as the blob of coconut-scented conditioner she'd managed to flick right into her eye blinded her. 'Shit.' Pulling back the shower curtain, she flapped her hands about until she made contact with the towel rail. Which was pretty easy, given that the bathroom in the flat above the Slug was small. Using the shower spray to douse the thick conditioner away from her face, she heard a noise. *A door slamming?* She stuck her head back out of the shower, gripping the curtain tight with one hand and reaching behind her with the other until she felt her fancy new loofah. The type that looked like a beige chunk of coral reef mounted on a wooden stick.

*Bang!*

There it was again! *Someone was definitely downstairs.* Heart thudding, she grabbed at the end of the wooden handle, gripping it tight. It was too light to do any real damage, but she felt better for having it in her hand. Tyler had no reason to come back, and Bradley was in Harrogate, right? He'd have called first, surely?

The water was still pummelling down on her back, dripping onto the bathmat as she slowly climbed out of the shower. Her toes had barely touched the floor before she heard footsteps up the stairs. Clunky, heavy ones. *It didn't sound like Bradley.* Wrapping a towel around her one handed, she raised the loofah behind her head baseball-bat style. 'This is not how I am going out,' she muttered through gritted teeth. 'Half naked with a loofah is not what I want written on my bloody obituary.' She'd kept the water on, not wanting to alert her would-be murderer that she knew they were there. She thought of who would find her in the morning. The cleaner had a day off, which meant it would probably be Tyler. *God no.* She was not about to let her best friend find her in a pool of coconut-scented blood with her tatas flying free. *At least I shaved my legs.* She gripped the bamboo handle tighter, giving it a little practice swing as she heard the footsteps getting closer. She would give whoever came through that door everything she'd got, and then leg it down the stairs. If she could just get to the control panel on the bar alarm, she'd have people here to save her.

Trying not to hyperventilate, she tilted her ear towards the door and willed her body to be still. The towel around her chest was jumping along with her racing heart as she waited for movement she hoped wouldn't come. If it was someone she knew, they would have called her name, she told herself. A break-in? She had the takings in the safe; did they know when she went to the bank? *God, I wish I hadn't left my phone on the couch.*

When she heard the unmistakable squeak of the floorboard outside the door, she held her breath. 'Come on,' she whispered between breathy pants. 'Give it your best shot.' How she kept the squeak from escaping when the handle turned, she couldn't say. She was too busy readying herself for battle.

'Die, wanker!' she shouted, and the second she saw a flash of black clothing, she bellowed like an angry bear and brought the loofah down as hard as she could. The second it made contact, it snapped in half. The dark shadow screamed, falling back out of the door with a high pitched 'Arrgghhh! Amber, what the—!'

'B-Bradley!?' She took in his crumpled form on the floor, legs half in the room as the steam from the shower enveloped him.

'Yeah! Of course it's me! Who else would it be?' He was looking at her like she'd grown an extra head. She saw his wide, blue eyes take in her weapon, his brows forming an incredulous frown. 'Is that a nunchuk?' The loofah head was totalled, leaving a rather smooth nub in her clenched hand, the pad dangling at its side by a single thread. 'What is... er... bur...' His words grew more garbled the lower his gaze got. It was right about then that Amber realised she'd dropped her towel during the fracas and it was now on the floor beside Bradley, who was open mouthed and bumbling nonsensical words.

'For God's sake,' she seethed, grabbing for the towel and covering her modesty. 'You've seen me naked before. You scared the shit out of me!'

'I know,' he leered back. 'But not all angry and wet.'

She scowled his way. 'You're an idiot.'

'Yeah.' He reached up for her hand at lightning speed, pulling her to the floor and into his arms. 'But I'm your idiot.' He brushed back a tendril of wet hair between two fingers, moving them to her chin and lifting her lips to his. He kissed her so softly, she almost forgot she was mad at him. He tasted like mint and Champagne. 'Forgiven?' he murmured when he pulled back. She was sitting on his lap now like side saddle on a horse, one hand holding the tenuous bit of towel tucked in under the seam. 'Come on, you can't be mad.' He kissed her again, a little more forcefully this time. 'I came to see you, didn't I?' He looked down at his rather damp suit. 'And took a beating. Look at my suit.'

He wiped at a spot of wet on his suit sleeve and she rolled her eyes.

'I'm sure your dry cleaner will be able to get a water stain out, James Bond.' She tapped his bow tie with her finger before getting to her feet. He rose with her, and they stood together in the tiny doorway. 'How did you get in, anyway?' He'd always insisted that they didn't need to swap keys. *Another sign you ignored. What partner doesn't have a key to their other half's place? Or want one?* She'd offered. He never had, and it was another brick in the wall between them.

'I used the key in the lock box.' He tilted his head to one side. 'Wait, are you mad I came?'

'No,' she scoffed, pushing past him to get to the bedroom. 'It's not that; you just scared the bejesus out of me. I wasn't expecting to see you. You also now owe me a loofah.' She looked at the clock on her bedside table. It was now nearly one in the morning. She had been hoping to have the big talk after she'd slept on it, worked out what she wanted to say. 'I have to be up for the brewery delivery first thing.'

'Sorry, babe. I thought you'd be in bed, all snug by now. I rang you on the way home; when you didn't answer, I thought you were either asleep or still annoyed with me.'

'I was.' She moved around her room, looking for something to sleep in. Her drawers offered two different options: her sexy nightie collection and a pile of comfy, flannel-type pyjamas she saved for cold nights and lazy days off. *Hmm. Definitely a flannel type of talk.* 'I am. It's pretty late, and you didn't reply to my message. After blowing me off again, I didn't exactly expect you.'

She felt him close behind her. Reaching for the black nightie, he pulled it out of the drawer. 'I had it on silent, baby. Please don't be mad.' He ran his hand over the material. 'Hmm. No granny clothing tonight,' he whispered against the shell of her ear, making her shudder. Not in the good way either. He really didn't give a shit that she was mad. Thought he could come here for some late-night booty call. 'I came straight here after the event, to see you.'

'Well, partners who care show up when they make plans. And if you'd bothered to ask for a key, I would have given you one. We should be doing those kinds of things by now if we're going to be together.' She ignored his look of affront as she went on. 'I mean, it's worth a discussion, right? If only to save my future loofahs from damage. Things can't go on as they are, Brad. I'm not happy.'

'Well,' he shrugged, starting to undress. 'I'm here now, and the lock box is fine.' He dropped his bow tie to the floor, starting on the buttons. 'See, no need for a discussion. I just want to see you. Less talking, more undressing.' When she didn't answer him, he rolled his eyes. 'I won't come next time if this is the reception I get.'

He was on the third button of his shirt before she spoke again. 'Yeah, well. Maybe you shouldn't.'

His fingers stilled on the button. 'Shouldn't what?'

'Come over.' His brows furrowed, and she cut him off before he could spout more fake platitudes. 'I just told you I wasn't happy, and you didn't even flinch.'

He sighed, dropping his hands to his side.

'It's late. I've had a drink. Can we just leave it for tonight? I'll make it up to you then.'

He went to undo the next button, and that's when she knew. The man she thought he was didn't exist. He wasn't going to change, because he didn't want to. Didn't feel the need to. He was not what she wanted. Not like this. She wasn't about to be anyone's afterthought a minute longer.

'I think you should leave.'

His laugh was like a slap in the face. 'What?'

'You heard me, Bradley. I'm not some late-night sex buddy. You either treat me as a partner or we call the whole thing off.'

He didn't say anything for the longest time. 'Has someone said something to you?'

'No,' she frowned. 'Should they have?'

'No, no,' he ran a flustered hand through his hair, ruffling it out of place. 'I just don't know where all this has come from all of a sudden. You were fine when we spoke earlier.'

'I was mad earlier, Bradley! I've been mad for a while, actually. I thought we were okay, but the more you're not here, the more you check out, the madder I get. I've been mad more than happy for a long time. You just don't notice! This is not what we planned. Since the eatery, I have to practically make an appointment to see you. It's changing me, and I hate that. I'm not this person, Brad; I'm not the girl who waits by the phone for a man to give her the time of day. I have my own life, you know. Stuff I want to do. I'm not getting any younger, and—'

'Oh,' his shoulders slumped in relief. 'You had me going there for a minute.' He huffed out a laugh, and Amber felt her spine stiffen at the noise. *He was laughing, when she was pouring her heart out.* 'I get it. It's your birthday making you feel like this. Turning thirty isn't that bad, babe. You still have a few good years left in you yet.'

*Nice.* She shook her head, wondering what she ever saw in the man. 'Thanks for that, and it's not about my birthday. Not only about that, but it's true that it's made me think.' She locked eyes with him. *Now or never. I don't have another loofah if he keeps talking like this.* She was still smarting from the derisive dismissal in his voice when she drew in a breath and spoke again. 'This relationship, if you can call it that, is not what I want. You have to choose, Bradley. I won't sit around for the next few months waiting for you to bother to spend time with me.'

She watched his brows furrow, his eyes taking her in as if he was seeing her in a new light. *Trust him to notice me now.*

'So you want me to choose between my business and you?'

'No, I want you to realise I'm part of your life! If I was important to you, it wouldn't even be a choice. We're all busy, Brad, but I still make time for you. For my friends.'

'Yeah,' he scoffed. 'And we all know your friends are not fans of mine.'

'That's not tr—'

'Yeah it is. Sharon isn't exactly subtle, and Tyler...' He bit at the inside of his cheek. 'Well, let's just say I know he's not a fan.'

Amber couldn't say anything about Sharon, but the Tyler comment surprised her. Sure, he'd said things to her, but he barely spoke to Bradley when they were together. Brad was always trying to talk to him about his next steps for work. Maybe that was it. He'd never seemed open to working for Bradley, sure, but showing he didn't like him? That was just Tyler's way. When he'd first started work at the Slug, he didn't speak if it wasn't connected to work. Hell, she wasn't sure she even liked him herself that first couple of months. He would just stare at her and stomp around the place. Coming from London, he never spoke about what brought him to

Yorkshire. Amber got the impression that he'd needed a change: little things he said about being burned out. He was a bit of a bear all around, huge and often bad tempered, and growly. Out of work though, Amber saw another side of him. Softer. He was funny. Caring, protective. She felt the need to defend her friends rise up.

'Sharon's heart's in the right place. You know how she can be blunt, and Tyler just doesn't want to work for you. You do tend to badger him about the eatery, and you know he's never been interested.'

Bradley's jaw clenched. 'Yeah, sure Amber. That's what it's about.' He stared at her intently. 'Lack of interest.' When she folded her arms across her chest with a sigh, he looked to the floor. 'I don't know what to say here, babe.'

Amber felt the stab in her heart like a knife. 'You do, actually. I'm asking you to put more effort into us, and you're blaming my friends. It's not coming from them. I have my own mind, Bradley. You know I want The Arms back, and you know I want a family. When I think about everything we'd planned, I don't get the same excitement I used to. You're like dating a ghost. It's a long-distance relationship without the distance. I am going to hit my thirties next month, and you might think it's just nagging but I mean everything I say.' She dropped her arms, feeling her spine straighten as she steeled herself for the thing she was about to do. 'Most of all, this side of me, the nagging, clingy side? I hate it, and I don't want to do it any more. It's not me. I've never been this type of girl, Brad! Things change, I get it. We both have things we want to do, but when we started this, they lined up.'

Brad wasn't moving. He was just standing there, frozen. She waited for the knife to twist in her chest, but she felt nothing but adrenaline coursing through her body. 'I think I know the answer to this, but I'm asking it anyway. Do you still want that, or should I just move on without you?'

## 3

Ticking off the order on her clipboard, Amber puffed out a sigh. It didn't seem two minutes since Tyler had helped her uncover the outdoor seating, and she couldn't believe another year was passing so fast. Summer was upon them, and she'd barely made a dent on her New Year's resolution to kick this year in the arse. Now, with half the year gone, she was further away than ever. After Bradley had left, she couldn't sleep. Couldn't get the look on his face when she asked him the question out of her head. He didn't even try to hide the answer that was written all over his face. His slumped shoulders. He looked upset, but his words said different. 'I think I messed all of this up some time ago, Amber. The truth is, I've been trying to be the man you met, but I've done too much to pull it back. I'm sorry, you deserve better, you really do, but I can't stop now. I've done too much to break away. Everything I have is on the line with the eatery.' He'd sighed, a flash of pained resignation across his face. 'I want you to have your dreams, Amber.' He'd walked over to her, run his hand down her cheek. 'I just can't be the man who gives it to you. Not any more.'

So that was that. He'd leaned in, kissed her cheek, and left her standing there clad in a towel with tears streaming down her face. A whole year with a man she'd thought was The One, and he'd just stepped away without a fight. He'd taken all of two seconds to give her the 'it's me not you' speech and click for an Uber. She wanted him to go to the mat for her. He hadn't even bothered to don gloves. She had her answer. Now, she just had to deal with it.

When she'd finally slipped under her covers, she remembered something Sharon had said earlier that day. About someone loving someone enough to be there. Bradley hadn't done that, he hadn't in a while. Sure, he was full of plans but no follow through. It was all just crap, big talk.

She hadn't even cried since he left. Since the few tears that spilled out when he basically told her he couldn't change like she wanted. Wouldn't try. She'd come to a conclusion when she'd woken up that morning. The tears she'd shed hadn't been from the loss of Bradley; they had come from embarrassment. The shame of putting a man first who everyone around her knew didn't do the same for her. Shouldn't she miss him? Want to talk to him, to try to salvage things? She didn't feel anything but shock. Not at him, but at herself. She had wasted time on a man that would never change. Bradley had shown her who he was again and again. She just hadn't listened. He was a man who talked the talk and didn't walk the damn walk. He was a magpie, obsessed with the shiny new thing, until he spied the next enchanting thing to chase. He'd been pulling away for a while, and she had clung to something that wasn't there in the first place. Because she wanted to have the family, the dream life. Now, she would be seeing in her thirties alone, and no further on than she was the year before.

'Way to be pathetic, Fitzpatrick,' she mumbled to herself, just as Tyler appeared.

'Coffee, madam.' A reusable cup appeared before her pinched face, and she reached for it like a child would a lollipop. Tyler slid the clipboard out of her hand, glancing at the truck parked by the back doors and the barrel chute.

'How much left?' he said with a tip of his head.

'Too much,' Amber grumbled, her body uncurling as the hot coffee passed her lips. 'Thanks Ty. God, I needed that.'

'I know,' he quipped, his lips twitching as he eyed her. 'You're like Satan's meaner cousin before your caffeine hits.'

'Says the John McEnroe of the kitchen.' She took another sip, smiling as the delicious drink chased away her fatigue.

'Touché,' he rumble-laughed back. 'It's your fault I'm up anyway. Who texts people at 6 a.m.? I'm pretty sure it's breaking some kind of employer-employee etiquette.'

'In my defence, I forgot it was early, and I texted Sharon too. I just wanted to get a jump start on work.' The truth was, she'd been woken by the birds singing through her open window and, not wanting to dwell on her failed relationship, she'd decided to throw herself into work. Mostly to stop herself from texting Brad and telling him what a prize dickhead she thought he was. *Hmm, anger as well as shock. I'm flying through the break-up stages of grief pretty fast.*

'Right.' His tone was laced with scepticism. 'Well, I'm pretty sure Sharon will have been laid face down in some bloke's chest at that time or snoring in her pit.'

Amber pursed her lips, but she couldn't argue with his logic. She was pretty sure he was right. One of the construction workers from the lunchtime crew had started coming in on an evening too and sitting at the bar. Earlier than when the rest of his mates rocked up. Amber just hoped Sharon knew what she was doing. These long-term construction types usually had someone at home waiting for them. *Someone like me, probably.* 'Maybe.' Tyler raised a sarcastic brow her way. 'Fine. Probably.' She smirked. 'I'm pretty sure Sharon only thinks that there's one six o'clock in existence, and it's definitely not in the a.m.'

Tyler almost snorted on his coffee. The delivery driver and his mate rolled another barrel past, and he moved the clipboard closer so she could tick it off. 'Sounds like a Sharonism to me. Why were you texting about the new specials that early, anyway? And why have you changed the lock-box code?' His face darkened. 'Wait, did someone try to get in?' His head snapped up to the windows, as though he was suddenly expecting to see carnage.

'No, nothing like that. Bradley used it. I didn't sleep much, and I didn't want either of you to be locked out. He came to see me late last night. I was in the shower, didn't hear him coming in 'til he was in the flat. I almost battered him to death with a loofah brush.'

'Almost?' he checked. She thought she heard him say something that sounded like, 'Shame'. Lower, under his breath.

She smiled then, thinking of Brad's face when she'd run at him wet through and angry. It was pretty funny, now she thought about it. 'It broke on his body.' She smirked. 'Anyway, the long and short of it is we broke up, so I changed the lock-box code. Not that I expect him to come back. It just felt right.' She felt Ty's eyes on her, his gaze burning a hole in her cheek. 'I don't really want to talk about it. It's done.'

Tyler rolled his lips, dipped his head into a slow nod. 'Fair enough. Do you need anything? Can I help, I mean?'

'Nope,' she huffed, feeling her shoulders tense up all over again. 'Like I said, I don't want to talk about it.' *I haven't fully processed it myself yet. Maybe that's it: I'm in shock. Perhaps that's why I don't feel anything.* Tyler was giving her a look that she registered as concern. Pity maybe? She couldn't bear it. Bradley might have been the one who did the dumping, but it was her ultimatum that had brought it about.

'You sure?' Tyler said softly. 'You know you can talk to me, Amb. I've been there myself, remember.'

She did remember. When he'd first started working at the Slug, he'd told her that he'd been through a bad break-up. One of the reasons he'd moved out of London, though he'd never gone into detail. Just like she didn't want to now about her recent dumping. It was too fresh, and she couldn't hear the 'I told you so's. Not yet. She held the pen out, ticking off the boxes of alcopops from the list when he brandished the clipboard her way. 'Just the bitter now, and we're done. I can take it from here. You didn't have to come in this early. Sorry for waking you too. It won't happen again.' He didn't move and, when she turned to him, he was already watching her. 'What?'

'You text me at the crack of dawn because you changed the code. I came because I was worried about you.' He ran a hand over his stubble. He'd obviously missed his shave that morning, and she felt a pang of guilt that she'd ruined his morning over nothing. 'You sure you're okay?' The clench of his jaw was hard to miss. 'Did you have a fight or something? Do I need to go have a word with Brad?'

'No,' she replied a little too quickly, lifting the coffee cup. 'I'm good, honestly. It was just a talk, and we're done. No need to protect me, Ty. I'm a big girl. Thanks for checking on me, and for the coffee.'

He huffed in his usual gruff Tyler way before heading indoors. As she ticked the bitter barrels off, she could hear him muttering to himself all the way to the back door.

'I can hear you, you know! I can read you like a book, Tyler Williams!'

He didn't stop, didn't look back. She didn't miss the way his shoulders rose, though, the way his gait coiled a little. 'If you could, Amber, we wouldn't have just had that conversation. In fact, we wouldn't be having a lot of the conversations we have.'

She was still trying to figure out what he meant when Ben arrived for his shift. When the deliveries were done, she'd opted for burying herself in filing in the office before opening time, enjoying the peace and the sit down before the rush started. For a little pub, they had a lot of foot fall and a sturdy set of regulars who felt more like family than customers. Sharon walked in, no doubt tipped off by Tyler that she was in a funny mood, and why. One look at her friend's face, and she knew she was being checked on.

'You're early,' Amber drawled.

'And you're observant. How was your night off?'

'Boring, then pretty eventful. I tried to decapitate Brad with a loofah. He surprised me when I was showering. I thought he was a burglar.'

'Nice!' Sharon tittered. 'Foreplay gets weirder and weirder these days. I take it you didn't hear him come in.'

'No, I was in the shower at the time. He used the lock-box key.'

*Hmm. Maybe Tyler didn't spill the beans.*

Her eyes narrowed. 'Why did you change it then? I got your text.'

Amber shrugged. 'We had a talk. I wasn't expecting him to show up, so I kind of attacked him half naked.'

'Promising,' Sharon giggled.

'Nope,' Amber sighed. 'It got worse from there. I spoke to him about how things have been lately.'

Sharon tutted. 'I'm guessing from your mood that it didn't go well. So did he come to talk too, or was it a pure booty call?'

'Was what a booty call?' Tyler asked, walking in brandishing some supplier invoices at the perfect wrong moment.

'Nothing,' the women said in unison. Tyler's face darkened, and Amber looked away before she met his searching eyes. Kept her hands busy, taking the invoices from his grasp without meeting his eye. 'Thanks for these. Kitchen ready?'

'Yep.' When she kept working, he turned his attention to Sharon. 'When's your next night off?'

'Why?' Sharon fake flirted, batting her lashes at him like a pantomime cow. 'Going to take me out?'

'Funny. We have that thing, remember? Details need to be finalised.'

'I know,' Sharon trilled. 'I'll text you.'

'Okay, but we need to get on with it.'

Amber focused on the filing cabinet as if it was the most interesting thing in the room, but she could hear them whispering.

'Get on with what?' she asked eventually.

The pair of them threw her a shifty look.

'You two can't whisper to save your life.'

'Pretty hard to do, with those big, flappy ears of yours,' Tyler smirked back. His phone beeped in his pocket. 'Oops, saved by the bell.'

When he'd sidled off back to his kitchen, Amber turned to Sharon.

'Spill.'

'We have the bar to set up.'

Hmm. Now Amber knew something was going on.

'You never say that, and it's mostly done. What's the tea?'

'No tea. I'll go finish the bar, but we are going to talk more about the Brad thing.'

'Sharon! You can't do that!'

'Watch me. Bye!' Her mate practically catapulted out of the door.

'Nice. Now those two are being extra shifty. Just what I need.' Shutting the filing cabinet and locking it up, she sat back at her desk. Checking the coast was clear, she brought up her bookmarks on the computer and began reading. She'd had enough weirdness for one morning. Time to have a little daydream about her someday plans before she had to go back to reality. It seemed everyone was getting on with life, and she needed to shake off the bad mood. She only had herself to please now. Nothing to wait for. Procrastination and break-ups didn't mix. She had her answer on the man in her life. Now she was single, she owed it to herself to get on with it. What she didn't want to do was listen to everyone whispering behind her back about getting dumped. If she was going to be the talk of Hebblestone, she might as well *give them* something to talk about that wasn't Bradley bloody Sloane. The old-new Amber Fitzpatrick was all about living her life to the full and getting what she longed for. If people had an opinion, then she'd be far too happy to care, either way.

Flicking through the tabs she'd bookmarked was a stark reminder of how things had changed in the last twenty-four hours. She went through each one. Bride directory. Deleted. Engagement-party inspiration. Gone. She deleted half a dozen more, until she landed on one that made her pause. Something that she'd been looking into before she and Bradley had had the marriage and baby talk themselves, and she'd shelved the idea. At the time, it had seemed like a last-resort plan, something she'd stumbled upon one day. It had started off innocently enough. She'd been looking for wedding ideas, and the Internet algorithms had worked their magic. Sucked her into parenting websites. From there, it was a downhill slope into everything from sperm donors to tips for single working mothers. From there, it was only a hop, skip and a jump to the IVF clinic she'd saved. Sperm donors sparked in her mind more these days than the perfect wedding dress, that was for sure. After the past few months of being bailed on and playing phone tag with the man who'd once stopped her in front of the jewellers' window and told her that, when the eatery was opened, the ring would be his next mission. Towards the end, she couldn't even get a day date with him unless she showed up masquerading as a pot wash at Sloane's. *Well, not any more. It's just me again.* Typing *30* and *single* into the search engine, she baulked at the depressing reading it made for.

Turning 30? Things to do before you die.

'What the hell,' she breathed out in a mutter. 'Early menopause – how much time do you really have to bag your dream man? Seriously, who writes this shit?' On a whim, she typed in *men turning 30.* 'Aww nice. *How to enjoy your prime years. Daredevil adventures to meet that milestone?* Are you frigging kidding me!' She stabbed at the keys, killing all the pages one by one. 'I hate the Internet. According to this thing, I'm basically washed up. Thanks Brad, for wasting a year of my egg shelf life!'

So that was it, apparently. She was too late. Research told her that she might as well start waxing her chin and stocking up on retinol supplements. She'd missed the winning-at-life medal, simply by turning another year older and daring not to be settled down in every aspect of her life. If the break-up wasn't depressing enough, the last half hour of surfing sure did it. Her biological clock was now giving Big Ben a run for its money.

'I am so getting drunk for my birthday.'

Deleting a pop-up about egg freezing, she noticed an advert.

'No way,' she breathed. Clicking on it, she read further. 'You can get it delivered to your door now?' She skimmed the legal text but it was legit. A real firm delivering baby batter with your morning pint of milk. Well, not quite. It wasn't exactly Uber Baby. 'Interesting.' She wouldn't need a man to have a baby this way. It was cheaper, private. Discreet. *I could just do it. I have no-one else to answer to. No-one else to think about. I have my savings. IVF is a fortune compared. Even if it takes a few times, this could be it. My chance. I could have a family of my—*

'What's interesting?' A deep, familiar voice rumbled from behind her.

'Shit! Tyler, again? You scared me to death!' She frantically clicked the tabs till her business plan was showing, just as Tyler leaned in to see what she was peering at on the screen.

'Sorry.' He laughed, putting a plate down next to her. 'I brought you some breakfast.' On the plate was an apple and cherry Danish, still warm from the oven. Amber's stomach gurgled at the sight of her favourite sweet treat. 'Glad to see you are back on your game.'

'Game?' she said, a mouthful of flaky, fruity deliciousness warping her words as she dived in for a bite. 'Oh my God, these are even better than normal. You really are a god in the kitchen.'

'Not just there,' he retorted, his lips twitching as he watched her eat. 'It's nice to see you back at the computer, that's all. You haven't talked about your business plan lately. I see they're still not doing anything with your gran's old place.' *Phew. He didn't see what I was researching.* Explaining that to Tyler would not go down well. He was the protective bear sort of friend, at least around her. He might think she was losing her mind. It was a little crazy, thinking about it. Having a baby on her own would be beyond hard, but the more she turned it over in her head, the less far-fetched it felt. She was already considering it a year ago, right? It wasn't some whim. She'd done okay without her parents, right? Sure, she would rather do the whole nuclear family, but maybe she didn't need the stereotypical make-up. People had babies in all kinds of ways every day. Ty's mention of the Arms, however, did summon up a stir of fear in her. That place was still the goal. One of the two things she couldn't live without on her to-do list for life.

'I know,' she said between bites of deliciousness. 'Breaks my heart whenever I pass the place. I just wish I had been in a position to take it on when she got sick.'

'Well, you were looking after her, and then grieving, and you had this place to run. And with the overheads, it would have been hard, Amb.'

'I know, my inheritance wouldn't have covered it.' *It still won't, even with the years of saving I've managed since.* 'It was just bad timing.' Her heart panged at her own choice of words. 'Not that there's ever a good time for your only remaining family member to pass away.' She felt some of the cherry juice drip down her chin, and before she could reach for something to stem the flow, Tyler was handing her a napkin. 'Thanks.'

'No problem.' His eyes shone with pride, and something else she couldn't decipher. 'You always tear into those things like you've never seen food before.' His eyes crinkled at the corners. 'In fact, with those panda eyes, you look like a wild racoon today.'

She balled up the napkin and threw it at him. 'Very funny. It's your fault; these little babies are addictive. I swear, you could do a mean side hustle as a takeaway bakery.'

'Yeah, sure the brewery would love me dealing desserts out of the back door like some drug baron.' He nodded to the screen again. 'Care to share? I would love to see your ideas. I think I could help too, with the kitchen side of things.' He threw her a cheeky wink. 'Come on, you have to show me it sometime.'

'No doubt you would have a lot to say, Mr Perfectionist.' She ignored his eye roll. 'I wanted to kinda go the traditional route, but Brad said no-one wants to eat old-style food any more.'

'Screw Brad. Old-style food? What does he think you're going to serve, turnip soup and soda bread? Let me have a quick look.' He twirled the monitor to face him and her hand reached out to slap him away. 'Hey! Come on!'

'No,' she protested, panicking as she tried to block his view. The company advertising sperm to your door was still bookmarked, and if he saw that, she would have a lot of embarrassed explaining to do. 'It's not ready!' Which wasn't exactly a lie. Her actual business plan wasn't finished. She'd stopped working so hard on it when things had got serious with Brad and now she was too fed up to even look at it. 'It's also private.'

'Private, eh?' Tyler teased. He lunged for the keyboard just as she hit the close button for the browser. Tyler's eyes bulged, and she stabbed at the power button on the screen. He went rigid at her side. 'I know what you're up to you know. You can't hide things from me.'

'You know?' *Jesus. He saw it.*

'Yep. Of course I do. You made it pretty obvious.'

'I did not!'

'You so did, looking all guilty when I walked in. You kind of gave yourself away. So, how long has this been going on?' She studied his face, but he just looked oddly amused. Teasing. *He can't know; he wouldn't be looking at me like that if he did, surely?* If she played along, maybe she could test her theory without giving herself away in the process.

'Nothing is going on,' she hedged, keeping her voice light. 'I was just looking, that's all. People look things up on the Internet all the time; it's not that radical an idea. I really don't want people knowing either, Ty.'

'Oh, I won't be telling a soul, don't worry about that.' He laughed out loud. 'You are a dark horse. I wouldn't have pegged you for the type.'

*Ouch. That stung.* 'Type?'

'Yeah, you know. I just figured it wasn't your thing.' He shrugged with an ease she didn't return. 'It's fine, it's not mine either. It's hardly realistic.'

'I wouldn't say that. I was always going to do it at some point.'

'Do it?' Tyler's eyes bulged. 'Really?'

'Yeah,' she bristled. 'I've wanted to forever.' She folded her arms, the pastry now a distant memory as a bad taste filled her mouth. 'You sound as if you think I might be bad at it, but it's really none of your business. Besides, I was just researching. A little.'

Tyler didn't answer for a moment, his eyes glazing over. When he spoke, his voice was deeper, almost rasping. 'I don't doubt you'd be good, amazing even, but the stuff in those movies is not real life. You don't need to research like that. I mean,' he ran his hand down his scruff, swallowing hard. 'Having a bit of variety is good, but I don't know. Some of it is just—'

*Hold the phone. What?*

'Movies? What the hell are you talking about, Tyler?'

He nodded to the blank screen. 'You know, that. You don't need to change, Amb. Any man who wants you to is an idiot. Is this about Brad? Did he say something to upset you?' His jaw clenched. 'Do I need to go have a word?'

'Tyler, I have no idea what you're going on about.'

'I'm just saying.' He shuffled from one foot to the other. 'You don't need to watch that stuff.'

'Watch what stuff?'

'Porn!' He half shouted; his face scrunched up.

'Porn?' *He didn't see. He thought I was hiding… porn?* She exploded with incredulous laughter. 'Porn! You think I was looking at…' His words played on repeat in her head. 'You think I was looking at porn.' The relief she felt in her hammering heart soon gave way to horror. 'Ugh, Tyler! I was not looking at porn. Really?'

Tyler was doing his best impression of a fish out of water. 'Er… no… well… I thought…' His brows were like two caterpillars break-dancing as he reprocessed the conversation. 'Well, it's doesn't matter what I thought. Sorry.'

She couldn't help it. She wanted to be mad at him for thinking she was in her office looking at well-endowed wangs but the look on his face was making it hard. No pun intended.

'It's fine.' She smirked, and when their eyes met again, they both snickered. 'I can't believe you thought that.'

Tyler ran a hand through his thick, black hair, sagging against the desk. 'I am relieved, I've got to say. I thought Sloane might have said something to make you feel bad. I dunno. I thought I saw something. My bad.'

She winced. 'Nope. Our sex life wasn't what broke us up, Ty. Well, the lack of one maybe featured.'

Tyler's jaw clenched, but he said nothing.

'Thanks though.' She grinned at him. 'I needed the laugh.'

'You're welcome.' He smirked, those brown eyes of his twinkling before he looked away. 'Well, I'm glad we got that sorted out. I better get back to the kitchen before I make more of an ass of myself.'

'I think that's probably a good idea.' He was halfway out the door when something he said replayed in her head. 'Amazing, eh?'

'What?'

She twirled around on her office chair, and she could swear he was blushing.

'You said, and I quote, "You'd be good, amazing even."'

'Did I?' He twiddled his hair between two fingers.

'Yep. You remember? A minute ago, when you thought I was looking for sex tips on the net? You said I didn't need to watch that stuff.'

'Er... well...' He looked away. 'I shouldn't have said that.'

'But you've thought about it.' She was enjoying this, teasing him back. It soothed the barb she'd felt in her chest when she'd thought he was talking about her being a mother. Pushed them back into their usual teasing banter. 'My amazingness.'

'I didn't... er... I haven't... not thought about it.' His blush was practically crimson now. Brown eyes flashed to hers. 'Haven't you...?' *Shit.* She was teasing, but now they were in new territory.

What could she say? He was her friend, her best male friend, but he was also sculpted by the gods. The gods that made Vikings, lumberjacks, Norse Gods. The man was fit with a capital F. Add to that his surly, burly ways, the little things he did for her, and... well, a woman would have to be made of stone not to let her mind wander once in a while. She'd have to be dead not to notice him. He was always just there, it seemed. When she was struggling with a barrel, or hangry behind the bar. He'd just materialise from nowhere, fix the problem. Shove food in front of her when everyone else recoiled from her snarling form. If a customer gave her trouble, he was the one who just seemed to appear at her shoulder. One look from him and the problem just... went away. Sharon used to joke he was her bodyguard, until Bradley came into her life. He'd retreated then, but she knew he was always there. Ever watchful, as if he was waiting for her to need him for something. And she kind of did, even though it was in this moment that she was acknowledging that. They'd known each other longer than her relationship had lasted, and having a male best friend was a little weird to some people. Brad had even asked her a couple of times early in their relationship whether they'd ever dated. She'd been mindful of that ever since, and she figured that's why Tyler had stepped back a little. It was nice to have him close again. Tyler Williams had this way of making her feel calm when her head was spinning.

She'd felt it the first time they'd met, when his deep-set, brown eyes had assessed her with that scowl he often sported on his face. She saw it, even now when he looked at her. His eyes were boring into her as if he wanted to stare the answer right out of her. She willed her face not to flush, remembering all the times she'd glanced more than once at his corded forearms, or at how the flannel shirts he always seemed to wear screamed with tension over his thick biceps. Oh yeah, she'd thought about it, but they were colleagues. If she ever crossed that line, the little things he did might get lost. The pastries full of cherries she loved, the way he always tried to push her to pull the trigger on her life. Before she'd met Brad, she'd thought about asking him to come with her to the Arms. To stay, work *with* her. But something had always stopped her from getting too close, like that. He was important to her, but she couldn't say the thoughts she'd had about him were always on a friendship level. He didn't even do relationships. The last one he'd had in London had wrecked him, from what little she could tell. So he'd become a friend, and one of her favourite people on the planet. Even if she had sometimes wondered what he would do if she ever tried to venture her fingers under that flannel...

*Oh God, stop thinking about it now! Answer him! It's Tyler, Amber. Tyler.*

'Answer the question, Amber.' His commanding tone skittered her thoughts apart, and she didn't give herself time to form a sensible answer before she was pushing words out on a slightly shaky breath.

'I... a couple of times, sure.' She felt her face redden, her mouth running out ahead of her. 'Before Brad, I...' *You what, Amber? Wanted to climb him like a wildcat up a tree? Stop talking!*

'You have?' His brows shot up to his hairline, his lips pressing together as his fists clenched at his sides. 'In what way, exactly, and when did you—'

Ben appeared in the doorway behind him. 'Morning, boss!' He saw Amber sitting at the desk, slack jawed and mind whirling. 'Morning, big boss.' Looking between the two of them with curiosity as they looked at each other as if he wasn't there. 'What's up with you two?'

'Nothing!' Amber trilled in a tone far too high pitched, in the same second Tyler growled out a, 'Leave' without looking away. Ben's brows rose and fell comically, his jaw bobbing as he looked from Tyler's rigid back to Amber's face. When she dropped her eyes back to Tyler, the look on his face made her stomach flip. The tension was radiating off him, and she knew Ben could sense it too.

'I'll er... just... yeah.' He turned on his heel and headed to the kitchen, and Amber turned back to her desk with a spin that almost sent her careening to the wall behind.

'I'd better get on—'

'Amber.' His voice was deep, sultry, but she was already out of the moment. Whatever that moment was in the first place. Her palms were sweating, leaving little marks on the leather desk protector in front of her. 'When—'

'Thanks for the pastry, mate. I'll let you get on.' She picked up some invoices for something to do with her hands and heard his irritated huff. When she finally looked up, he was still standing there. Watching her. She searched for something to say, but her words were stuck in her throat. She shouldn't have said anything. Her relationship was barely cold. She didn't want to lose any people. Not again. Tyler's eyes roamed her face, and she felt bare before him. Whatever he saw looking back at him made his lips roll together.

He pointed at the screen before her. 'It's quiet out front. Use the time to get your stuff done. Worst thing in the world is waiting too long for something. Trust me. I'll bring you some lunch later.'

She watched him leave, his whole body tensed up like he'd been stung.

'Thanks,' she called after him, but all she heard in response was the door to the kitchen slamming shut. 'Shit,' she sighed. She'd gone and done it now. Dropping the invoices back onto the pile, she brought the computer screen back to life. *Why did I say that?* She'd never meant to say anything to Tyler, but his reaction had stunned her. Did she imagine it? Had he been thinking about her that way? *No. No way.* It was Tyler; he didn't date. He didn't bother with women full stop. Sharon and her had teased him about it, tried to set him up. The guy wasn't bothered. He was making a joke, and she'd blurted out that she'd thought about him. *That way.* The poor guy was shell shocked. That was all. The moment they'd imagined was in her head. The way he'd growled at Ben to leave, though. It didn't make sense... unless. He was embarrassed. *Oh Christ, I've embarrassed him.* She'd been dumped less than twelve hours ago, and now he thought she was some desperate, porn-watching, horny singleton. He was covering for her because he'd thought Ben had heard their conversation. Her cheeks heated as she replayed it in her head.

'Oh God,' she groaned, leaning her head on the desk. 'I'm such an idiot.'

**4**

'Strike!'

Ben punched the air in triumph, turning from the fallen pins and flexing his biceps in a muscleman pose. Amber's giggle barely suffocated the collective groans of Tyler and Sharon.

His score came up on the screen above them, knocking Tyler and Sharon's team back into second place. 'Suck it, Ty-Ty.' Ben came back to sit next to Amber, laughing as he reached for his pint. Tyler's eyes narrowed to slits from the opposite bench.

'Don't call me that,' he grumbled, turning to Sharon at his side. 'Take him down, Shazza, or he'll be insufferable.'

The bowling alley was quite full for a Sunday evening. The families had drifted off, leaving more couples and adults on the other bowling lanes. When it hit seven o'clock, the lights had lowered, and the music decibels had risen. It gave the place a party feel, and also hid Amber's discomfort. Sharon had come with her in the taxi there, Ben and Tyler making their own way, and when they'd first met up, it had been beyond awkward. Sundays were the one night they all got off. The kitchen closed, Mary and Mick from the village ran the quiz night, leaving them free to do their own thing. Which was why they were all here bowling; Sharon's way of cheering her up since the break-up. It was either agree to this or, as Sharon had put it, Bradley was to get a friendly nut punching. So Amber had chosen to bowl, and endure a slightly awkward night out with her friends and colleagues.

Since the moment in her office the other day, Tyler had been distant. Not weird, or nasty, but he wasn't himself. He'd brought her lunch later as promised, leaving it on her desk with a gruff, 'Make sure you eat it all' thrown before he'd bolted again. Since then, he'd only spoken to her about work, and there had been no memes that he found funny sent her way. Even Sharon had asked her on the way over if they'd fallen out. Amber had brushed her off, and she seemed to buy it, but the energy was definitely off tonight.

Sharon left two pins standing on her next shot and, when she turned back to Tyler, he high-fived her. 'Nice one, Shazza.'

She eye-rolled him. 'We needed a strike. We lost!'

'Damn right you did,' Ben chipped in. 'Good thing you have another game to redeem yourselves, losers.'

'It's a game, not the Olympics,' Tyler cut in, draining the rest of his pint like it was thimble-sized. 'Shall I get the drinks in before the next game?'

This was it: her chance to address the elephant in the room. 'I'll come with you.'

They left the other two ribbing each other and headed to the bar. As they waited for their turn, she tried to think of a good way to start the conversation. He broke the ice first.

'Did you get your plan for the Arms done yet?'

'Not yet.' She'd hidden in her office for another hour and then given up on her new life for another day.

'So what's holding you back? You were all guns blazing a few months ago.'

'I still am, I just...'

'You're still waiting for things to change, Amber. They won't unless you change them.'

She felt her head rear back as if he'd slapped her. 'Ouch. Say what you mean, Ty. It's not like I just got dumped or anything. Give a girl a minute.'

'I mean it.' He turned to face her, his eyes lasering in. The barman interrupted them, and Tyler ordered another round. When she went to get her purse out to pay, his meaty hand covered hers. Everything stopped.

'I'll get it. You need to save your money for bigger things.' She barely heard him. The second his fingers cradled hers, she felt it. Through her whole body. Her head spun to look at him, but he was staring at the point their hands met. *Did he feel that? It registered as a seismic event on my end.* 'I... I made it awkward, the other day.' He swallowed, and she felt his fingers squeeze hers, just for a second before he pulled away.

'No, you didn't.' The barman left the drinks on the bar, Tyler tapping his card on the reader without even a glance. 'I did that. I shouldn't have said it. You're my friend, Ty. I don't want you to feel awkward at work.'

'No,' he rumbled back. 'I don't feel awkward. I just wish you'd said something sooner.' She waited for him to burst into laughter, tease her about porn again. He didn't do any of that. In fact, he looked like he meant every damn word. 'I wanted to say something myself, but I didn't know if—'

'Hey.' Sharon made them jump, reaching between them for the drinks. 'Second game needs starting; we only have the lane another hour.'

He didn't take his eyes off her. Amber wanted to tell Sharon to give them a minute. She wanted to hear more. *He was going to say something? When?* Why didn't he say something when she met

Brad? Before? Why now? Why couldn't she look away? Her feet felt like they were stuck to the carpet.

'Hello,' Sharon sang, clicking her fingers in front of their faces. 'What the hell's going on with you two?' *Good point, Shaz. This was Tyler. My employee, my friend.* She needed to get a bloody grip.

'Nothing,' Amber replied finally. 'We're coming now.'

She watched Tyler bite the inside of his cheek before grabbing the pints and striding back to Ben.

Sharon pulled her back. 'Hang fire a minute.' *Fine by me. I need a hot minute to get my shit together.* 'I don't know what's happening tonight, but you are acting off.'

Amber headed back to the lane without answering. Sharon reached for her arm. 'Amber, talk to me. You've been weird for days.'

One look at her friend and she caved.

'I know. I'm kind of going through something. I had a weird conversation with Tyler.'

'Good!' She folded her arms. 'It's about time he said something.'

'Er... yeah. He said something. Wait, what do you know about it?'

Her expression softened, and she hooked an arm under hers and walked her right back to the guys. 'Are you kidding? It was my idea. Well, I helped.'

They were almost within earshot now. Amber hit the brakes. 'What do you mean, you helped? How long have you known about this? I mean, I didn't have a clue. When we were in the office the other day, we got to talking.' She gripped Sharon's hand. 'I actually really need to talk to you about this. You know, a woman's perspective. The thing is, Tyler—'

'He let slip about the party. I knew it! He said I would be the one to crack!' She cackled to herself. 'Well, actually, we thought Brad would ruin it, but—' She paused, wincing. 'Sorry, but at least you know now. I felt so bad for whispering around you. Tyler was the one who wanted it to be a surprise party. I said we should just tell you, but he's been planning the thing for weeks. He also said if I told you, he would make me do all the cooking for it.' She shook her head, laughing. 'And he caved! What a loser, eh?'

Amber glanced across at their lane. Ben was talking to Tyler. Who was staring right at her, a rueful look on his face.

'Tyler planned a whole surprise party for me?' No-one had ever done that. Not since her grandmother. Bradley would never have even thought of it. 'Why would he do that?'

Sharon rolled her eyes theatrically. 'You kidding me? Ty knows what a big deal your thirtieth is to you. He knew things weren't good with Bradley.' She linked arms, pulling her back to the guys. 'And it's Tyler, come on. You know he's a big softie when it comes to you.'

'He is?' she muttered, but it was swallowed up by the music as they hit the lane.

The second they reached Ben and Tyler, Amber could feel their eyes on her. Tyler stood first.

'Everything okay?' he drawled, and she met his eye with a happy smile she didn't feel. Her mind was trying to fit things into neat little boxes but everything was suddenly the wrong bloody shape.

'Yeah, everything's great. Let's play; they'll be turfing us out soon.'

Ben clapped his hands together. 'Game on, eh Amber? Ready to thrash them again?'

'Amber's on my team this time,' Tyler cut in. Heading to the ball rack, he passed her the pink one she always used when they came. 'You're up first.'

Sharon laughed, slapping Ben on the arm as she took a seat.

'Looks like it's you and me, Benny Boy.'

The second game was decidedly more high stakes than the first. When Amber went to take the ball from Ty's hands, he leaned closer. 'Let's knock that smile off Ben's face, Cherry. I am not losing to him again. He'll be insufferable at work tomorrow.'

Despite herself, him using the name he sometimes called her made her grin. He'd once said she would end up looking like a cherry pie, after one shift when she ate five of his pastries. He'd called her Cherry after that, when they were messing about. He'd not said it in a while. Since Bradley, she realised with a jolt. *Were there other things I'd missed, being with Bradley? Like the fact my chef and close friend is actually kinda hot? Scratch that. He's totally smoking hot. Henry Cavill level of hot.* Maybe it was the baby fever. That was it. Her uterus was throwing her at the nearest available male specimen. It wasn't like she'd just noticed him. *Oh Jesus, take the wheel. I'm losing my damn mind.*

'Oh, come on!' She shrugged, giving herself a mental cold shower. 'Sharon doesn't care about the game. You men and your sports.'

Sharon was three vodka and cokes down already and drinking her fourth. She threw them a hearty thumbs up. 'You're right there. Benny my boy, you don't need me, right? I thought you were the king of pins?'

'Yeah,' he huffed. 'Well, let's just get on with it.'

Turning to bowl, Amber walked straight into Tyler. His hands were there instantly, steadying her, and there it was again. That jolt. The second he put his hands on her bare arms, it was like she'd been zapped. When their eyes met, he was staring at her as if they were the only two people in the world. She could swear she felt his fingers clench around her arm.

'You good?'

All she could do was nod dumbly up at him.

'Yep. Yeah. Sure. Definitely. All good. Thanks.'

With a twist of his lips, he released her and went to sit next to Sharon. Amber's arms were jelly and goosebumps. It took all of her muster to not drop the ball on her damn foot as she headed to the pins. Taking a deep breath, she launched the ball with everything she had.

'Strike!' Tyler yelled as the pins skittered away from the impact. She heard Ben curse, Sharon laugh and Tyler's roar of joy almost drowning out both. Turning on a heel, something warm and solid brushed up against her. Turning to look up, she found Tyler's face was right there. He lifted her off the ground and twirled her around. 'Perfect!' He whooped, his arms tight around her.

Laughing, she pointed at their opponents. 'Suck on that, losers!'

Tyler laughed again, giving her a high five.

'That's my girl,' he rumbled, lowering her only to tuck her under his arm. Amber's stomach flipped like a pancake.

'Yeah,' Sharon slurred from behind them, slapping Ben on the back. 'We're going to need another round.'

## 5

The taxi pulled up to the Slug an hour before last orders. Ben having gone home to see his wife, it had been down to her and Tyler to corral Sharon into the car. Which was probably just as well, because the energy between the two of them was positively crackling. Amber had been zapped with a shock when she touched the cab door to get out, and she was pretty sure it was the air around them sensing the tension between them.

'Ouch,' she yelped, yanking her hand back as Tyler helped Sharon to the pavement.

'What?' he asked, his concerned gaze snapping to her.

'Electric shock,' she laughed, reaching back in to grab her bag. It was vibrating and, when she pulled her phone out, her face dropped.

'I need a little coffee,' Sharon hiccupped.

'No shit,' Tyler laughed, propping her up against the lamppost as he paid the driver. 'I'll get Mary to put the kettle on.'

Amber held up her phone. 'I'll be there in a minute, okay?'

She waited until they were inside to answer.

'Bradley.'

'Hi.'

'Hello.' She toed at a tuft of grass growing in a pavement crack.

'How have you been? I haven't heard from you.'

'That's how break-ups work,' she quipped. 'Did you not read that part of the manual?'

He laughed awkwardly. 'Er, no. I guess I probably should have. Listen, I wondered if we could talk.'

*Wow. The irony.*

'About what?'

'Us. I don't like how we left things.'

'Well, we broke up. I don't think there's anything left to say really. Nothing's changed, has it?'

'Well, no – but... could we meet up? I could come over.'

Amber looked at the Slug, full of the usual regulars. 'Er, no, I don't think that's a good idea.'

'Tomorrow then. I have some things I want to say. I was a bit hasty the other night. You caught me off guard, babe. Please?'

'I don't know, Bradley.'

'Please. Ten minutes. I could come over to the Slug tomorrow? For me?'

'Bradley, you already gave me an answer. I really don't think there's any point.'

'Will you think about it at least? I'm sorry. You took me by surprise, that's all. I didn't really think things through. I just want to see you, Amb. Come on.' *Why now? Why had it taken him days to bother to call me? He dumped me, he made his choice. I was moving on, damn it!* She thought of her life, behind those doors. The life she wanted. One he had already walked away from.

'Come on? Brad, I don't know what this is about, but it's too late.'

'Too late? What do you mean, too late? We haven't been broken up a week! Don't you at least owe me a conversation?'

A conversation? That was all she'd wanted to do for weeks. Months if she was honest. Sharon was in her head, the words had stuck in her grey matter hard and fast.

'I'm not sure I do, no. If you wanted to stay with me, you should have tried harder. If a man wants you, he shows you. Goodnight.'

'Amber, come on! I—'

She cut off the call and headed inside. Walking into the warmth of the Slug, she was assaulted by the voices of the patrons around her. The familiar smells and sounds felt so comforting her eyes filled with tears. She belonged here, in a place like this. The second she'd walked through the doors, she'd felt less alone than she had standing outside listening to Bradley's attempts at talking her round. Blinking rapidly, she pushed a smile onto her face, and her ex out of her mind.

Sitting at the end of the bar, perched on a stool that looked like a kiddie seat under his large, brooding form, was Tyler. His eyes followed her as her feet moved to him automatically. *Why is my heart beating out of my chest? Why do I feel calmer, just by seeing him? This thing, it hasn't always been there, right?* She felt elated and pissed off all at the same time. She couldn't get Bradley to walk through the door when they were together, and here Tyler was. Again. Gazing at her as if he knew something she didn't and was waiting for her to catch on. Breaking eye contact, she took in the busy bar. It was a typical Sunday and there was a steady stream of people waiting to be served. 'Where's Sharon?'

Tyler nodded his head over to the window, where Sharon was sitting with a guy from the construction site. They looked pretty cosy and Sharon was laughing at something he said. He had his arm around her, his nose close to her neck as he spoke into her ear. She looked different to normal. Like she'd melted into the man cradling her. She watched him lift a mug to her lips. 'She's fine,'

Tyler rumbled. 'Mary made her some strong coffee. I think he was waiting for her to come back.'

'Good for her.' Amber smiled. Maybe her ice queen love 'em and leave 'em friend was mellowing. It was nice to see, but the tenderness between them was a little hard to watch. Being single seemed to amplify every happy couple in her orbit. It made her heart clench.

'Bradley coming over?' Tyler's voice pulled her attention back to him. 'I'm guessing it was him on the phone.'

'Nope, and yeah, it was.' She sighed, pulling up the empty stool next to him and dropping her bag at her feet. 'What ya drinking?' She was already reaching for his glass, tipping the contents straight down her throat and feeling the burn as it went down.

'Neat whisky,' he smirked as she pounded at her chest. 'Take it easy!'

'Needed it,' she rasped out.

'I bet. Take it you didn't sort things out then.'

'He said he wants to talk. I didn't think it was a good idea. No point.'

'Right.' Tyler didn't sound convinced. 'Two more, Mary, please.' He called to her as the older barmaid came over. Mary gave him one of her mothering smiles and turned to the optics.

'There's a queue,' Amber teased. 'What is it with you and the ladies around here, eh?' She lifted a finger and swirled it in the air. 'One bit of Williams charm and they all fall at your feet.' Her smile died when she saw his stony face staring back at her.

'Not all of them,' he muttered. 'It wouldn't matter anyway.'

Amber felt her throat dry out. 'Of course it wouldn't. I forgot, you don't do relationships, do you?'

Mary brought their drinks and Tyler handed her a note. She practically fanned herself with it before getting back to the others. Amber was mid-sip of her whisky when his voice rumbled again.

'What makes you say that? I've had relationships.'

'Not while I've known you,' she countered. 'You shun every date we try to set you up on.'

'Doesn't mean I'm not relationship material. Just means I know what I want.'

When their eyes met, that damn spark fizzed again. Like an electric current arcing between them unseen. She took another sip, turning to stare at the back of the bar.

'So, are you going to talk to him?'

The huff burst from her chest before she could stop it. 'Nope. I think I've done enough talking for the both of us. Didn't get me anywhere, did it?' She tapped her finger on the side of her glass, running her tip along the curved edge as she remembered what she'd felt hearing his voice. *Nothing. No butterflies, no stab of regret.* Just the familiar burn of something in her chest. Like indigestion from a bad burrito. 'To be honest, I have no idea what he wants any more. I don't even know why he bothered to call.'

'What about what you want? Does that even count?' His voice was strained, as if he was trying to calm himself down. 'He was an asshole to you, but I also know he can spin a good tale when he wants something.'

'I don't really want to talk about it, Tyler. I can't.' She forced herself to meet his eyes. 'Not with you.'

His brows shot up, his face growing cautious. 'Why not me?'

'I...' She watched his eyes search hers. What was she going to say? That she'd started comparing Bradley to Tyler, and found him lacking? How Bradley out there, stressing out and trying to build his future, had actually turned her off? How desperate she was to have a baby of her own? He wouldn't get it. 'I just feel weird about it.'

'Why?' His tongue peeked out, ran across his bottom lip and her eyes tracked every millisecond of the movement. *I wonder if the jolt I've felt around him lately would be there if we kissed.* 'Amber, tell me why. Please, Cherry. I have to know.'

His little nickname for her was almost enough to make her blurt everything out, but she squashed it down. She needed things to stop, just for a minute. She felt like she was on the carousel at the fair her grandmother always took her to when it came to Hebblestone. Her head was swimming, and the faces of everyone she held dear were zooming around her as she was spun around. Gripping on for dear life, she drew in a breath. Now was not the time to jump into some half-cocked feeling of lust, not when her mind was so chaotic. She couldn't afford to waste any more time. Risk something else not working out. Plus, it was Tyler! He wasn't some rebound. It was far too messy, far too soon. She needed her head clear, and her bed empty.

'Because we're friends.'

Tyler's jaw closed tight, and she could see the muscles in his bare forearms flex as he tightened them around the glass he was holding. 'That it?'

'Isn't that enough?' She drained her glass, welcoming the numbing amber liquid as it hit her body. 'It's over with Brad. Being single is better for me right now.' *Wow.* That last part even sounded lame to her own ears. 'I just want to enjoy my birthday next week, worry about the rest later.'

Tyler huffed. 'So that's your plan?' He turned his hulking frame on the stool, pinning her knees between his. 'Just let your life get away from you? I thought you were better than that, Amb. When I first started, you were full of big ideas and stuff you wanted to do.' He leaned closer, pointing a finger at her chest. 'Where's that girl, eh? Cos that girl wanted to get back to the Arms, make it her own. She wanted a big, full life.'

'She's still here,' Amber pushed his hand away, but he grabbed for hers. 'Just licking her wounds, that's all.'

'Yeah?' Pushing her palm against his own chest, he covered it with his broad palm. 'Well, my heart beats for that girl, and it's fucking breaking right now seeing you like this. If you let him, he'll worm his way back into your life. He doesn't pissing well deserve you, and I—' His voice fell away, and she felt the frustration roiling through her. She had no right to his words. She was denying this new aspect of them herself, but his hesitation still stung. Another man who couldn't just say what they meant. *If a man wants you, he'll be there*. Her quota of waiting for the opposite sex was full for the year. 'I—'

'You what, Ty?' They were causing a scene now. Her voice had shot up, and Tyler was so het up, she could feel his snarl under her palm. She ripped her hand away, leaning to get her purse and almost knocking the stool away in her haste to put some distance between them. 'I'm sick of all these little comments. Men! You never say what you damn well mean!'

His hand was still on his chest, as if he still felt her touch. 'I'm not the one *with* someone, am I.'

'No,' she replied hotly, feeling her face flush and her eyes sting with the threat of tears. *No way am I crying here. Not a damn chance.* 'No, Tyler. You're not. I'm not with Bradley, and yeah, we had our issues, God knows, but at least I tried with *someone*. You haven't been on one date since we met, so you're hardly an expert on relationships. I will make my dreams happen, man or no man. It's just not that easy.'

'Bullshit,' he rasped back, standing and coming to meet her chest to chest. Well, not exactly. With his size, she was pretty much hate-eyeing his pecs right now. In fact, she was so het up, she could probably reach over and nipple twist him to death if she wanted to. 'You let Bradley put you on hold, and you deserve more, Cherry. So much fucking more. You need to do your own shit!'

'Don't Cherry me, Master Chef!' She was shouting now.

Glancing around, half the pub suddenly looked away to study the wallpaper, the beermats, anything but look in their direction. Sharon was staring at them both, a look Amber didn't understand clouding her face. She looked almost... amused? *Nah*.

'Mr Master Chef if you don't mind, and I'll Cherry you as much as I like!'

Her head whirled around to laser focus on him again. His jaw was so tight, she thought his teeth might pop.

'And, anyway, if you're so good, why are you still here?' She jabbed her hands towards the kitchen. 'You could have gotten a better gig months ago. You didn't want to work with Bradley, you turn down offers all the time! You hark on about me being stuck, but you're still here too!'

'Yeah,' he fumed. 'I am, and it's a good job too, because you need someone to give you a kick up the behind! No-one else will do it, will they? You're on your own, Amber!'

'I DON'T NEED YOU!' she shouted back. That last comment had cut through her like a chuffing samurai sword. 'I'm fine on my own! I've been on my own most of my life, Tyler.'

He took a step back, his body draining of anger before her. 'Amber, I didn't mean that. I meant—'

'Oh, I know what you meant.' Her voice had dropped to a raspy whisper. 'And we're done talking. My relationship with Bradley is none of your business. What I do in my life is my problem, not yours.' Her chest was heaving with frustration and hurt. She was so upset, so hopping mad and embarrassed that she couldn't get a breath into her lungs deep enough to quell everything within. Gripping her bag to her like a life raft in the sea of watching faces, she headed straight upstairs to her flat. She knew she was being rude, but she was done. For once, she wasn't the nice woman who made everyone else feel welcome. Quite frankly, right now she wished that they'd all jog on. The problem with living in Hebblestone was that everyone knew your business. Before now, it had never been an issue. Maybe it had helped that Bradley didn't live here too, but she couldn't think about that right now. It just reminded her that he'd left rather than staying to fight for their relationship. That, sooner or later, everyone left.

She got to her flat door when she heard him.

'Tyler, just leave it. Please.'

Her stupid key wouldn't fit in the lock. Her shaky hands were rimming the metal, and she grabbed it with her other hand to steady it enough to push it home.

'I'm sorry. I didn't mean that.'

Her door opened, and she faced him with a weary look. She felt exhaustion running through her entire being.

'Yeah, you did. And you have a point with most of it, but I just don't want to talk about it any more.'

'What if I do?' She drank him in as he stood there. Halfway up the steps, his face contrite, stricken. 'I have more to say.'

'Whatever you have to say doesn't matter. I meant what I said.' She bit her lip. 'I've been feeling weird around you lately, and it's not right. I'm still getting over Bradley, and I have my own stuff going on. We just hurt each other, in front of everyone? Can't you see that?'

He looked devastated.

'I know.'

'That's not us, Tyler.' She laughed, but it was thin, strained. 'I need you in my corner, like before. You're right, you do look after me. Too much, probably.'

'I like taking care of you, Cherry.'

'Don't call me that.' Her eyes slammed shut as she tried to pull her thoughts together. 'Listen, Bradley is going to get the eatery open. You'll leave. Things will change and, if I don't do something, I will still be here, living this life. I don't want to lose you—'

'You won't,' he growled. 'Ever.'

Her heart did that flip-floppy thing it had been doing lately when he spoke to her like this. She really needed an ECG or something, because it felt like the damn thing stopped for a split second and then raced to catch up with itself.

'Good,' she started to turn away, not wanting to face him. 'Because you're a good friend. I wouldn't want that to change when so many other things might. I have to follow my own path.'

'Friend,' he echoed as she half hid behind the closing door. 'Right.' *Did I just hear him swallow?* 'Got you.' The door was open a crack now. She felt like when she was a bitty thing and her parents would get her to hide behind the couch so the rent collector couldn't spot them through the window. *Guilty, sly.*

'Goodnight,' she pushed out, hating herself.

He didn't reply until she'd locked the door behind her.

'Yeah. Goodnight, Amber. Sleep tight.'

# 6

The Slug patrons were pretty rubbish at hiding their intrigue as Tyler stomped back to his seat. Mary pushed a stiff double whisky in front of him, patting his hand. 'On me, love.' She smiled, before heading back off to help her husband start the bar shutdown. Sharon appeared at his side. He'd crossed his arms on the bar, was staring at the carpeted floor. When her pink-painted toenails came into view in her peep-toe stilettos, he groaned.

'I know, you don't have to say it.'

'Well, I will anyway. What were you thinking, saying that?'

He huffed, feeling the pop in his neck muscles as he dragged his tired body upright. Sharon's lip was curled up at one side as she looked at him. Well, through him. She was still pretty sozzled.

'I was trying to help. He called her, you know. Trying to talk his way back in. I want to knock his damn teeth out.'

*Still might, if he breaks her heart again.* One of the biggest mistakes he'd ever made was letting him chat her up on that night out. The first was not asking her out the second he'd got his head out of his arse and realised his new boss was the woman of his dreams. By the time he'd recovered from his own shitshow of a London love life, it was too late. Enter Bradley sodding Sloane.

He'd heard about his flash ladies' man reputation, and regretted his hesitation ever since. He'd never thought that Amber would look twice at a man like Bradley Sloane. Why would she? He was the opposite of everything she was. When Bradley and Amber had got talking that night, Tyler felt as though he'd been punched in the gut. He'd wanted to stride over there, pick Amber up and take her back to his cave and guard her from him. But then he'd seen how happy she'd been after. Bradley, to his credit, had changed too and he'd become almost worthy of her. Almost. When they'd talked about their business plans, he thought it might spur her on. He knew she was scared of not getting The Bingley Arms, but she'd been working every hour, telling him about her ideas and plans. He knew she could do it. He could see her, in that life. Having the family she wanted, back in her happy place. Hell, it was one of the reasons he'd stayed at the Slug so long: for the chance to see her pull it off. Maybe he'd even harboured the dream that she'd ask him to work there *with* her. He would have done that in a heartbeat.

But Bradley, the stupid prick, had taken one look at her and decided that she was the woman he'd wanted. He'd changed, been a good boyfriend, so Tyler had just let it happen. It wasn't like he could do much about it anyway. Couldn't offer her everything she wanted. He still bore his own scars, after all.

He'd been friend zoned pretty quickly. For the first few months of working there, Tyler had been broken, and then so tongue tied and love drunk around her, he'd been a big, gruff, monosyllabic idiot. By the time he'd gotten his bearings, they were friends, good friends. And then he'd waited some more, because he loved being her friend, loved being in her life. Amber Fitzpatrick was a woman who took care of everyone around her. She bought toys and treats and took them to the animal shelter every Christmas, because she said she couldn't bear the thought of the dogs waiting to be adopted not getting anything to play with. She ran a library book service for the regulars, going there once a week to collect and drop off books. She'd done the round trip ever since the mobile library had been forced to stop due to budget cuts. Bill's wife adored her for it, and Bill was always dropping off little lists of books his wife wanted, along with her signature fruit cake. A cake, incidentally, that Amber didn't even like. Every time she ooh'd and aah'd over the cake, and never said a word. He knew for a fact that she dropped it into the food bank bag she dropped off in the village. She even knitted woolly hats and scarves in winter for the old blokes who came to the pub for God's sake. When Tyler had asked her about it, she'd shrugged. 'Well, I don't want them to be cold,' she'd said. He'd bought her a tonne of wool balls the next September. Could still see the look on her face when she realised he'd remembered. How shocked she'd been because someone had thought of *her*. Even though she didn't quite understand the real reason he'd done it. He still had the hat and scarf she'd knitted him as a thank you. He'd smelled like her for a few days, with that creation around his neck. It had driven him half crazy, inhaling that scent on something she'd made just for him. Who didn't want to be there for a woman like that?

'Earth to Tyler,' Sharon flicked him on his forehead.

'What?' He jumped, pulling himself out of his stupor.

'I said, what's the plan?'

He grunted back at her, but she wasn't having it. 'Words. I need actual words. It's her birthday party next week. Are we still doing it or what?'

'Hell yeah, we are,' he nodded. 'Everything's on track.'

Sharon folded her arms, looking back at her date and giving him a 'five minutes' gesture before rounding back to him.

'Yeah, and how's that going to work, if you're not talking to her and her and Bradley are still talking? What if he shows up?'

'I don't give a shit about Bradley. He's not part of this. We planned it. If he comes, he comes.' *There's a bin out back with his name on it.*

'Ok-ay,' Sharon drawled. 'But what about you two? What's going on?'

'Nothing,' he grabbed for the whisky as Mary rang the last-orders bell. Drained half of it without blinking. 'We're friends. I apologised. We'll be good.'

Sharon sighed, taking the stool next to him.

'Yeah, but for how long?'

Tyler played with his glass, shooting her a blank stare.

Her sculpted brows lifted to her hairline. 'How long are you going to pretend you're not totally in love with her, eh? You just going to look after her and hope one day she realises? Doesn't sound like a good move to me.'

'I... don't...' Sharon shook her head at him, and he sagged further on his stool. 'How long have you known?'

Her returning look was full of pity. 'I've known pretty much the whole time. Why do you think I got her to help me arrange all those dates? I thought it would give you a push.'

'You did that even after Sloane came along.'

Sharon shrugged. 'Yeah well, it was funny too. There's not that much to do around here.'

'You're the worst,' he huffed. 'Does she know?'

She nudged her elbow with her own. 'Sorry, big guy. She doesn't have a clue.'

His head dropped to the bar with a thunk, making a couple of the nearby pub goers jump. Sharon yanked him back up by the hair, pulling off a beer-soaked coaster that had attached to his face.

She laughed, warm humour wrapping her words. 'If it's any conso-lation, she's been looking at you a little differently lately.'

Tyler wiped beer foam off his cheek. 'Yeah?' His chest warmed with something akin to hope. 'Ya think?'

Sharon's eyes narrowed. 'I think she tried to tell me tonight, but I didn't twig 'til I saw the two of you going at it.' She nodded to their surroundings. 'And shouting at her in front of this lot about her unfulfilled life is not the way to go. She's stubborn, you know that. Now Bradley's gone, she'll dig her heels in. It takes her forever to trust her own mind, let alone her heart.'

'I know,' he groaned, the ember of hope fizzing out in the thun-derstorm that rolled in his chest. 'I fucked everything up.'

'Not quite. You're her best friend. Aside from yours truly, of course. So do that. Be her best friend in your usual Williams way. You fire her up and she needs that, if she's going to shut that voice of doubt up and finally go for it.'

He rolled his lips together, feeling the dread slide over him. He felt like a bear in a cage. 'I don't know if I can do that. Now I know she might feel something.' He pulled at his own hair with a frustrated movement. 'Fuck, Sharon. I don't think I can just go back to that.' His lips curled when he thought of watching her with Bradley again. 'And that little shit doesn't deserve her. We can't let him crawl his way back in.'

Sharon leaned in, throwing an arm around him in solidarity. 'Oh, don't worry about Bradders, my angry little friend. She's not stupid, our girl. Let's just stick to the plan, throw the party and see what happens.'

'And be her friend,' he added. 'You really think it'll work?'

Sharon's look was fire. 'One thing I know about Amber Fitz-patrick is that she knows what she wants from life, and he's not it. Maybe when he was trying to woo her, but now the real slimy toad's peeked out? He might have been the one ending things, but only because she finally spoke up for herself. So, yeah, I know it will work. We have to let her figure it out, and be there. Be her friends, and love her.' She smirked at him, booping him on the nose with her index finger. 'And I know you can do that. Right?'

Sharon was right. This was Amber. Big-hearted, caring, beautiful Amber. The woman who lived with her dreams in her head, and her heart on her sleeve.

'Right.' He nodded, feeling the steely edge of determination flow through him. It wasn't over yet, if he had anything to say about it. Now she'd shown him she cared, hell – he'd walk through cut glass every day if he could get the chance to make her happy again. His words earlier had meant to put that passion back into her, not snuff it out. He would bend the world in half to get her what she wanted, even if she strode off into the damn sunset without him at the end of it. 'Friends.' He raised his fist, and Sharon bumped it, her face curling into a grin. 'I'll be the best damn friend Amber ever had.'

'That's the spirit!' Sharon laughed, patting him on the back.

---

## 7

'Don't get blue,' Sharon stage-whispered from the corner of her mouth. Amber barely heard her over the noise of the chair she was lounging in. The combination of the massaging motion under her, with the warm soothing water lapping at her feet, left her practically boneless.

'Eh?' She turned lazily, her head sitting between the massaging head rest. Sharon peeked at the beauty therapist, but she was off gathering lotions and bottles of gel polish in a little caddy.

'I said, don't get blue on your nails.'

'Oh.' Amber could feel the knots being slowly pummelled from her body. As birthday eves went, this one was shaping up to be better than she'd thought. When Sharon had arrived that morning, bearing balloons and gifts, she'd been about ready to pull the covers over her head and sleep the last day of her twenties away. Not that she could, given that she had a not-surprise surprise party to get ready for. Sharon whisking her off to a fancy salon in Harrogate was a nice distraction. They had a whole spa day planned, all booked and paid for, and she was so grateful, she'd almost burst into tears on the spot. Sharon had got her to pack a bag with some bits in it – flip flops, her charger and phone, a bikini for the massage, and told her she had precisely ten minutes to get ready and get downstairs.

She replayed what Sharon said in her head. 'Why not blue?'

Sharon flashed her a serious look, waggling her fingers. 'Dead people.'

Amber tittered, but Sharon's face didn't change. 'Dead people?'

'Yeah,' she nodded, pulling a face. 'You know, when you die – your nails go all blue.' A shiver ran through her, making Amber want to laugh again. 'Gross. Don't get blue.'

Amber shook her head, practically moaning as the therapist came and poured some minty smelling potion into the foot bath her feet were currently resting in. 'You watch far too much of that crime channel.'

Sharon shook her head. 'And you don't watch enough.' At Amber's critical gaze back, her lips finally tugged upwards. 'Get coral, suits you.'

The massage chair stopped for a second, and then their magical little cogs started whirring in the other direction. She melted further into the leather. 'Thanks for this, mate. Just what I needed.' She thought of the stack of gifts back at the flat and felt a pang of guilt in her gut. 'But you shouldn't have spent so much.'

Sharon winced. 'Well, to be honest, I didn't exactly pay for this.'

Amber's relaxed muscles coiled tight. 'What?' she hissed, her eyes darting around. If she had snuck them in here...

'Relax, it's paid. I'm not that bad!'

Amber's brow lifted. 'Oh, not that bad? Remember the Avril Lavigne concert we went to? That security guard practically carried us out of there. I knew I should have checked the tickets.'

Sharon laughed, slapping her hand on the leather arm. 'Oh my God, yeah! I'll give you that one.' She belly laughed, jabbing a finger in her direction. 'I swear, that other bloke with the hi-vis vest,

I thought he was going to throw you like a javelin when you went all tense on him.'

'I thought he was wrong!' she protested, face flushing as she remembered locking her body up as the burly security guard tried to eject them from the venue. At one point, she could swear she heard Avril laugh. The whole crowd was watching her. 'How was I supposed to know you'd snuck us in there with that shady roadie! You told us they were VIP!'

She groaned. 'Oh... Victor. Don't remind me. You know I think he'd used that one before.'

Another therapist came past, giving them a glass of Champagne and a selection of gel-polish samples on a key-chain-looking thing.

'No rush ladies, take all the time you need to decide.'

'Thanks.' Sharon raised the glass at her. 'Bubbles as well, eh?' She held her flute out to Amber's. 'Happy thirtieth, mate! Tomorrow's the big day!'

Amber chinked her glass, taking a long sip. 'Thanks. I think I'll need thirty of these to get over the shock.' Her eyes narrowed. 'So, who did pay for this then?'

For a moment, she thought of Bradley. Maybe he'd done it before the break-up. He hadn't sent her a card, or been in touch. She was hoping that he'd just leave it alone now. She had daydreamed that he'd give her a ring for her birthday, once upon a couple of months ago. Now, she just felt relief that he wasn't going to be there, or stand her up like he usually did. She wanted her thirties to be Sloane, and drama, free.

When her friend didn't answer, she turned to scrutinise her. 'Who paid for this, Shaz?'

'Tyler.'

'Tyler?'

Sharon nodded.

'Yep. Paid for both of us, the whole day.' She raised her brows. 'The full package too.'

Amber felt her heart throw itself against her rib cage. 'When?'

'Does it matter when?'

Amber thought of her friend, back home in the kitchen, working away with Ben, and smiled. 'No. Not really.' Her gut twisted when she thought of their fight. The way he'd pushed her to fight for her own life. When did she stop fighting for it herself? She'd screamed at him, pushed him away, and he'd still come after her. 'I feel bad now.'

'And why is that?' Sharon's face was all knowing, and Amber had to drain the rest of her glass before replying.

'You know why. I was awful to him the other night. He's been nothing but nice since, and I feel like a prize dickhead.'

He had been more than nice. The day after the bowling alley, he'd snapped back into being her friend. The grumpy, scowling hulk of a gentle giant she knew and...

'That's Tyler for you. Mr Dependable.' Sharon leaned back in her chair, pressing a button on the control and moaning like a porn star at the increased pressure. 'Oh, dear Lord, that's better than sex.'

Amber huffed. 'Yeah, well it's as close as I'm going to get these days.'

Sharon tutted at the side of her. 'Well, that's what parties are for. Maybe your luck will be in sooner than you think.'

'Not a chance. No more men for me. I don't have time for all that now. I have to get serious if I'm going to get the Arms.' *And the baby.* 'I'm good single.' Sure, she felt a pang of... something whenever she saw her friend these days. All week, he'd been the usual Tyler. Master of the kitchen, bringer of pastries. He'd fallen back into his easy pattern, their easy pattern. Before all the lustful looks and snatched conversations that left her breathless and wanting to hear more. But she had a plan and, after her birthday, she'd resolved to get on with it. She was going to fix the business proposal and have faith that everything would come right in the end. It had to, right? Tyler would go and work somewhere else; their sexual tension would fade. She'd have everything she wanted.

'So, that's it? You're just staying single?'

'Yep. Easier that way. No wasting my time, no waiting for someone else to show up. I can just do my own thing. Master of my own destiny.'

'Sounds lonely,' Sharon pointed out.

'Yeah,' Amber sighed. 'Well, I'm a hell of a lot less lonely since I got dumped, so riddle me that, Batman.'

'Aww honey,' Sharon reached for the polish samples, selecting a dark, dull-looking blue. 'Not all men are like Sloane. You and Bradley were like blue polish on toenails.' She gave her a pointed look, holding up the navy-blue thumbnail. 'Looked good in some lights.' She stuck her tongue out of the side of her mouth, shutting her eyes comically. 'Dead when you look closer.'

# 8

Hours and a heavenly few treatments later, and Amber was back outside the doors of the Slug, Sharon's arm linked through hers.

They got changed at the spa, and Amber felt amazing in a pretty, peach-coloured dress she'd splashed out on on their recent post-break-up shopping trip. 'It looks great with the coral,' Sharon had winked when she saw it on, and Amber had felt a huge wave of affection for her friend. She might not have family, or a partner she could rely on, but she did have her. This place, and the people in it. And Tyler. The thought of seeing him tonight, out of their work relationship for the first time since the bowling fiasco, churned her gut. She didn't quite know what she was going to be walking into. Or what she would feel when she saw him. Over the past week, Tyler Williams had been running through her head so many times, her grey matter felt like it had run a marathon.

'So, you ready?' Sharon beamed. 'Tonight is the start of your new thirty and fabulous life!'

Wow. That hit Amber like a sucker punch. She was right. Tonight was the last night of her twenties. Tomorrow, she would wake up thirty years old. She'd been thinking of this for months.

Planning on how she was going to make her next decade count. A few months ago, she thought she might be getting engaged soon. Starting her life with Bradley. *The time is now, Amber. If you are still here this time next year, single – floating through life and running the Slug – you will only have yourself to blame.*

'Amber? You okay?'

'Huh?'

Sharon came to stand in front of her, rubbing her shoulders.

'Sorry. Was just thinking about... something.' She caught her bottom lip between her teeth. 'You ever think about having a family, Shaz?'

Her friend eyed her for a long moment, her eyes boring into her. 'Sometimes,' she admitted. 'Since mum moved away with husband number three, I've been thinking that maybe it wouldn't be so bad to have someone. I dunno.' She shrugged. 'I know you want more, Amber. It will happen. Just because things didn't work out, it doesn't mean that the next thing won't.'

Amber shrugged. 'Maybe. If my eggs will hold out that long without a freezer.'

'Eggs?' Sharon asked. 'As in fertile eggs? You've really been thinking about it that much?'

'A little.' She bit her lip. 'A lot, actually. I don't want to have to date someone else for a couple of years, you know. That whole scene is depressing, and I'll be so busy with the business. Finding the time to even find someone half decent takes time. And then what if he doesn't have the same goals as me? You know what men are like: half of them have the attention span of a sandwich. Women who go into relationships all baby crazy aren't exactly snapped up.'

'I had no idea.' Sharon squeezed her tighter. 'I think you have time, though; you never know what's around the corner.'

Amber shrugged. 'Yeah, well – maybe some things just need to be done instead of waiting for the perfect situation that might never come.' She thought back to the site, just waiting for her to place the order that might just make her a mother.

'Have you told anyone else about this?' Sharon asked, fiddling with her bag. 'Tyler maybe?'

'Tyler doesn't need to hear about my baby fever, Sharon. He already thinks I should be focusing on the Arms now Bradley's gone. I can't see him being on board with this, and I don't need anyone's opinions.'

'Huh.' Sharon didn't look convinced. 'Still, I think it might be worth a conversation. Tonight, maybe.'

Amber thought of the guy waiting inside for them. A vision of Tyler popped into her head, lifting a toddler into his broad, muscly arms. Teaching a cute little kid how to make cherry pastries. *Shit. Stop that. Shut it down. Friend, not baby daddy.* 'Nope. Not tonight, it's party time. Just ignore me,' she said, shaking herself out of it. 'Birthday blues, I think.'

Sharon smiled back, but there was something in her expression that told Amber she wasn't going to let this drop for long. 'I have a cure for that.' She thumbed at the bar behind her. 'Let's get pissed, eh? Get your surprise game face on.'

Linking arms, Sharon pulled her towards the pub doors. It was eerily quiet, and just for a second Amber's heart thudded. She steeled herself for what she was walking into, and felt Sharon push her through the entrance.

The first thing she saw was not people, but balloons. The whole ceiling was full of them, all kinds of colours. And then the place exploded. 'Surprise!'

The opening bars of Stevie Wonder's 'Happy Birthday' blasted out from the speakers in front of a DJ stand, and the whole pub was there. Everyone from Bill and his wife, Mary and her husband

Mick, Ben and his wife, the staff from the dog shelter, Grandma's old crew. She jumped at the noise, despite herself, her hands flying up to cover her squeal. 'Happy birthday, Amber!' they all shouted together, laughing and clapping at her shocked face. Party poppers went off around her, and Sharon shouted 'Yes! Paaarrrrty!' behind her. At the bar, she could see Sharon's construction guy waiting. *Hmm, interesting.* Next to him, though, was someone who made her heart stutter to a shuddering stop.

Tyler strode across the room, the now animated crowd parting for him as he batted away well-wishers and came to a stop in front of her. He looked... lickable. There was no flannel tonight. *No sirree.* He was wearing a peach-coloured button-down shirt that only served to show off his thick, muscled chest, and a pair of black dress trousers that looked like they were stitched onto his body by tiny little angels. In his huge hands, a bunch of her favourite blooms were wrapped in tissue paper and fancy, gold-tinted cellophane. His hair was freshly washed, though she could see from the sides he'd run his hands though it a few times. There were tiny little cowlicks sticking out of it, which only served to make her brain rearrange him in her head further. This was Tyler, but tonight, he looked... better. No, not better. That wasn't right. He still looked like him, but it was as if her eyes were truly seeing him for the first time. It took her a hot minute to remind herself where she was, who she was standing in front of. To breathe.

He held the flowers out to her, and her hands somehow started working well enough to reach out for them.

'Thank you,' she managed to croak out. 'This is... amazing.'

'Group effort. Happy birthday, Cherry.' He grinned. She didn't miss his eyes, looking her up and down lazily. His cheeks heated. 'You look...'

'Thirty?' she cut in, trying not to combust on the spot. Even in the crowd, it felt like they were the only two people in the world. Everyone around them was getting drinks in, settled in for the party. Others were leaving gifts in a little pile on a table by the bar. 'Although, after our spa day, I do feel a little less decrepit.'

His smile tugged at a corner of his full lips, forming a dimple she'd never spotted before. She wanted to put her finger in the little dip. She clenched the flowers a little tighter. Nodding at his shirt, which was a shade akin to her dress and nails, she smirked. 'We match.'

'Glad you had a good day.' His eyes dropped to her mouth, and it looked like it cost him to pull them back to her eyes. 'Sharon picked out the shirt. Told me if I wore flannel tonight, she'd burn all my clothes in the car park.'

Amber giggled. 'Sounds like Sharon.' After a pause, she added, 'I like your flannels, lumberjack.'

His eyes crinkled in the corners. 'You look mesmerising, Amber.' She was about to shrug him off, but he stepped closer, and her rebuttal died in her throat. 'Prettiest woman I've ever seen.' His gaze turned heated. His jaw ticking with what looked like... arousal, and then it was gone. His face dropped back into her best friend once more. 'Enjoy your party,' he said, leaning in. For the briefest slice of time, she breathed in his aftershave, like sea salt and the ocean, and her head lifted to meet his automatically. His gait was tight, and then she felt his lips brush against her forehead. 'See you later,' he huffed out, as if the touch of his mouth hadn't just branded her skin. He left her standing there, swallowed by the crowd as they descended around her.

By the time she made her way to the bar, Sharon already had a drink waiting for her.

'Peach is my colour, eh? I could kill you,' Amber threatened, but Sharon knew she was full of it. 'Thank you, mate. I mean it. This is great.'

'You're welcome.' She beamed, passing her a shot glass. 'It was nothing. Well, it wasn't nothing... but it was mostly Tyler, if I'm honest. If he ever gets bored of cooking, he'd make an awesome party planner.' She waved a hand at all the decorations, the little touches around the place. There was even a photo wall. Some of the puppies from the shelter with their little gifts, and what looked like a police line-up photo. Leaning forward, she saw it was some of the regulars, all posing with their hats and scarves. 'He's been planning it for a while,' she added, following her gaze. Amber looked around the place, her heart full.

'I can't believe he did all this.'

Sharon clinked her shot glass against Amber's. 'Can't you? I swear, sometimes you don't see what's right in front of you.'

'Come on, I know he likes me. I'm getting that, but it's Tyler. He doesn't do relationships.'

'I think he'd do you,' Sharon retorted, just as the shot hit the back of Amber's throat. It made her cough. 'Oops!' She necked her own, sucking through her teeth as the alcohol hit. 'You know what I meant.'

'We're friends.'

Sharon's brows shot up.

'Okay, okay.' Amber laughed. 'We're friends who fancy each other, but it's not going anywhere. He's leaving; I have my thing. I just got out of a relationship, and if I'm going to do the baby thing, I need to get serious.'

Sharon reached for the tequila bottle. 'Mate, baby schmaby. A man like that does not put all this work in for a friend. Tyler's a good mate, yeah, but he doesn't look at me like that.' She nodded behind her and, when Amber turned, Tyler was there. Talking to Bill and his wife, but his gaze was locked on hers. 'I'm just saying, maybe things happen for a reason. You're single now, and he did all this when you were with Bradley. The man didn't even send you a damn card, Amber, and he's not here.'

'A man will show up when he wants to,' she echoed, her eyes still on Ty. He raised his pint glass towards her, and she blushed a grin back.

'Exactly,' Sharon said. 'Now drink this, and let's have some bloody fun for once.'

# 9

A couple of hours later, the party was in full flow. Customers and friends were all living it up. Bill was dancing with his wife in the corner, seemingly unaware of their surroundings as they slow danced to a song that no-one else could hear. It made Amber's eyes sting watching them. Knowing their love triangle back story made it all the sweeter, and she couldn't help but lament the fact that she might not ever get that. Bill had been married at twenty-five. She was already well behind in the game of love.

*Prettiest woman I've ever seen.*

Tyler's words pierced through her thoughts, drowning them out. It was laughable really. Her best male friend, the man she'd come to rely on as a friend, the one who didn't date, and he was the one who'd hit her with the one line she would take to her damn grave. She knew those words by heart now; her eyes had recorded the way he'd looked at her. The smouldering gaze he'd focused on her as if she was the only woman in the world. God, she'd still be thinking about that when she was eighty years old and sitting in an easy chair in her bed socks. Even then, it would keep her warm just to think of it. Just when she'd decided to go it alone, in every sense of the word. Just when she had decided that God and fate willing, she would be a mother by her next birthday. This night kinda sucked. She had everyone around her, but she still felt alone. Like someone up there was having a laugh. Sending her Tyler at a time when she couldn't do a damn thing about it. Just like she and Bradley had been, they were on different paths. It wouldn't be fair to stop Tyler from having his plans. As soon as he got the right job, he'd move on. What was she going to do: tell him she liked him, but wanted a kid? It wouldn't be fair. She didn't even know if he wanted kids. He'd never talked about wanting a girlfriend, so a baby was a bit of a far-fetched stretch.

'Shazza.' She nudged her friend and nearly toppled her off her bar stool. They were propping up the bar like a couple of middle-aged lushes. 'How come people want different things all the time? I mean, whatever happened to just meeting someone, falling in love and making a life together, eh?'

Sharon stopped chewing on her straw. 'Are you thinking about that knobhead? I knew something was eating you!' She pounded her fist on the bar, missing and smacking herself on the thigh. 'Ooh! I'm going to murder him. I was going to let it slide, but that's it now. Upsetting you on your bloody birthday. I am going to murder him, and Tyler is going to chop him into teeny little bits in the kitchen, and then I'm going to stick *those* bits into a wood chipper and splat him. All over Sloane's' front window.'

'Stay off the crime channel, Hannibal. It's fine.' She giggled at the vision of Brad, red misted all over his fancy restaurant front. 'I'm not talking about Bradley. I just mean in general, you know. You make plans, and then some... thing comes along that you didn't even see coming. But you can't really have that... thing, but it's all you can think about. And it's so handsome and funny, and makes you feel things you forgot a person could feel, and it feels so nice, and comforting...' When she looked across at her mate, Sharon's jaw was dragging on the bar.

'Some... thing, eh?' She was trying to raise a sceptical brow, but with the tequila they'd enbibed, it was more of a gurn. 'Does this something wear flannel and plan surprise parties?'

'No.' Amber winced. 'And I'm not upset. Just philosophical. I'm having a great time!'

Sharon reached for her arm and swung her seat around to face the revellers. Now the karaoke session was over, which had been hilarious, the DJ was spinning discs, and most people were on the dance floor. The rest were all drinking and laughing, chatting in the buffet line. She smiled, watching them all. They'd all come for her. 'Tell your face that then. Look at how much fun people are having! Everyone here loves the bones of you. I wish you could see that, and not get stuck in what ifs. New life, new year, remember?' Leaning in, she added, 'Go and talk to Tyler. Tell him what you just told me. You like him, and that's okay, Amber! This is your year. Go get what you want for once.'

Did she want Tyler? *God yes.* She wanted to see what these feelings were. To see where he stood. What would be the harm? Technically, she wasn't thirty yet. It was kismet. She could talk to him, see where the land lay. By the time she woke up tomorrow, she would know what to do. 'You're right,' she finally said. She turned to face the bar, catching her reflection in the mirror behind the till. 'Oh God,' she exclaimed, seeing the panda eyes her mascara had left from rubbing her eyes. 'I look like roadkill.'

Sharon reached into her purse, and a minute later, she was doing things to Amber's face. Amber let her, sitting still like a child would while her mother cleaned her up. She let herself gaze off into the distance as Sharon brandished brushes and wands and wet wipes. If she stopped the voices in her head, the doubts, she knew tonight was perfect. A chance to gauge where they were at. Help her decision making. They needed to have this out, once and for all.

A movement from the back caught her eye. Tyler was just coming out of the kitchen, his homemade pizza cut into slices on the silver platter he was carrying. He chatted to a couple of people along the way to the buffet table, laughing as someone in the queue said something to him. He'd been milling around all night she realised, making sure the food was ready. *Keeping his distance,* something in her head spat out. Maybe he was confused too. He was still there though, her Tyler. Being all Tyler-like, taking care of people in his quiet, broody way. Checking everyone had a drink. Ben was working the bar tonight with his wife, Shayla, who was on the payroll and often helped out ad-hoc when they needed some extra staff and Mary couldn't cover. The pair of them looked happy too, at home behind the polished wood as they served drinks and still seemed to be enjoying the festivities.

She saw Ty taking some empty trays back to the kitchen, and he winked at her when he caught her watching him. He disappeared through the kitchen doors, and she sighed involuntarily. The conversation they'd had in her office sprang into her head. All the little conversations they'd shared lately. If Ben hadn't walked in that day, she would have confessed to the huge crush she'd had on him when they'd first met. Back when they first started working together at the Slug. Both still fresh faced and idealistic about their chosen vocations. Perhaps if they hadn't become such fast friends, things might have been different. She'd thought he would never be interested, she remembered. He never seemed to string a sentence together when she tried to talk to him, and then she picked up on the fact he didn't date. The way he rolled his eyes when Sharon mentioned him going on a date. She had often thought he just needed to meet the right person, but he never had. Once or twice, she thought she'd seen something behind that scrunched-up face of his, but then the cement set as friends. Good friends. A friend she couldn't in all honesty live without.

So, she'd never said a word and the little flutters in her tummy had dissipated quickly as he became one of her best friends. One of her favourite people in the world, as it went, and Lord knows she didn't have many of them. Still, in her semi-sozzled state, the sight of him in that peach shirt tonight had woken a butterfly or two. *Who am I kidding?* After that wink, his words earlier, the contents of her stomach were a lepidopterist's wet dream.

'Beautiful,' Sharon suddenly announced, bringing her out of her daydream. Amber smiled at her before looking into the bar back at her reflection. Wow. She did look good. The panda eyed look was now a make-up artist level smoky eye. Her puffy eyes were hidden beneath plumped up, dark lashes, and her hair looked tousled and styled at the same time. She looked... great and, turning to her friend, she pulled her in for a hug. 'Thanks mate, I love it.'

Sharon squeezed her back. 'When you feel like shit, looking great on the outside helps. I'm going to check on the rabble, and then we are getting well and truly sloshed, birthday girl. Deal?'

She nodded, blinking hard against the grateful tears that threatened her perfect make-up. 'Deal.'

Sharon slid off her stool and into the throng, leaving her alone with her thoughts. Bradley wouldn't have fit in here. The thought hit her from nowhere. It was true though. When he did come into the pub, he didn't make an effort with the customers. They were punters to him, she knew. He only sucked up to the wealthier set of his customers at Sloane's. She'd seen it for herself first hand. The Slug clientele was more family than bread and butter. He would probably have spent half the night on his phone anyway. Tyler would have been there, on her arm. Giving her little kisses as they chatted to people. He'd have spoken to everyone, as he always did, not because they could be a tool to something better, but because he was generally interested in other people. He'd have been attentive. Maybe even got her a gift and given her it in front of everyone. He'd paid for a whole spa day and sworn Sharon to secrecy instead. Caring for her from the sidelines yet again. Right now, she wished that she'd been braver sooner. Realised what was in her kitchen all along. She had a prince for a best friend, and she'd spent a whole year kissing a damn frog.

'I'm back.' Sharon smiled, bringing her out of her daydream. She set a tray of shots on the bar, and Amber necked hers without hesitation. 'All sorted. Everyone is happy, and I've told the DJ to not overdo the karaoke later. That first session made my ears bleed. Also,' She smiled kindly, 'I've told him no sappy love songs unless one of the regulars request them.' Amber watched her friend scan her face. 'Well, you look miserable from your expression, but your make-up is amazing.'

Amber couldn't help but grin, checking herself out again in the mirror. 'Not miserable, just thinking. I do look good. It actually suits me. And the dress.'

Sharon grinned. 'You look good, right? I've wanted to give you a make-over for a while. Your bone structure is killer.'

'What's killer?' Tyler appeared behind them, a whiff of his aftershave enveloping them. 'The food's all out, everything's off. I thought I'd come for a drink. The clean down can wait 'til tomorrow.' His eyes narrowed when he looked at her. 'What's up with your face? Hey! Don't slap me!' Sharon had swiped him on his tattooed arm. Amber could make out the peep of dark ink under his shirt cuff.

Sharon pulled a face. 'Don't be a dick, then! I gave her a little make-over! She looks good! Sexy!'

'Yeah,' Amber agreed, dropping her voice to sound sultry. 'Sexy.'

Tyler's brown eyes bored into her. She tried to focus on them, but it was a bit too much effort.

'I didn't say I didn't like it. I was referring to your Eeyore expression.' His features hardened. 'You're drunk.'

'Nope,' Amber refuted, selecting a blue shot and beckoning Sharon to do the same. 'But I will be soon!'

Tyler turned to Sharon. 'What the hell happened? You were supposed to be watching her while I got the food done!'

Sharon shrugged, and Amber stuck out a rather blue-tinged tongue at him. 'She was looking after the place. I don't need a babysitter. Fine on my own, remember?' *Oops.* Her nerves were mixing with the tequila and making her snarky.

She was pretty sure she heard Tyler curse under his breath but couldn't be sure over the now pulsing dance music. His hand snaked out to grab the next shot before Amber necked it, but she was quicker.

'Eugh, cinnamon!' She gagged at the taste. Tyler appeared bar side and swept the rest of the shots out of the way. Ben and Shayla wisely kept their distance, shepherding the customers to the other end of the bar to be served. Tyler gave Ben a nod. *God, he was annoyingly hot when he was being all protective. Always looking after things. Bleurgh. That shot was rank.* 'Tyler! Gimmethoseback!'

'Nope.' He placed a large glass of ice water in front of her. 'Drink that. Sharon, don't let her drink any more.' He was looking over Amber's head at something, and she turned her head to try to see what he was looking at. She could make out a couple of men-shaped blobs, both puffing their chests out at each other in an unmistakable 'fight me' way. 'I won't be a minute.'

'And where is he going?' Amber looked at Sharon, but she could see two of her. 'I'm drunk,' she stated unnecessarily. 'Not a fun drunk, either.' She rested her head on the bar top. 'I just bit his head off, not a great start, eh? God, why is it so hard to tell someone you fancy them?'

Sharon wasn't listening. She'd already wandered off. She thought she saw Tyler out of the corner of her eye. *Shit. Did he hear that?* Deciding that the water might not be a bad idea, Amber turned on her stool, watching everyone have fun around her. 'Oh, that's where you went.' Sharon was sucking face with construction guy. She made a mental note to quiz her about him later. Sharon didn't do relationships, but she seemed to be gravitating to this guy. The fact she hadn't talked about him spoke volumes about it being something different. She looked away, feeling like a creep on a private moment. She people watched for a while, and when no-one seemed to notice her there, she headed upstairs. Tyler was nowhere to be seen and given that she was finding it hard to string a sentence together, perhaps that 'talk' would have to wait. The lack of food she'd eaten had mixed with the alcohol pretty quickly, and she needed a minute on her own. She had snacks upstairs, and a bottle of cheap Champagne she'd been saving for a special occasion in her fridge. Since it wasn't her actual birthday for a few more hours, and her whole life seemed banal, she figured it was time to open the sucker. The new year, new me stuff could wait just a little longer.

# 10

'So that's where you got to.' Tyler found her a few hours later, laptop and half empty bottle of Champagne open on the coffee table. He nudged her legs, which were currently hanging over the end of the couch. 'Shift up.'

She groaned, turning to sit properly as he flumped down next to her. 'How's the party going? It's been pretty quiet.'

Tyler nodded to her stereo, which was currently playing her favourite best of the nineties playlist. 'Well, I'm surprised you could hear it over the blasts from the pasts you've been playing.'

She poked him in the ribs. 'Hey, you love this playlist! Don't think I don't hear you using it in the kitchen.'

'Damn you, shared Spotify account!' He shook a fist dramatically. 'Everyone went home. Sharon says she'll come give you a hand in the morning. Just give her a ring.' He chuckled to himself. 'Hey, I think she took that building-site guy home, you know?'

'Never!' Amber gasped. 'Back to hers? She never does that!'

'I know. I think she might actually like this guy.'

'Wow,' Amber breathed, sitting back against the cushions. 'Even Sharon's moving on with her life. Nice.'

She felt Tyler's arm come around her, and she leaned into him automatically.

'You've had a bad couple of months. That doesn't mean your life's crappy, Amber.'

'Doesn't it? I mean, what else is going right exactly? I don't have the pub; I still live and work here—'

'Hey! It's not so bad here, right?' He turned her to look at him. 'It's just a bad day, Ambs, not a bad life. You make this place. The regulars come here because of you, the atmosphere. The brewery know that, deep down. You're only young still, plenty of time for your five-year plan.'

'Not all of it,' she muttered. 'I might not have many eggs left to put in my basket.'

'What?'

'Nothing. I suppose you're right really, and tonight was great. Everyone I love under the same roof, getting on and having fun.'

'You did have that; all of your friends left gifts and cards. When you disappeared, they were all concerned. I had to strong arm half of them out the door.'

'They are pretty great, aren't they. Thanks for tonight, Ty.' He shrugged, but she covered his hand with hers. 'I mean it. It's nice knowing I have you looking out for me.'

'Always.' He grinned. 'And, for the record, I'm glad that you're not with Bradley any more.'

Amber swallowed. *Not as glad as I am right now.* 'We were too different. I should have seen it a long time ago, but, when you want something to work out, it's easy to ignore the alarm bells.'

His jaw clenched. 'He never saw what he had, Amb. You need a partner in life, not someone who only makes time for you when he feels like it. He should have been there. Done more to show you how special you are.'

'I don't think a guy like that exists in real life.' *Yes, he does, and he makes a damn fine pastry.*

'Of course he does,' Tyler refuted before she'd even finished her sentence. 'Trust me, there's a guy out there who would worship the fucking ground you walk on. Who would move heaven and earth to give you what you want. What you need. A guy who wouldn't have you sitting alone at your own damned birthday party. He would make sure you knew exactly what you were worth to him, and everyone you love. No man would ever hurt you again once he knew you were his. No-one would get near you, Amb. A guy like that would make it his one fucking mission in life to make you smile every single day. A man who would never stop making sure your body and mind both knew how beautiful you are, inside and out.'

*Wow.* She didn't want him to stop talking. She wanted to hear more about this guy Tyler knew so much about, but the air was already thick with his declaration. And that's what it had sounded like. It wasn't some casual conversation. What he had just told her felt like a solemn vow from someone who'd thought a whole lot about the subject. Someone who sounded like the perfect person to have in your corner. The longer she sat in stunned silence, the tenser she felt his body become around her. 'Well,' she said, clearing her throat when the word came out as a raspy croak. 'Maybe I should hold out for him, then.' She was still in the nook of his arm, his muscled bicep enveloping her.

'Yeah, maybe you should. Maybe he was an idiot for not speaking up sooner.' He paused and Amber couldn't breathe. As if all the air had been sucked out of the room. 'I never thought Bradley was good enough for you.'

It was her turn to stiffen. 'I still remember him in the beginning,' she confessed. 'He was kinda that guy you're describing.'

'He's nothing like the guy I'm describing,' Tyler spat back, his whole chest rumbling with the conviction of his retort. He sat up, pulling her with him. Grasping her gently by the chin to turn her to him. 'Don't you get it, Amber? You're the fucking prize. Nothing else comes close.'

With her eyes locked onto his like this, seeing the want and need swirling in those irises was unavoidable. This was another moment between them, she knew. Another step that blurred the lines between friendship and... whatever this was. Lust? Want? *More?*

She'd thought about him naked before, but the curiosity was freed by the alcohol. Zipping to the surface. She wondered what his tattoos would taste like under her tongue. What he was packing under his drawstring chequered chef's trousers. They'd been swimming together before. She still dined out on the memory of that bulge in his swim shorts as they'd mucked about splashing each other in the water. The way he'd said he'd be out after another couple of lengths. She'd wondered at the time if he was really waiting for his own length to cool down, but then in the car on the way home, it was business as usual. Mates hitting the burger drive thru and talking about the merits of burger relish over ketchup. There was so much in her head, so much to say to him. To ask. She wanted to comb through the last few years and ask him everything she'd wondered about over their friendship. The times he'd said little things, done little things for her. She wanted to know what made Tyler Williams' heart beat in his chest. What came out was something she never expected.

'I want a baby.'

He was so still at first, she started to doubt she'd said it aloud. His eyes crinkled in the corners, his determined stare turning to a bemused grin, before it fell away to nothing but confusion.

'What?'

She licked at her lips, trying to get some moisture back in her mouth.

'I... I've been thinking about it a lot. Years, actually. With the break-up and everything, I've been thinking about how much time I've wasted.'

She watched as he looked to the ceiling, saw the column of his throat work as he swallowed. 'I didn't know you and Bradley were at that point.'

'We weren't, not really. We talked about it in the beginning, but that was all it was. Talk, I mean. Now I'm single, I don't want to wait any more.'

'I... don't think I understand. You're thirty. You have plenty of time.'

'That's the point, though.' She smiled ruefully. 'I don't want to wait. It's 2024. I realised I don't have to. I could just do it, and once the idea was in my head, I can't get it out. I could do it. The Arms, have a baby. I don't want to look back later and have regrets.' His brown eyes were searching her face, but it was one of those rare times that she couldn't read him. 'Haven't you ever thought about it? Having a family?'

'No.' No hesitation there. 'Not for a long time.'

'What changed?' she asked, feeling her heart break. *I mean, what were you expecting? Him to offer up his bloody sperm?* She felt stupid. Her Champagne-loose tongue had scared the shit out of him. They hadn't even kissed, for God's sake. They hadn't even laid their cards on the table about what they were to each other. Still, the biological ticking clock wasn't something she could hit the snooze button on. Even for the man in front of her. He knew now. It was out there. 'Was it because of your ex?'

'That was a lifetime ago,' he muttered. She felt something shift between them, fall away. His jaw clenched tight, fingers sliding away from her chin. He turned away, hands dropping to rest on his lap as he hung his head. She mourned the loss of his heat as he pulled away from her, and the moment. 'It's late. I should go. I'll be in early for the clean-up.'

'Ty, I—'

The feeling of helplessness grew with each step he took away from her. Even in their close proximity, she'd never felt as far from him as she did right now. The space between them was an ache, tangible in her chest. He paused in the doorway, his fists clenching at his sides. 'You know, sometimes I really regret being your friend. I regret a lot of things I can't seem to take back.' His eyes flashed with something she'd not seen before. Resignation? Pain. Then it was gone. 'Drink some water, please.'

'Tyler.'

He shook his head, a small smile not quite hitting his lips. 'I'm good, Amber. Don't worry about me. I just want you to be happy. To get what you want in life. Drink that water.' He went to leave but turned back at the last minute. 'Happy birthday, Cherry. You really did look beautiful tonight. You always do to me. Sleep tight.'

She sat there, sobering up as she listened for him leaving. When the back door closed behind him, she finally let out the breath she'd been holding. He'd called her Cherry again. It had been a while since he'd used his nickname for her freely as he did now, in honour of the cherry Danish he had started making, just because she'd told him it was her favourite. Now he used it all the time, and she loved the sound of it. Waited for his lips to utter it daily. She was so restless right now, sitting there in Tyler's wake. She could smell his aftershave on her clothing. It lingered like his parting words. The look on his face when she'd told him what she wanted. Did she really expect anything different? What kind of man would have any other response, really? They weren't even together. Sure, she liked him. A lot, but it was new, and fragile. If she was going to do this, she needed to go all in. Make the smart choices and, at least this way, it was easier. Tyler didn't want kids. Hell, he'd practically run out of the place at the thought. Maybe his ex had done a bigger number on him then she'd imagined. *What was her name again? Lauren? Laurel?* He never spoke about her, apart from alluding to the fact that the break-up had been messy.

Either way, it didn't matter now. He'd gone, and she hadn't changed her mind about her plans in the last half hour. She couldn't go on like this. She knew she wouldn't sleep. There was no chance of that, with her mind whirring. Looking at the clock on the shelf, she saw it was just after midnight.

'Well,' she said to the empty room. 'Happy fecking birthday to me.' When she spotted her laptop, she took a swig of water, and fired it up. She was going to hit her thirties running.

Opening up her business plan, she read through what she had written months ago. It was pretty good; even with her tequila goggles on, she could see it was going to be hard for the bank to turn down. She felt excited, until she decided to read her emails. There was one from the council and, when she opened it up, her heart sank. When her grandmother had passed, her friend Denise, who worked in the planning department, had pulled her aside at the funeral and told her that she would do anything she could to make sure that the Arms would be there waiting when she was ready.

She read the words over and over, willing them to make sense, to disappear.

So happy to hear you're finally doing it, but I was surprised that you don't plan to keep it as a pub. I'm sure your grandmother would be happy, either way. An eatery sounds swish! Good luck to you and Bradley! Planning don't have a meeting until the end of August, so I'll be in touch. Remember, you didn't hear it from me.

Have a great birthday!
Love, Denise

'What the... Bradley is going after the Arms?'

She read it over and over, wracking her brain. Why the hell would he do this? They had never talked about the Arms being anything but hers. She thought back to the last few months. His pulling away, furtive phone calls. He'd been struggling to find a good venue for a while, wanting something in the heart of Hebble-stone. Well, he'd obviously found it. He'd strung her along until he got the planning go ahead. Once he had that, the investors would pony up the money... and the Arms would be his.

She thought of his face when she'd given him an ultimatum. The way he'd walked away so easily. Talked of things he couldn't pull back on. He'd just assumed she'd go along with it, because she'd listened to him about holding off on her plans.

'He... played me. He strung me along 'til it was too late.' He'd never cared what she wanted. He'd just looked at the Arms as an opportunity. For him. 'God, I took him there. I'm so stupid!'

Pulling up a fresh email, she clicked on his address and started typing.

This is war, Sloane.

## 11

'A bit to the left,' she shouted up the ladder. 'Shazza, hold it tight, I can see it wobbling!'

Sharon groaned, gripping the tall, metal ladder tighter as Tyler stood at the top, a banner in his hands.

'Under New Management' was written across the white canvas in huge, golden font, matching the metal sign above it.

Fitzpatrick Arms – fine ales and home-cooked food

'That's it!' She grinned, and Tyler tightened the rope.

'You sure?' he bellowed down to her. 'Cos I've moved it twenty sodding times!'

'Yes, yes!' She laughed, standing back as her two friends came to join her. 'Look at it,' she beamed. The place was perfect. Colourful hanging baskets hung from evenly spaced hooks around the wooden trim, making the cream rendered walls look all the better and brighter. The banner finished off the look, with the gold and silver balloon arch around the door and the sandwich chalk board off to one side. 'Opening day specials' *was written across the black surface, Tyler's neat hand detailing the deli-cious-sounding dishes underneath. 'Can you believe it?'*

*Sharon laughed, wrapping her arms around her shoulders. 'I can, mate. You deserve this, after everything. You've worked hard.' People were starting to walk up to the entrance and, as Sharon pulled away, she shot her a wink. 'I'll go see to them, get the drinks sorted.'*

*She was left outside with Tyler, taking in the people she'd known for years, and new faces, all talking and laughing as they headed into her new home.*

*'Proud of you, mate.' She turned, and bumped into him in more ways than one. 'Oh! Sorry. Geez, you'd think I'd get used to being a wide load.' Her pregnant belly had well and truly popped, and she cradled her bump out of habit. Tyler laughed, putting his hand on her tummy and pulling her in for a gentle hug.*

*'You look beautiful. You always do to me,' he breathed into her ear. 'Amber?'*

*'Yeah,' she said, lost in his embrace, the tickle of his aftershave and scented words in her ear.*

*'Amber,' he said again. She could hear a banging noise in the distance. Bang bang bang, like rapid fire.*

*'Yes, Tyler?'*

*Bang bang bang bang.*

*'Are you going to open the fecking door, or do I have to break it down?'*

*'Eh?'*

Bang bang bang bang bang. Amber's eyes opened, and her world was sideways. Her brain scrambled to gain some kind of purchase on what she was seeing. The pub had gone, Tyler. She was looking at her TV, which was frozen with an image of Hugh Grant on it. *Sense and Sensibility,* by the looks of his period garb. The banging noise came again, and she could hear Sharon.

'I don't think she's in; could she have gone somewhere?'

She shot up and fell straight off the couch. Banging her shin on the coffee table corner as she scrabbled to get up, she cursed and ran to the window. *OhmyGodmyhead.* Throwing open the curtains, she looked out of the window. Tyler and Sharon were both standing there, ready for work. His dark eyes narrowed as he took her in, his shoulders coming up to meet his earlobes. *Shit. What time is it?* Tyler motioned for her to open the window. She pulled the sash window up, immediately regretting it when the sounds of traffic and the smell of the fresh Yorkshire air hit her. She had to try hard not to vomit out of the window.

'I'm sorry, I must have slept in. Why didn't you use your key?'

'We tried. You deadbolted the doors, and your phone's off.' Tyler's brows were knitted together tight. 'Did you drink more after I left?'

There was no point lying. She was pretty sure she was still drunk. The rage was still there. She could feel it coursing through her veins with the alcohol.

'Maybe.' She winced. His pupils turned black, or maybe it was just her squinting eyes. 'I'm coming down; give me a minute.'

Shutting the window, she went to the mirror above the fireplace. 'Jesus,' she groaned. 'I look like an Alice Cooper tribute singer.'

Her hair was up at all angles, her beautifully arranged curls from the night before now matted and full of knots. She looked like she'd spent the night in a mosh pit. The pretty glow from the make-up was a distant memory now; she just looked gaunt. Pale *and* green, which was something of an achievement. She was still wearing her dress from the night before, the front now covered in cheese dust from the family-sized pack of Doritos she spotted on the floor. Right next to the empty bottle of champers.

Sharon's face was a picture when she finally threw a robe on and went to answer the door.

'Je-sus,' she whistled. 'You look as rough as a hedgehog's arse.'

'Cheers, yeah.' She sagged against the door as the pair of them walked in, followed by Ben and Irene, the cleaning lady. 'Oh shit, Irene. I haven't cleaned up from last night.' Irene waved her off, yellow duster in hand.

'Don't worry, you need a coffee or something. Leave me and Sharon to sort it. Your day off, remember? Happy birthday, duck. Sorry I missed the party.' She thrust a gift bag at her and carried on chatting to Sharon as they headed through to the bar area. Ben was standing behind Tyler looking uncomfortable to be standing next to his boss, who was positively vibrating. Tyler was standing there, arms folded in his usual bullish way. His face was hard to look at without flinching.

'What?' she sighed, finally looking at him.

'What happened?' He noticed Ben standing there and nodded towards the kitchen. 'We're late for prep, mate; you get cracking – I'll just be a minute.'

Ben slumped with relief and tootled off.

'Nothing. I finished the Champagne, had myself a little after-party.' She groaned, reaching down to plug the phone cable back in. She had a vague memory of pulling it out of the wall the night before when it had started ringing shortly after her emailing sesh. Right about the time she locked the doors shut in case the slimy weasel showed up and cracked the key lock box. The second she pushed it back into the socket, it started ringing. 'Oh Christ, my head.' She picked it up. 'Good morning, the—'

'Hello? Amber?'

It was Bradley.

'Drop dead, dickface.' She hung up. It rang again. Tyler put his hand out, but she answered it, waving him off with a shaky hand.

'Good morning, the Lazy Slug. How can I help?'

'Hi, I just want to talk.'

'No,' she spat back. 'I don't have anything to say, Brad!'

It rang again the second she hung up, making her headache clatter to a whole new level.

'I can't,' she groaned, putting the phone back into its cradle. It rang off eventually, falling silent. 'If he rings again, don't answer it. Or tell him I moved. Or died. Your choice. Either way, I'm not here.'

Tyler didn't move. He was studying her, and she felt exposed under his gaze. 'I knew I shouldn't have left last night. What happened?' His eyes dropped to the food debris on her chest, and she flicked it off half-heartedly. 'Did Bradley bother you?'

'You could say that. I don't want to talk about it, not yet. I can't, too mad. You got any tablets? My head's pounding.'

'I'll get you some,' he grumbled. 'And some water. But I want to talk, Amb. I have some stuff to say too, about last night.'

'Yeah, okay.' She waved him off, feeling like her legs were made of noodles. 'I need to get ready to open.' She pushed her feet into her favourite fluffy slippers and, giftbag still in her hand, walked through to the bar. She could hear Tyler hot on her heels.

'Your day off. So you have time. What happened? You were okay when I left. You look like you lost a fight with a bottle of vodka.' Sharon was taking down the balloon arch. Every balloon popping sounded like mortar fire. 'She looks rough, doesn't she?'

Amber almost threw the gift bag at her. If only to make her stop stabbing rubber.

'Thanks. You're lucky I'm not holding the scissors.' Sagging onto one of the stools, Tyler came through, passing her some tablets and a large glass of water. He gave her a look and went back into the kitchen. 'Great, now I've pissed him off again.'

'Again?' Sharon asked.

'Don't ask.'

She sat the gift bag on the bar, wiping a stain away with one of the beer towels. Sharon resumed her popping, and then Irene started up with the hoover in the pool room. 'My God,' Amber groaned. 'I think I might actually die today. Or kill someone.'

'Go back to bed,' Sharon urged. 'We've got this.'

Amber thought about crawling into her bed, but she knew she wouldn't sleep. The after-party was not one of her best ideas, but, when Tyler had left, and she'd seen the email, she'd felt so weird about everything that drinking more felt like a great idea. Her liver was strongly disagreeing with her now, and hearing Bradley's voice hadn't helped. What the hell did he want? They had nothing to talk about. She'd already told him just what she thought of him.

'No,' she groaned, leaning on the bar for support while she winced at the chalky tablet taste. 'I'll be fine just here.'

Eventually, the bar was returned to normal. All signs of her birthday party were gone, and her headache had lowered to a dull roar. More water and some dry toast Tyler had wordlessly shoved at her earlier saw her through the worst of the lunch rush, and by three in the afternoon things were calm. Everyone was in a good mood after last night, the customers ribbing her about being hungover. If she ignored the fact that Tyler was in a weird mood, and her ex was a conniving little shitbag, she could just about cope. She was where she felt safe, grounded. Behind the bar, with people she knew and trusted around her.

'Can I have a Jameson on the rocks please.'

*Spoke too soon.*

Amber felt her muscles lock up at the sound of his voice behind her.

'Sorry, we're all out.'

'Jack Daniels then.'

'Nope, out of that too.' She made herself turn and look Bradley in the eye.

'There's a full bottle on the optic.'

Turning, she pretended to be surprised. 'Oh yeah, so there is.

What do you want, Brad? More insider information?' Turning back to face him, she inspected her nails and tried to look bored. The coral colour reminded her of Tyler's shirt.

'Amber.'

She didn't acknowledge him.

'Amber. Look at me.'

When she met his eyeline, his face brightened. She hated him for that. He should be crawling back under the rock he slithered out of.

'I've been ringing your phone all day. I rang the pub line, but Sharon told me if I called again, she would castrate me. Your cell phone's off.'

'It's upstairs,' she countered.

'Right,' he nodded. 'I know I have a lot to explain, Amber—'

'How long?'

His head snapped back, manscaped brows uniting in confusion. 'How long what?'

'How long were you scheming to take the Arms for yourself? When were you going to tell me? Opening night? You know how I feel about that place. I put my own plans on hold for yours, and you decided what? That my childhood home was yours for the taking? I honestly can't believe that you have the brass neck to even stand here. Is this why you wanted to talk?'

'No, I—'

'How long, Bradley?'

'Let me—'

'Were you ever going to tell me? I mean, we broke up, so you don't owe me anything, right?'

His face was bloodless at this point, and her stomach lurched.

'Right,' she nodded, a grim realisation crystallising in her brain. 'Thought so. You weren't going to 'fess up. That's why you were so distant, blowing me off. You wanted your ducks in a row. I just forced your hand with my little ultimatum.' Her lip curled in disgust. 'I can't believe I ever saw any good in you. You really are a selfish, slimy little pig, aren't you?'

He went quiet. As had the rest of the pub. Looking around, Amber could see most of the regulars were pretending not to be listening. Sharon was suspiciously nowhere to be seen. Probably telling Tyler, which meant Bradley's time on Earth was going to be short. Bradley had noticed the attention too; she could tell from the awkward foot shuffling.

'You're wrong about this, babe.'

'Don't. Call. Me. Babe,' she snarled. 'I'm not wrong, Sloane. I found out about the planning application. That's why you're here. Because you were found out. Nothing else. You strung me along and knew exactly what you were doing.'

'It's not like that. The eatery would have been for us, b— Amber. I was struggling to find premises. My investor and I got chatting one night, and I mentioned your plans for the Arms.'

'Bet you did,' she fumed, folding her arms to stop herself from launching herself at him like a cornered cat.

'It just kind of snowballed from there. The location's perfect, and the layout wouldn't need much renovation. You weren't doing anything about it, and—'

'I was waiting for you! For your plans to happen first.' She covered her face with trembling hands, giving herself a minute to let that truth sink in. She'd been so... weak. She'd waited for a man, instead of blazing her own trail like she'd planned. And now, she might just have lost everything. Taking a deep breath, she levelled him with a death-willing stare. 'I hate you for this, and I'm not going down without a fight either. That stupid girl you knew, that waited for you to give her attention? She's gone, and I am going to fight you on this every step of the way. Now get the hell out of my pub, and don't come back.' She poked him in the chest, hard. 'I wish I'd never set eyes on you.'

He cast a sheepish look behind him, aware of all the ears listening to his every word. 'Listen, I know you're mad, but...'

'Hah!' she barked at him. 'I was way past mad hours ago.'

He dropped his head. 'Look.' He side-eyed the hostile crowd. 'I know I fucked up, and this looks terrible, but if we could just go somewhere, talk.'

'Why? So you can explain why you fucked over the woman you supposedly loved, for a business deal?' She felt herself get emotional and bunched her fists together to quell it. 'I got it. Now leave, and good luck getting Hebblestone to eat in your poncy little place, because people around here know a snake when they see one.'

Bill hissed from somewhere behind, another regular shouting, 'You tell him, love.'

'I know, it looks bad, but it's the investors! I promise, it's like I said. Sloane's is sunk without the money they're offering. I'll be wiped out. Done. I was going to tell you; I rang to talk the other day, remember? I will make this right, I promise. Now you know, maybe we can sort this all out. Run the place together, like I was going to tell you! You could run the bar!'

Amber snorted. 'Are you kidding me? I would rather burn the place to the ground!'

Bradley's shoulders dropped another inch. 'I know, I'm sorry. I just got caught up; I have so much to lose. If you just give me ten minutes, I have my car outside. Let me take you out for lunch. For your birthday. I'll explain everything. Please.'

'She's not going anywhere with you,' came a growly voice from behind her. 'Get out now, Sloane.'

For the first time since he walked in, Bradley's expression changed from weak and contrite. Amber watched him glare at

Tyler, who had taken his chef's hat off and looked like he was about to jump over the bar.

'This is none of your business, mate.' Bradley spat. 'It's between me and Amber. Get back to your microwave.'

Amber felt Tyler move closer, his arm snake around her waist, and she leaned into his warmth. Brad's eyes flicked down, narrowing at what he saw. 'You're making a scene in my place of work, Brad, and after what I just heard, you have a nerve even showing up. She doesn't want you here. Leave. Now.'

'I'm trying to have a conversation, actually. And, after what I've just seen, you have more than a job at stake here. Stop trying to get in between us, Ty. I've had just about enough of you being her shadow.' Bradley huffed, turning to Amber and dismissing him entirely. 'My car's in the car park; how long do you need?'

'Are you deaf?' Tyler shouted, coming to stand in front of Amber. As if the thick wooden bar wasn't enough of a barrier between them. She tutted, pushing him out of the way. Or tried to. The man was built like a side of beef. He hooked his arm around her, locking her into place at his side. This made Bradley's nostrils flare like a hippo in a water hole. 'Leave, before I make you.'

'Here, here,' Bill's table chorused. 'You're not welcome here. Upsetting our Amber.'

'Yeah, bugger off,' and, 'Sling your hook' came from other tables, making Amber stand that little bit taller. The whole place knew what was going on. The whole community now knew that, not only had she been dumped, but played too. Hebblestone was a close-knit place, and she felt that love now as her regulars grew restless. Bill looked positively fatherly, foot tapping on the carpet while he sat glaring a hole in the back of Bradley's coiffed head. Their clear support made her feel that bit stronger. Muted that sting of shame that fizzed in the pit of her stomach when she saw him.

'You heard them,' she told him firmly. She felt Tyler's arm squeeze her tighter. Brad's narrowed eyes tracked the movement. 'You're upsetting my customers.' Leaning forward, she added, 'You're also barred.'

A few whoops and scattered clapping rose up around her, and when Bradley's shoulders sagged, she knew he was beaten.

'Fine.' He gave her one last long look. 'I can see you're angry, and I get it. This is not over, Amber.' Tyler let loose a snarl at the side of her, and Bradley shook his head at him. 'Call me when you want to talk. I'll be waiting.'

The doors swished closed behind him, and she leaned into her mate as cheers went up around them.

'Good for you, love,' someone said. She heard Bill mutter something about taking the trash out, and supressed a smile.

'Thanks for being a neanderthal,' she joked when things died down and she managed to catch her breath. 'I thought you were going to physically chuck him out of the door.'

Tyler turned her to rest against his chest, stroking her hair. 'Nah. I was planning to fold him up like a pretzel first.'

She laughed then, but it soon dissolved into little sobs. He shouted for Sharon, whispering, 'Not here' into her ear and taking her out into the hallway. When they got to the bottom of the stairs leading to her place, he wrapped her back into his embrace and just stood there. Let her cry it out, until her tears dried up to sniffles. Smelling his ocean scent through her teary sobs.

'Can you believe him?' she asked finally. 'He didn't even look guilty. Am I wrong about this?'

'Nope. You should have called me last night.' After a beat, he asked, 'How did you find out?'

'Denise from planning. She thought that Brad and I were applying together. If the council agrees to this, I've lost the Arms,

Ty. Just when I'd got my act together. I feel like such an idiot. I never should have waited. I wish I'd never gone out with him.'

'This is not your fault.' His voice was a low rumble that vibrated through her body. His hand rubbing slow circles on her back. 'He was never good enough for you. Idiot. Why didn't you call me last night? I would have been there for you, Cherry. I hate the thought of you here alone, drinking by yourself.'

She pulled back, wiping at her face. 'I didn't want to hear a bunch of I told you so's, and I didn't want to have to find a new chef because you were in prison for knocking him out.' *And I didn't trust myself around you.*

'You should have called me. I would have come back, looked after you. I'm sick of you thinking you're alone in all this.' She thought of his face the night before, when she'd declared her need for a baby. She would be alone in that; she needed to stand on her own two feet. Having a man in the equation hadn't exactly worked out so well lately. So she did what felt safer. Pushed him away. 'Do me a favour, Ty. Spare me the lecture for now, please? My head's pounding, and I feel like I licked a birdcage bottom.'

His laugh surprised her. His smirk all knowing. As if he knew what she was up to. *It's hard to hide from someone who always sees you.* 'Okay, fair enough.' He lifted her chin, dipping his head to meet her eye. 'Am I really that judgemental?'

'I don't know. Lately, our energy has been a little off.'

His jaw ticked. 'I know, but I would still have been there for you last night. I'll always be there for you, Cherry.' He pushed a tear-stained tendril of hair out of her eyeline. 'Sharon's got the bar covered. Before you do anything, take the day. Please. Go upstairs, have a shower. Get some sleep. You'll feel better.'

She nodded, blindly agreeing. It did sound good. Her hangover was still giving her a headache, and crying hadn't made it any better.

'A shower and a nap sound pretty good right now.'

She dipped her head and felt his touch. *Did he just kiss my forehead again?* He'd stepped back before she had a chance to process it. 'Get some sleep, okay?'

When she dragged her sniffling behind up the stairs, she noticed that all the gifts had been stacked up in the living room. Her phone and laptop were still on the coffee table, and someone had cleaned up her depression clutter from the night before. God bless Irene. Picking up her phone and turning it on, she saw that the battery was almost flat. There was a myriad of notifications on the screen. Banking, emails, missed calls, messages. Even looking at them made her eyes cross. Her printer, sitting on a side table in the corner of the room, looked like it had vomited a load of paper overnight. Tutting, she headed over, neatening the pile. Her business plan. Looking at the frozen image on the screen, a dim memory flashed back through the half dozen brain cells she'd killed with alcohol the night before. She'd done it. She'd gone all drunken planner. The last time she did this, she ordered a load of business books and fancy highlighters from Amazon. This time, she'd seemingly tweaked her business plan. Taking it back over to the coffee table, she plonked herself on the sofa and put it into a neat clip from her stationery box.

'What else did I do?' she asked herself.

'You talking to yourself now?' Tyler's voice made her jump. He held his free hand up in surrender. 'Hey! I come in peace. I brought you some food.' A delicious steaming hot plate of burger, chips and his legendary coleslaw. Her mouth watered before the shock had a chance to wear off. 'You should be getting some sleep.'

She tossed the business plan to one side and reached for the plate as he came to sit next to her. He frowned when he saw the image of Hugh on the TV screen. She clicked the off button on the remote and moaned as the first chip passed her lips.

'Mmmm, I didn't even realise I was so hungry.'

Tyler didn't say anything; he was looking at the laptop screen on the coffee table, which had come back to life when she put the business plan down. She was just about to bite into the thick, juicy burger when she saw his stony face.

'Cherry, what the hell is that?' She was mid bite when he lunged across the keyboard and clicked on the bookmark labelled 'sperm'. The website popped up, on a page marked *order confirmation*. 'Amber, what the fuck is this?' The food turned to ash in her mouth as she saw Tyler's scowl. His eyes darkened as they darted over the words. Swallowing audibly, she leaned in. *Shit. Shit. Double shitty shit shit. She'd gone and done it.* Drunk her really had hit the nuclear button on the whole 'life begins at 30' thing. Her hangover had suppressed the memory of it all. *I really did it.*

'Tyler, I—'

'You ordered sperm on the Internet? Are you freaking kidding me? What the hell's going on?' He was out of his chair and across the room. His eyes were scanning the place frantically. 'I thought it was just drunk talk last night. You can't be serious, Amber. Cancel it. Now.'

Even while she was still reeling on the fact that she'd actually done it, his tone and utter shock well and truly raised her hackles.

'Don't tell me what to do!' She slammed the laptop lid down, slamming the plate down next to it. The coleslaw slid off the plate as she rose, landing in her lap. 'Shit!' She grabbed the sticky mess before it hit the carpet. 'Give me a minute, okay?' Stomping off to the bathroom, she left him standing there like an angry sergeant major, hands on hips. She could hear his foot tapping as she cleaned herself up. 'I was drunk, okay?'

'No shit. I knew I shouldn't have left you alone after the party.'

His eyes tracked her from the second she re-entered the lounge.

'I am a grown-ass woman, Tyler. I know what I want.'

'Says the hungover woman with a wet patch on her trousers. You can't even eat a meal without making a mess. This is just a reaction to last night. Cancel it. It's not too late.'

'So, I can't have a baby, right?'

'What?' His brows crashed together. 'No... of course not... but you can't do it like this! Ordering baby batter to your door, I mean who freaking does that? You were drunk, upset about your birthday. Pissed off. Confused, even. I get it. Turning thirty has always been a big thing for you. I know you've been beating yourself up about the Arms. This isn't the answer, Amber. Take a breath. You don't need to jump into everything right away.' His eyes fell to the business plan. 'Go for the Arms; the rest can wait.'

'Are you telling me that or guessing? Because I didn't just google having a baby, Ty. I have had that bookmark a while. Actually, I have been looking into having a baby on my own for ages. I had my eggs checked months ago, and it's time! With or without a man, I want a family!' She grabbed the business plan, thrusting it into his hands like she was handing him the answer. 'I also did this. I finished my business proposal; you're not kicking off about that!'

He barely glanced at the papers in front of him, shaking his head like some kind of buffering robot. 'The two things are a bit different, and you know it. This is not the way you start a family, Amber. You have better options.'

She seized on his word. 'Exactly. Options. I have options, and this is one of them. That site was bookmarked for a reason. I can do this, and maybe I don't need to answer to anyone. I keep telling you, I'm fine on my own. I might not have done this quite so quick, sure. I was upset, and pissed, but this was not me ordering five pairs of shoes while on tequila.'

'And what did you do with those shoes, eh?' He countered, moving closer. 'You cancelled the order the minute you realised, so think about it. Just for a minute, and then consider whether you might just have buyer's remorse.'

Ben's voice rose up from the staircase. 'Er, Tyler? Getting pretty busy down here, mate.'

'I'm coming,' he roared back. 'I've got to go.'

'Don't let me stop you.' She scowled.

'I'll come up later, once my shift's finished.'

She went to the door, holding it open in a way that would give him the message. 'Don't bother.' She thumbed towards the stairs. 'And before you overstep again, don't forget that, while you are at work, I'm the boss. I don't and have never needed an assistant to run my life. Stick to the kitchen from now on, and butt out.'

His jaw tensed so hard, she half expected his teeth to crack into pieces.

'We are more than that, and you know it. One day, you might just stop trying to bend to everyone else's will and see that.'

'See what, Tyler? We fancy each other, sure. I can admit that much. And you're right, I am sick of bending over backwards for people.'

'I've never asked you to do that, not once. I don't want to change you!'

'Don't you get it, Ty? That's what would happen. I'm sick of it. Trying to please everyone. You, me – us? It wouldn't work. You will leave one day, and I'll be alone again. We want different things.'

'It's not that simple,' he protested, reaching for her.

She stepped out of his orbit. 'It is, Tyler. I can't afford to waste any more time, and I can't lose any more people. I just can't.'

'You won't.' He took a step towards her, but she moved closer to the door. 'Not the right people.'

'You don't know that. And it's too late, it's done. Ben needs you,' she pushed out, wanting him to go and stop looking at her like she was going to smash into a million pieces. She'd done it. She'd ordered it. Even in her shock, she couldn't bring herself to feel the shock Tyler did. Maybe it was right. Drunk her had pulled the trigger, but they were her plans. She dimly remembered doing it, now the fog was clearing. She wanted this.

'Can we at least talk about this?'

He looked so upset, standing there, but she remembered his reaction to her news last night. Her dreams didn't align with his. She couldn't let anything start between them, not if she was going to be a mum. Remembering her dream last night confirmed it. This way, Tyler would still be in her life. A good friend, someone she could trust. Without all the hurt and worry. Dragging Tyler along for the ride would only end one way. Badly. For both of them.

'I'm tired,' she muttered with a shake of her head. 'I know what I'm doing, Ty. I don't need anyone changing my mind.'

'Fine,' he growled. 'Message received, Amber.'

Slamming the door behind him, she heard him slam the bottom door leading to the bar and stamped her foot in frustration. Heading back to her seat, she picked up the lukewarm burger and started to eat. She finished the food, and promptly burst into tears.

\* \* \*

A couple of days later, she finally told her friend.

'You didn't!' Sharon, usually not one to shock easily, looked positively, well, shaken.

'I did, and what's more, I don't regret it. I've decided, I'm going to do it.'

'Seriously?'

'Yeah! Why not? You know what they say, drunk people always show their true intentions.'

'When they pee off the side of buildings or arrange booty calls, yeah! Especially after a break-up. Have you spoken to Tyler about this?'

She felt the pang when her friend mentioned his name. That was the one thing that was bothering her the most about this. She'd been getting closer to Tyler but he didn't want kids. There was no point in trying to force another relationship to fit her plans. At least, this way, they could just get over their weirdness. Go back to being friends again, eventually. She thought of his stricken face, the way he reached for her. The tingle she'd felt when her body wanted to fold itself into his. If only to rid him of that look. Feel his arms around her before things changed yet again. She really did need to book that ECG; her heart flip-flopping was getting a bit much.

'Amber! Are you still hungover or what? Your eyes have glazed over.'

'Sorry! Sorry.' She shook herself out of her inner debate. 'What were you saying?'

'I was saying that you need to take a break, before you decide your next big life move. People need a minute to recover from stuff like this, Amb. Cutting their ex's clothes up or keying their car, maybe. Even getting under another man to get over the one who broke your heart I can roll with. This is extreme. You don't decide to have a baby the same fortnight and order the... the... juice! I mean, I've ordered drunk before. Remember that life-sized cardboard cutout of Clint Eastwood I ordered after that time we drank Pernod?'

'Yeah.' Amber laughed at the memory. 'I also remember your disappointment because you meant to order his son.'

'Exactly. It was a mistake!'

'You also kept him. He's still in your closet. We freaked your neighbours out last Halloween pretending to cut his head off in the window.'

'Oh yeah,' Sharon laughed, distracted from her rant. 'I wondered why his head was taped together.' She shook her head like a wet dog. 'That's not the point. My point is people don't just decide to have a baby on a drunken whim.'

'Shazza, half the people we know were probably the result of a drunken whim. I told you, I want to be a mum. Just because I don't bang on about it 24/7 doesn't mean it's not there. Not everyone plans a baby; it's not like I went out and found some random penis!'

Bill came to the bar at precisely the wrong moment. 'I didn't hear that. Usual, Sharon my lovely.'

'Sorry Bill.' Amber blushed.

When he was safely back in his seat, pint in hand, she tried to explain.

'Listen, yeah, sure. It was a kneejerk reaction to finding out about what Brad was up to, but it's not something I haven't thought about before. A lot. I had the site bookmarked on my laptop. I've been reading parenting blogs for the past two years. My biological clock was ticking like a bomb long before my birthday. Bradley and I talked about it when we were together. I'm thirty. I have no man.' She paused, thinking of how good she felt when Tyler was around. 'After possibly wasting the last year of it, I don't want to join the dating pool again. I don't have the time or the heart for it. Besides, it's 2024. I don't need a father for my child. I never knew mine, not really.'

'Yeah,' Sharon said with a pained look on her face, 'and your mother went from one bloke to the rest, trying to find someone to share her life with for the rest of hers and left you behind.' Her face fell. 'Shit. Sorry. You know I didn't mean it like that, but—'

'But it's true,' Amber rebuffed, Sharon's comment stinging her a lot more than she let on. Thinking of her mother always did that. 'She did, and my grandparents had the kind of storybook marriage that all the love songs are written about.'

'And Tyler?'

'What about Tyler?' Amber whispered. 'We haven't even kissed. Sure, we've flirted, but he doesn't want kids. He hasn't even said he wants a relationship, and it's too hard. We're good friends. I don't want to lose that. He's leaving, so in a few months, it will be a moot point anyway. I've seen both sides of the coin, Shaz. I choose not to flip it any more.'

'Flip what?' Ben asked as he rounded the corner.

'Nothing.' Amber glared at Sharon to shut up. 'Just chatting, you know.'

'Cool. Tyler said we need to put an order in for those steaks again from the butcher. We're nearly out. He's also in a raging mood again, so heads up if you cross his path.' He filled two glasses with ice and coke before heading off again.

'If you're so happy about your little plan, why not tell Ben, eh?' Sharon folded her arms in a 'huh?' move.

'Don't fold your arms like that at me!' Amber laughed. So, Tyler was still mad then. Well, so was she – so they were a pair of snarling bookends. Fine by her. 'There's nothing to tell yet, is there? It might not even work.'

'Or you daren't tell your best friend you didn't cancel the order.' Sharon snorted over her shoulder as she headed down the bar. 'Because you know he'll try to talk you out of it. You two need to talk; you make my heart spin.'

Luckily, Sharon was too busy to see her wince. She was right on the money on that one. Tyler was going to pitch an absolute fit when she told him she hadn't changed her mind. Plus, she didn't want the two of them joining forces in some kind of baby intervention. She was already stewing over Sharon's comments about the family she was born into. It was true, she had seen both happy and sad. Her grandparents really had been two souls very much in love, even when death had parted them. Stroking the glass photo frame on the back bar wall, she looked at her smiling grandparents and sighed. 'I wish you guys were here. You'd be happy for me, right?' She was still looking at the snap when she heard a smash from the kitchen, and Tyler's irritated growl reverberate through the place. 'Time to get out of here,' she muttered to herself. 'Try and salvage some of my sanity.'

\* \* \*

'Jasmine, put that down! Jasmine! I swear, this kid!'

Amber watched the mother in the park chuntering to herself as she sped over to a toddler. Presumably Jasmine, who was currently eating dirt with a huge grin on her face. Watching her mother scold her, pulling wipes out of her bag to deal with her mud-smeared face, she waited for the panic to set in. *Will my kid eat dirt? Will I be able to deal with it? Will I have the wipes at the ready?*

'Jas, honey. We can't eat dirt, okay?'

'Why?' Amber heard the little girl ask as her mother knocked the dark soil off her clothing.

'Because it's not food. It helps the plants to grow, and the carrots.'

'I like carrots!'

The mother laughed, picking the child up and settling her on her lap. As she wiped the rest of the forbidden snack from her fingers, the pair of them laughed together.

'I know you do, baby. So, let's not eat the dirt any more. Leave it to the carrots, and the flowers.' She checked her watch, her eyes meeting Amber's. 'Come on, darling, let's go meet Daddy for lunch, all right?'

'With carrots?' the little girl asked as they headed over to their stroller.

The laugh that came from her mother was so free, so full of joy, it made Amber's heart clench.

'Double carrots,' she trilled back, and Amber watched as she carried her little girl away from the play area. When they came alongside the bench Amber was sitting at, the woman turned and gave her a knowing smile. 'Kids, eh?'

Amber laughed. 'Worth it, though, right?'

'Mum, carrots!' the babe trilled in her arms, grabbing her by the cheeks and turning her away from the conversation. The woman laughed and pulled away long enough to grin at Amber.

'It's exhausting, stressful, expensive. You can't have a conversation with another adult longer than a second.'

Her daughter was currently smushing her cheeks together in an effort to stop her talking and shouting, 'Carrots, carrots, carrots' at the same time at the top of her tiny lungs.

'But, yeah, it's totally worth it. Have a good day.'

Amber waved them off, watched the pair of them head to the car park. Utterly raptured and engrossed by the other. Amber sat there long after their car had pulled away. She sat on that wooden park bench, watching the children play. Half listening to the parents as they chatted together on the fringes of the bark chippings. She could hear them talking about how work was moaning about their time off, about how little time they had to themselves. How little Billy had kept them up half the night. How their other half had slept through the whole thing. How they had considered suffocating them with a pillow in the middle of the night. She heard them talk about getting new teeth, about how their little one had learned to take their first steps the day before. How they would never let *their* child be the one scoffing on mud pies in the park.

For most of her adult life, she'd been on the fringes of conversations. The silent interloper, privy to their sorrows and successes. Listening to what they wanted to do, wanted to change in their lives. She'd been there when they celebrated births, engagements, marriages. Heck, even the odd divorce. She'd watched them fall in love, cheat, and fight. Years she'd listened and observed the minutiae of life. Now she was here again, single, and finally going on her own journey.

'Totally worth it,' she echoed. Looking at the tired parents, the laughing kids. The one in the corner digging a worm out from the flowerbed. She wanted this. She'd always wanted this.

She thought about Tyler. Angry at work. He felt rejected; she knew him well enough to know that. He thought she was acting rashly, but she felt calm about her decision. It felt right. If she ignored the gnawing gulf in her stomach when she thought about not seeing where things could go. She fancied him more and more, but there was no future to it. She felt the sting of rejection too, in a way, irritational as it was. It's not like she expected him to act any different. She had known where he stood all along. It just felt cruel, that they had their chance but, once again, the timing was all wrong. So, no Tyler, and she didn't want to try and find someone else. Her heart wasn't in it. Even if she waited to date, it could be years before she met another person she could consider sharing the rest of her days with. One thing she did know was that she didn't want another relationship where she was second. She didn't want to be the girl who was woken up for what essentially amounted to a relationship booty call. Dating was exhausting. Even the thought of it made her feel tired. Exhausted. Plus, she'd been around enough drunk people to know that the truth was usually elicited by alcohol. People fought; they said what was on their mind. They broke up, drunk-dialled old loves. She'd seemingly taken tequila's advice and kickstarted her life. Sober her was cautious; drunk her was all action. All guns blazing, all in. She'd ordered sperm online, had even discovered from her email trail that she'd booked a business meeting with her bank, all fuelled entirely by birthday cake, rejection and hard liquor. She'd even emailed her boss, asking for that pay rise she'd been moaning about for months. The thing was, he'd agreed. She was on more money, just for asking for what she wanted for once. It had only strengthened her resolve on the other things.

Her phone rang in her bag, jolting her from her children watching. Which was probably a good thing, as her coffee was long gone and childless strangers who hung out all day in parks were usually frowned upon. And locked up for being creepy.

She headed to the front gates, pulling her phone out of her bag as she pulled her jacket around her. Tyler. He'd been ringing her periodically since she'd left the Slug. She couldn't avoid him forever. She knew she'd have to speak to him at some point. Even knowing that, her finger still hovered over the green button without landing on the screen. He rang off, and seconds later, a message popped up.

> Amber, where are you? Talk to me. If you don't ring me back in half an hour, I'm coming to find you.

She headed out of the gates, dumping her empty cup in the trash bin as she passed by. Her phone beeped again.

> Amber, come on. Ring me. Everyone is worried. You are not on your own. Talk to me. This isn't like us.

*Us.* Her gut clenched. It sounded so good when he said that. Maybe she owed him a conversation. Maybe, if she could make him understand, they could go back to normal. She could stuff her feelings for him down. She'd done it before, right?

Another message beeped.

I know I'm mad about the other thing, and we need to talk more about it, but I swear if you are off somewhere crying over that fuckwit I will track him down and pummel his face in. Then I'll come track you down and bring you home. Please, stop hiding. Not from me, Cherry.

She sighed reading it. She wanted to be mad about his reaction to the baby thing, but his words deflated her anger like a popped balloon. He was right. She was hiding, and that's what she'd been doing for far too long. Hiding behind a crappy relationship, hiding behind big dreams that she never reached for. She wasn't alone. She had a family at that pub, but it wasn't enough any more. She needed to take action. For once, she wanted people to see her live her life. She would have a baby, and go all out for the Arms. Crush Bradley's little scheme and get her happy ever after. Her grandmother had run the place *and* raised her. Another Fitzpatrick woman had already shown her it could be done. She had to been taught to stand on her own two feet, and she needed her decks clear for her new life. No more hiding. Tyler would have to wait. Firing off a text, she headed for a showdown of a different kind.

\* \* \*

When she arrived at Bradley's place, he was already outside, waiting.

'Hi,' she said, walking over to him. He was looking as polished as ever, a light-grey suit tailored to his body, but she could see the bags under his eyes. The way his face pinched when he looked at her.

'Thanks for coming,' he breathed. 'Talk upstairs?'

'I'm good here, thanks.'

She saw the shame on his face. 'I am sorry, Amber. One thing I didn't want to do in all this was hurt you. I'm guessing I'm the talk of Hebblestone.'

'What's wrong? Worried about your reputation?'

He shrugged but didn't deny it. 'I'm a businessman; reputation matters.'

'Yeah, well, the Slug is hardly the *Daily Mail* news desk, Brad. I'm sure you'll be fine. Although, I wouldn't show up there again if I were you.'

'Tyler wouldn't hold back, I'm guessing.' His eyes grew hard. 'Finally made his move, did he?' He cursed under his breath. 'I always kind of guessed he liked you, but he never said anything. Even denied it when I asked. Said he wasn't looking for a relationship.'

'He's not,' she confirmed, even as a stab of something hit her chest. 'He's not one to settle down.'

'But he does like you, right?'

'That's none of your business.' She pressed her lips together. 'We got close lately, that's all. Working together so much, you were off doing your own thing. I've never cheated on you.'

He waved her off, as if it didn't matter. 'I know that. I still think we can sort this out. Now you know—'

'Now I know just how much of a wanker you are?'

He huffed, pulling his tie loose from its binding. 'I deserve that. And more. I never meant for it to happen like this.'

'So call it off. I am going for the Arms, Brad. I will not let you just swoop in and take it, and Hebblestone is not going to welcome you with open arms if you win. You can still stop this. Walk away. Find another place.'

He winced, swallowing hard. 'I'm in too deep to pull out of the eatery now. I have to push through on this. The investors are... pushing for me to get things moving. I had to do it.' He didn't look entirely happy with the prospect. 'I know I've changed,' his eyes grew soft. 'But I did change for the better when I met you, Amber. You made me better, I just... forget to be that man sometimes. It's cost me, more than you know. I've lost you for good, haven't I?'

It would be funny if it wasn't so tragic. Looking at him now, she couldn't imagine a time when she ever had feelings for such a person. Tyler might not share her dreams, but he had never made her feel anything but supported. Even now, when he was mad, he was still there – looking out for her.

'You lost me a long time ago. You just didn't notice. I'm going to fight you on this, every step of the way. You're not crushing my dreams to get what you want. Not any more.'

He nodded, a strange look clouding his face before he came to stand in front of her. His head bent to meet hers. His lips brushed hers for the briefest of moments, before he pulled back. 'I never deserved you, Fitzpatrick.'

She smiled fully for the first time. 'Tell me something I don't know, Sloane.'

## 12

Tyler opened the back door while her key was still in the lock.

'Jesus! Stalk much? Your shift finished half an hour ago.' He was on his night off. She thought he'd have been gone by now.

'Hmm, I wonder why you waited for that to come home.'

*Busted.* She should have been embarrassed for being caught out, but the way he'd been waiting for her, still all antsy and irritable, raised her heckles. She'd banked on having more time to get her thoughts together. She'd already said goodbye to one man today. Speaking to Tyler, having the talk, wasn't something she relished. Seeing him now reminded her of how gutted she was to be ending something that had never had a chance to start. She should just rip off the Band-Aid, cry alone later. Instead, she decided to go the childish route, and pick a fight.

'Oops.' She yanked her key out of its housing and stomped straight up to her flat. 'Sorry Dad, am I grounded for missing curfew?'

'Don't be cute. Where have you been?' he demanded.

'Out,' she huffed, realising the second he strode into her flat behind her that she wasn't going to be able to shut the door on him.

Dropping her keys on the hook, she fished her phone out of her handbag and headed into the lounge. 'Sharon said she would cover.'

'I know that.' He glared as his eyes fell to the phone in her hand. 'Your phone obviously works too. You could have let me know where you were.'

'Not that it's your business, Ty, but I agreed to meet Bradley.'

'You did what?' Tyler's face was contorted by confusion. 'Why the fuck would you do that?'

'To tell him where I stood, and can you not shout? I don't need you in my face like this, Ty. Okay? I told him I'm going for the Arms. It's done with, we're done with. I've made an appointment with the bank; I have my plan. I don't want to fight, okay?'

Tyler ran his hands through his hair, leaving little stuck-up tufts in their wake. 'Okay. Fine. I don't want to fight either. I'm not exactly loving this side of me.' He sighed, his chest heaving with the effort. 'Can we talk about the other thing?'

She steeled herself for what was coming. 'I haven't changed my mind about that, either. I want a baby, Tyler. I haven't cancelled the order.'

'So that's it?' His voice was high pitched, disbelief on his face. He looked like she'd told him she was planning a one-way trip to Mars. She might even take that offer right about now, if it meant avoiding this. And the way Tyler looked at her. Their dynamic had changed so much recently, she wasn't sure what she felt when she looked at him; being close to him wasn't as clear cut as it used to be. It was all the possessive, protective stuff, she reasoned. It was kind of nice feeling like she had her own grizzly bear looking out for her, but the confessions, the way they seemed to irritate and gravitate to each other? It was confusing, trying to marry up what she felt with their differences. He was here, but they were friends. He didn't do relationships, even though he looked at her sometimes like he wanted to either shake her or kiss the ever-loving crap out of her. Bradley's comments had made her think too. He knew Tyler didn't do girlfriends, but he'd still picked up on the way Tyler was with her. It was driving her crazy. Sometimes, she wished she could swap parts of each of them to make one man. If she could take the commitment of the Bradley she first met and shove it into Tyler, would that work? *No. Look at his reaction to the baby idea. He was shocked to hell.* She needed to forget about the last few weeks if she wanted to keep Tyler. She needed his friendship, needed him on side. The thought of them not speaking again churned her insides. If she could just stop thinking about him naked, it would be great. Especially when he was all alpha male in front of her like this. As much as it irritated her, it was also a turn on. Feminists still loved muscular protectors. *So sue me.*

She used to say to people who asked the nature of their relationship that they were besties, almost brother and sister. Thinking of him as some kind of adopted sibling now felt utterly wrong. At odds to how her body responded around him. She needed some distance. She was already reeling enough from the meeting with Bradley.

'Amber?' Tyler pulled her attention back from her thoughts. 'I know you want a family. I get it, but it's not that simple. You can't just order spermsicles on the net and think that's the way to go.'

'Yes, actually, I can. I've made my mind up, and I really hope you can respect my decision. I need to see it through.'

'See it through? Jesus, Amber – it's not some puppy you picked from a shelter. It's the next eighteen years of your life.'

'That's not fair, and I don't need a lecture. Stop being all squeaky!'

'Squeaky!' he squealed before clearing his throat. 'I'm not squeaky,' his voice now a low rumble as he started to pace.

'You were,' Amber huffed from the sofa as she sagged into it.

She suddenly felt like she could sleep for a week. 'And now you're wearing a hole in my rug.'

'Yeah, well, wait 'til you have a baby running around. You'll have a lot more to worry about than a worn rug. They puke, you know. You really think you'll have the energy for a baby and a new business? Especially if the kid is from some guy who used to sit in the freezer next to your vodka?'

'Don't be mean, and I know kids puke. So do drunk people.'

He resumed his pacing. 'And they poo everywhere.'

'So do drunk people.'

'And they cry, and never sleep.'

'So do—'

'Stop it, you know what I mean. You don't have drunk people in your flat, do you, and that's another thing. How are you going to work the hours you do?'

'The brewery has plenty of families as employees, Ty. The landlady at the Wine Lodge in town has three kids. And, if I have my own place, I will plan for it. Take maternity leave, I have a little saved up. I could get a slightly bigger business loan. I just got a wage rise from this place; I can make it work. I have to try at least.'

He huffed, and she knew he couldn't argue with her logic. 'Fine. That could work out. What about the school runs?'

'Tyler, I don't even have a baby yet. School runs are, like, five years away.'

'Five years won't take long to come, and there's other things too. You work downstairs most nights.'

'Yeah, and I also have staff, and baby monitors nowadays do just about everything but feed the baby for you. Why are you so mad about this? Do you think I'll be a bad parent or something?'

'I'm not mad. Of course you'd be a great mum. I just want you to wait, concentrate on the business plan. Get your life back first and then think again. I'll stay here, help you. I'll stop looking for another job.'

Amber was still in her coat. The second she'd walked in the back door, Tyler had ambushed her. She was glad for it right now, found herself snuggling deeper into it as a shiver ran through her. Tyler's tone had sent a cold jolt down her spine. She was messing everything up. Tyler was getting caught in the crossfire. Staying here with her was not an option. Tyler had his own dreams; head chef at the Slug was a waste of what he could do. She wouldn't do that to him. Not a chance was she going to stop someone else going after what they wanted. She knew how it felt. If Tyler grew to resent her one day? She couldn't bear it. She'd rather lose him altogether.

'No, Tyler. Staying here is not what you want.' She pulled off her coat. 'I don't want that for you either. You're being such a good friend, but I want the best for you.'

'Back at you. Which is why I am helping you now. I want you to just think about it some more, before you do something you can't take back.'

Amber folded her coat over the arm of the sofa, settling herself down for what looked like a long talking to. The serene afternoon at the park felt like days ago now she was back in reality.

Her phone buzzed. Sharon had sent her a text.

Do you need an escape plan?

She laughed before she could stop it and Tyler, who was back to pacing and muttering to himself, stopped dead in front of her.

'Laughing, really?'

'Yeah, really.' She tapped a text back.

I'm fine. Thanks bud.

*I've just got to push the one guy away I never wanted to lose. No biggie.* 'I've done nothing *but* think about it. I didn't do any of this on a whim.'

'Tequila-fuelled depression is more than a whim.'

'Careful, Tyler,' she chided. She could feel her heckles rise. 'You're my friend, but I don't need your permission to do this. Nor do I want it. I don't dictate what you do with your life, and my work status is not your concern.'

'Not my— Amber, this is going to be hard!'

'I know it is!' She was on her feet before it even registered. Banging her shin on the coffee table, however, did. 'Ow, shit!' Tyler moved the coffee table away from her, but she held up a finger at him. 'Don't! Don't you dare; I don't need your help!' She rubbed at her smarting leg. 'In any of this! I can do what I like, so just go, will you?'

'Fine,' he huffed, getting to the door before rounding on her again. 'I care, Amb. That's all. I think you need to take a minute.'

'That's all I do, Ty. That's the point. I want my life to start. This is about what I want, and it's not a whim or a reaction to Bradley. He showed me who he was. He kept showing me who he was, over and over. I just didn't listen. Everyone else tried to warn me that he wasn't The One, and the truth is...' She sighed, rubbing her arms to try to give herself some kind of comfort. 'The truth is, I knew he wasn't the perfect one for me, but I was trying to make it fit. I do that: try to make little pieces fit together to make a life. To try to convince myself that it's enough, and it's not. Not any more. Yeah, I got hurt. I turned thirty. Yes, all of those things suck, but this is not the reason for my decision. Decisions, actually. I realised that I was relying on Bradley to make things happen, but I should have been doing it for myself. Either way, I am going for all my dreams. Baby, business, the lot.'

She could see her friend wrestle with his emotions. His jaw was pulsing, a full-blown muscle spasm across his cheek.

'You kicking off like this doesn't help. It makes me feel like a child, not a grown woman planning to have one. I don't need my hand holding through this, Ty. It's not your job. I know you don't want children.'

'I know that, but—'

'But that's the point.' She felt the tears sting her eyes. 'I do. I don't want to wait for something to change. I know you don't get it, and that's fine.' She felt her lip wobble. 'I'm not asking you to do this with me. It's my choice. It's my time.' She led him to the doorway. 'Now, if you don't mind, I'd really like to have a long bath with a good book and enjoy the rest of my time off. Tell Sharon I'll come down later to help her lock up if she needs it.'

'Amber—'

'I'll let you get back to your kitchen,' she said dismissively. 'Ben will be flapping by now.'

'Yeah,' Tyler grumbled over his shoulder. 'He's not the only one. I hate this, Amber.'

She had to lift her head to look up at him, and her heart broke when she saw his expression.

'I'm sorry,' she blurted out. 'I've been awful to you, and I hate it when we argue. We never do, not like this. The truth is, I've been so confused by you lately.'

His brows shifted. 'You have?'

She shot him a 'dur' look. 'You know I have, and I'm sorry for it. All of it. I need you in my life.'

His lips pressed together as he gazed down at her. 'I need you too.'

'Good.' She half smiled. 'Because I need someone in my corner, okay? I need someone to just be there for me, and I know the waters are muddy, but you're my friend. I still want that at the end of... whatever this is.'

For a moment, he looked as if he was going to tell her to go to hell and walk out. Instead, he pulled her into his arms and dropped a whiskery kiss on the top of her head. 'I would never walk away from you, Cherry. I don't think I have it in me.'

'So don't,' she breathed, wrapping her arms around him. As selfish a move as it felt, she still didn't stop herself from inhaling his ocean salt scent. Storing it up. 'Just trust that I know what I'm doing, even when you don't agree with it.'

He gripped her tighter. 'Whatever you need, I'm here. I think we both know I won't walk away from you. Your friendship is the best thing in my life.'

Her heart squeezed. *God, sometimes I wish he did want more. Much more. He was there all this time. I ignored all the good things I had. Maybe if I'd said something sooner, things might have been different.*

'Thanks, pal.'

He chuckled around her, and she knew that whatever storm was going on with them, it had at least calmed for now. Even if she had to have him at a distance, it was better than not having him in her life.

'Anytime, mate.'

## 13

Things settled into a rhythm again in the days that followed. Sharon was happy that Amber hadn't fallen back into Bradley's arms and Amber didn't miss Sloane one bit. The longer she was away from him, the less she thought about him. Well, other than wondering if voodoo dolls actually worked. She could probably knit a realistic enough looking douchebag to test the theory if she put her mind and her needles to it. Thoughts of murder and maiming aside, he didn't take up space in her head any more. The feeling of dread and unease she felt when she was with him had disappeared, leaving space for nicer things. Now, she was excited about her own plans again. She was starting to feel like the old Amber again.

When she woke that morning, she felt happy. Settled. She had a day shift to run, and then the night off. For once, she was looking forward to it. She didn't need a date for the evening; she was just looking forward to life again. The only sticking point being that she couldn't quite stop thinking about her best friend. Naked. Dressed. Saying those nice things to her. The way he'd folded her into his huge body as if he would gladly shield her from the world with his bare arms. But that was fine, right? She just needed to shut the little 'doesn't want a family' box in her head. Once she'd managed to shove him into it for good. Still, she had work to do.

Putting her game face on, she headed out of her flat.

Tyler was waiting for her at the bottom of the stairs.

'Morning, Cherry.' He grinned, waggling a wad of papers at her.

She lifted a brow. *Why does he have to look so good?* 'Morning. We're nowhere near opening time. What are you doing here so early?'

'Couldn't sleep.' He was looking at her like he'd won the lottery.

'What's got you so happy?' Then, she saw her business plan in his hand. 'What are you doing with that?'

'Well, I haven't stopped thinking about it since you showed it to me. I figured you had time to give it another tweak before you had your first meeting with the bank.' He was like a toddler, vibrating with energy. 'Come with me.'

Leading her through to the kitchen, she gasped.

'What the— what did you do, come in at dawn?'

'Pretty much. I went to the fish market first.'

'Hebblestone has a fish market that opens at dawn?'

'Ah, young Padawan, much to learn have you.' He reached for her, pulling her to the crammed counter. There were dishes on there that looked like they belonged in a Michelin restaurant.

'Holy pollock, it smells gorgeous in here.'

Tyler was preening like a proud peacock, his laugh huffing out in one amused breath. 'So, we know that pubs on their own don't cut it on the viability front these days. I know in your plan, you planned to do the basic pub grub, but I decided that we could do better. Really smash the eatery bullshit out of the water.'

She pushed her lips together. 'We?'

He shrugged those huge shoulders of his, flashing her an adorable little grin. 'Yeah. Any decent chef can follow my menu. I mean,' he bumped his body against hers, 'it won't be as good, but I'm amazing.'

She huffed out a laugh. 'And modest.'

'You forgot sexy.' They locked eyes for a moment. *I didn't forget that. That's half the problem.*

'So.' She focused her attentions on the dishes, willing her cheeks to stop combusting with heat. 'What do we have?'

He passed her one of the menu sheets. He'd written *Cherry's* on the top. She felt a warm feeling in her stomach, seeing his nickname for her. Ran her fingers along the scrawl, till she saw him watching and dropped her hand.

'For starters, we have the usual – prawn cocktail, mini appetisers like quiche and salad, fresh-made soups with crusty bread.' His hand landed on the small of her back, as he moved her along. The box in her mind popped open a little more. *Down, girl.* 'Mains, we have a fish dish with traditional chunky chips, a kick-ass chilli, and—'

'This is amazing,' Amber cut in. It really was. Every single dish looked like it was perfectly made, riots of colour on each plate. 'It also makes the Slug's food look it came from a rat-burger van.'

'Hey! That's still my food, cheeky!'

She giggled.

'You know what I meant. This stuff is great.' There it was again: that cute little smirk of his. 'You're great,' she blurted out. 'At this I mean.'

She heard him swallow audibly before he spoke again.

'So, dig in.'

She picked the chilli, spooning in a mouthful. The second it hit her lips, she moaned. Tyler, who had been watching her, turned away.

'Good?' he asked. His voice was thicker than usual.

'Amazing,' she said on a groan. 'I can't believe you did all this.

You really think the Arms could pull this off? To be honest, I wasn't thrilled with the thought of just doing pie and chips and the like.'

'Well, now you don't have to.' He reached for the business plan he'd left on the side. 'You know, this plan is pretty amazing. You should be really proud of yourself.'

'Yeah, turns out my drunk drafting is pretty solid. Although I think it's a good thing I only had to tweak a few bits. Thanks for this, really. It's great. More than great, but what are you going to do with it all?'

He shrugged. 'I have the dog shelter coming to get it before we open. I figured those guys could make use of it. I send them leftovers from here from time to time.' When he caught her surprised look, his shoulders lifted. 'What? You feed the dogs; the humans need a treat now and then too.'

His eyes locked with hers, and time shuddered to a stop.

'You should let more people see this side of you.'

'What side?' he asked softly.

'This side,' her fingers reached up to touch his chest, but she stilled them before making contact. 'Everyone thinks you're this grumpy, scowling, quiet lumberjack, but you're an absolute softie underneath it all. You care, Tyler Williams. More than you let people see.'

He covered the back of her hand, placing it on his chest for a moment before letting it go.

'If you tell anyone,' he whispered theatrically, 'I might have to put you in a pie.'

She laughed, using the hand that still tingled from his touch to tap him on the chest. 'Well, thanks. I'd better start opening up.'

She got to the door of the kitchen before he called her name.

'Yeah?' she asked.

'You're off tonight, right? Any plans?'

'Nope. Well, I was going to look at some baby stuff on the 'net.'

He nodded, his eyes narrowing before his face dropped into an easy smile.

'Why?'

'I'm off too. Leaving Ben to run things solo for once, and I've had another idea, if you fancy it?'

'Oh yeah?' She wrinkled her nose. 'It's not a fish market, is it?'

His laugh filled the kitchen. 'No, definitely not.'

'Then I'm in. It's nice this: us talking again. I like it.'

He grinned, and it was positively infectious, seeing him like that before her. Maybe if she still got little pieces of him, like this – she could cope without the rest. No-one ever got everything they wanted in life, right? Two out of three was still pretty good.

'Good, me too. It's a date then.'

When she got to the bar, she played the words over in her head. *It's a date.* She'd never corrected him. She could have, but something in her didn't want to. *Stop it,* she told herself. *You have sperm ordered. Actual baby-making schedules to start.* The thing was, the only thing that wasn't ruddy frozen was her heart.

## 14

'Any good?' Tyler gave her the thumbs up, but his puckered-up face told a different story.

'Really?' She raised a sceptical brow. 'Because you look like you're about to throw up.'

Tyler shook his head, but the motion turned his complexion green. Holding up a finger, he tapped at his chest and swallowed audibly.

'I did. In my mouth.' He grabbed at the bottle of water on her kitchen counter. 'Kinda regretting my suggestion to work on a drinks menu right now. We should have gone bowling or something instead.' His lips quirked up. 'Save my pride at least, and probably my liver.'

'That bad, huh?' She sniffed at her own glass. To be fair, it did smell rank. She could practically feel her nose hairs singeing.

After draining half the water bottle, he sagged against the counter. 'Even the vomit didn't improve the taste. You can't serve that.'

'Come on! It can't be that bad.' She lifted the cocktail to her lips, but Tyler reached across and pinched the straw shut between his fingertips.

'Don't. That shit will take the lining of your stomach and, if you're going to be a mother, you're going to need it.'

She eyed him for a moment over the glass and threw the drink down the sink. It was the first time he'd mentioned anything to do with her motherhood plan since their blow up. It made her feel funny, warm inside. Like he might just accept this. Heck, that it might actually be a reality some point soon. Tonight, here in her little place with Tyler, making cocktails – it was the most fun she'd had in a while. His effortless smile when he'd turned up earlier in his usual flannel shirt and jeans looking like some kind of stocky Yorkshire cowboy, she could see he was lighter too. It was as if something had sparked within him, too. She'd miss him being so close to her. When she thought of serving his menu at the Arms, without him behind the stove in the back, it didn't feel as exciting somehow. Still shiny, but duller somehow. Perhaps she should have told him not to look for that job after all. She pulled herself out of the feeling of dread that washed over her, back to the night she was enjoying.

'Fair enough. Nice to see that you're coming around to the whole baby thing.'

He finished the bottle, still rubbing at his chest. 'Good Gordon Ramsay, it burns. And I wouldn't say that.' He said it in a grumpy huff, but the heat from before wasn't present. It gave her hope.

'Oh, give over, you know it will be cool.'

He rolled his eyes, still rubbing his chest. 'Cool is not how I would describe it. Surprising, definitely. Difficult, maybe. It's not what you think it will be, you know. It will be harder.'

Amber rinsed out the jug, throwing the rest of her death cocktail concoction away down the drain and reaching for fresh ingredients. 'Wow, Uncle Tyler is going to be a real bummer.'

'Uncle, yeah.' He threw the empty bottle into the recycling bin a little harder than was necessary. The gruff lumberjack was waking up. 'Well, I guess that's better than nothing. I never did tell you why I don't want kids, did I?'

Amber ignored him in favour of chopping fresh watermelon into small chunks.

'Nothing to say? Not curious?'

'No, not everyone wants a family. I get it. Do you think almond milk would work? We could do some milkshake-type cocktails maybe?'

'Almond milk, sure. Nice way to change the subject.'

'Yeah, well – this is what I want to focus on.'

'Fine.' He shrugged, but she could tell he wanted to say more. 'We can do that.'

They both reached for the fridge door at the same time.

'Sorry,' they said together.

Tyler's brow knitted tight. 'I am sorry, actually. I didn't mean to be snarky.'

'Again.'

'Eh?'

'Snarky again.' She opened the fridge, passing him another bottle of water and reaching for the carton of almond milk. 'You've been like this since you found out.'

'I know. I have my reasons. Which you don't want to talk about.'

'So, I don't want to talk about it tonight.' She flashed him a bright smile she didn't feel. 'It hurts when you act like this, Ty.'

His lips pressed together, but he didn't speak.

'I thought we were past this. You're my friend. My biggest supporter, as it goes. Since I have no family. You are my family, you and Shazza; our regulars are all like my friends, but you are family. Both of you. Sharon hasn't given me half as much stick. She's the one who always said she'd rather stick pins in her eyes than be a single parent, but she's been pretty laidback about it. In fact, she was more bothered about the fact I might have given in to Bradley than becoming a mail-order mum.'

'She told me.'

'She did?'

Tyler nodded slowly, reaching for the carton in her hands and leading her over to the counter.

'Yep. She threatened to punch me in the nether regions if I didn't stop it.'

'Good old Shazza.' She nudged his arm playfully with her elbow. He didn't even move. It was like bumping up against a solid wall. 'She'll be a good auntie.'

'Oh, yeah, sure,' Tyler scoffed, taking the lid off the blender and pouring the milk in. 'She'll teach your kid to neck shots and avoid traffic tickets by flirting.'

Amber laughed, scooping the thin slices of melon in. 'Hey, don't knock it. They're not bad skills to have. Remember that awful stretch of road near the hospital? I once got away with doing forty in a thirty by crying and flashing a bit of cleavage.' Tyler's shocked face made her laugh all the harder. 'Don't mock, it worked. I got to her bedside in time to hold her hand while she passed, too.' The silence that fell around them settled like a heavy, scratchy blanket. Thinking of her grandmother in her last moments used to make her sad, but, now, that last interaction was a cherished one. 'You know, the great Norma Fitzpatrick wasn't afraid of anything. Even when it was her time, she was still...' She thought for a moment, trying to find the right word. 'Happy, I guess. She was almost excited, to see Grandad again. I was always more like her than I was either of my parents. I wanted to be her when I grew up. I still do.'

Tyler's hand was on her shoulder before she'd finished her sentence. His thumb tracing small, comforting circles on the bare skin above her sleeve cuff. When he caught her watching the movement, he dropped his hand.

'I suppose there could be worse things than having a fun aunt.' Tyler's voice was soft, gentle. 'I do get why you're doing it. I've thought about it a lot. Actually, I've thought of nothing but.'

Amber measured some sloe gin and tipped it in. 'It's not because of my grandparents.'

'I know—'

'No, you don't. You think I'm some sad, lonely woman staring at her thirties and panicking about the future. I'm not doing this because I feel lonely, Tyler. I'm doing it because I want to. I've always wanted to: the business, the child of my own. That's all I've wanted for as long as I can remember. And, yeah, when I get to Nana's age, I want to be like her. To have all that love and happiness around her. To make people happy, and feel like someone's there. These old pubs are a dying breed. They're closing all the time. The working men's clubs are seen as archaic. Old patrons are dying off far faster than new members join. Community used to be something, you know? My nana was at the heart of it. It's not all just pies and pints.'

She cut off his reply by turning on the blender. He put his hand over hers on the power button. Huffing, she turned it off and side-eyed him.

'I get it. I do. I know how much you've changed this place. The Arms would be fantastic with you there as the owner.' He smiled. 'You'd be great at everything, Cherry. I just worry that you're reacting. After everything. I get it. Believe me. Back in London, when everything happened, I reacted. I upped sticks and left everything. Started again. Closed myself off to a lot of things.'

'Do you regret it?' she asked, suddenly fearful that he would go back there. A new job could take him anywhere. 'Leaving?'

'Not that, no, but I have other regrets. This whole baby thing, it kind of spun my head around. I just want you to be sure, and not react quickly. Which is pretty hypocritical I guess, coming from me.'

Amber sighed. 'I am reacting, but not without thought.' She poured out a shot of grenadine and added it to the mix. 'I was upset, sure. And angry. At myself. For thinking that a man, and our relationship, was the cornerstone of my life. I am the cornerstone, Ty. Before Bradley, I never needed a man to build my life. I can make things happen on my own. Which is what I should have done in the first place, not hanging by the kitchen sink like some obedient little housewife. I knew what I wanted. I just forgot to keep building. Yes, I was drunk when I went on my little Internet quest, but I don't regret it. I just actioned things already primed. I haven't cancelled a thing. I don't want to.' She sighed, shaking her head. 'If I'm honest, the more time I'm not with Bradley, the more I see what I put up with the last six months, and I'm not going back to that. I can do this, and if you can't accept it—'

'I can,' he butted in. 'I'm here. Hand me a trowel, I'll get to work. I want to help you to have your dreams. I never did. I shut everything down, ran off. I guess I'm a little in awe of you, Cherry. Anything you need help with, I'm here. I'm just sorry I didn't handle things very well. I just had a different plan, I guess.'

'I know,' she breathed. He looked so conflicted, like he was rethinking his life. She wanted to know what had hurt him so deeply. Take it away. 'What did happen, in London? Is that why you don't want a family?'

His eyes searched hers. 'Yeah. It was.' His gaze dropped to her lips. 'I think you were right, though. It's a story for another day. In fact...' He walked over to the phone dock and tapped a few keys on his phone.

The tension popped in the room as he shot her a cheeky grin.

'What are you doing?' She laughed.

'Breaking the tension. I hate it when you get that little frown line on your forehead.' He bit at his lip, and her eyes followed the motion automatically. 'No more future talk. Tonight was supposed to be fun.' The second he docked it in the holder, music began to play. Familiar music. 'We're making cocktails for your new place. I think we should make a night of it.'

'"My Girl", really?' Her heart swelled. He looked like he could hold up the world on one shoulder but, man, the guy loved his cheesy pop songs. He also never missed a trick. It made her heart beat faster. Another part of not having Bradley around was this. The part she didn't expect. The fact that her friend, the gentle giant she totally fancied and always depended on, took her breath away. For a moment, she wished he was the one she was doing all this with. She pushed the thought away. Life was complicated enough. She couldn't let anything else get in the way. Not now she was so close.

Tyler wagged his finger at her, moving away from the counter with a sway of his hips. 'It's your favourite and you know it.'

She groaned, turning on the blender and adding ice. She could hear his laugh even over the motor. He turned up the volume, clicking his fingers as he moved around the kitchen, humming. She watched him, crooning away to the song her grandmother used to dance around her kitchen to. Having him here felt right. *Like home.* She turned off the blender and poured it into two cocktail glasses. The whole counter was filled with fruit, bottles of different and exotic alcohol, chocolate pieces and maraschino cherries, olives on sticks. Watching the man before her dance around, she knew she was where she wanted to be.

The song ended, and Tyler set it to shuffle. When Roy Orbison's 'Only The Lonely' started up, she squealed.

'I love this song too!'

'I know.' He shrugged, heading over to take one of the glasses.

His salty aftershave surrounded her, and she felt that pang all over again. *Your plans don't involve Tyler. He isn't up for being some insta baby daddy. He deserves to get a better job. He's not yours to try to keep, Amber. Don't drag him any further into your mess.* Tyler was looking at her latest creation, a relaxed smile lighting up his face. Utterly unaware that her mind was spinning right next to him. 'I pay attention to everything you like. It's important. This looks like sludge by the way. Gin and milk?'

Christ, if he kept saying things like that, she might cave anyway, ask for *his* sperm. She mentally shook herself, pouring the drink into two glasses. *It's a night with two friends,* she reminded herself. *Fun.*

'Just try it. What radio station is this?' A lame question, but she felt the urge to keep talking.

'Playlist,' he replied, eyeing the cocktail with a wary gaze. 'Well, I'm not dying alone. Come on fellow guinea pig, drink up.'

He held out his glass and clinked it against hers.

'Bottoms up,' she said, trying to be breezy. Reciting *friend, friend, friend* over and over in her head.

'Yeah, I think this might come to that,' he grimaced. 'This stuff looks like it could explode your colon.'

They both took a tentative sip. *Eugh.* The milk was already curdling in the glass. 'Mmmm,' she faked, swallowing it and trying to look impressed.

'Mmmm?' Ty looked like he just sucked a lemon. 'It tastes like that bad goat's cheese starter we ate that time. Call yourself a landlady?'

She remembered that. Bradley had dragged them out to some new opening. They'd all been sick the next day. Tyler had come over and held her hair back while she vomited. The memory combined with the cocktail make her stomach flip.

'Yes!' she defended. 'It's not that bad.'

'Your customers are going to throw up all over your brand-new furnishings the second this crap touches their lips.' He took the glass from her and tipped them down the sink. 'My turn. A classic.'

He got to work as she watched, taking in the music as she swilled her mouth out with a drink from her own water bottle. He passed her a shot glass. 'Here, Slippery Nipple. Down the hatch. Get the taste of that nut milk off your palate.'

She shook her head, smirking as they necked the shots.

'Ahh,' they said in unison. 'Better.'

They cracked out laughing the second they clocked their unity. 'Fair enough.' She nodded. 'One to you. Another? I have an idea for a twist on a Tequila Sunrise.'

'Ooooh, that could work. People love the classics. More music?'

Another song she liked had started, and she shook her head. 'No, I quite like this album. It's pretty eclectic though, what's it called again?'

'Playlist, I told you. Want some help? I can wash some of this stuff up?'

'Sure.' She thought about how much he'd helped her lately. He'd given her so much of his time recently. 'You sure you didn't have plans tonight? Your nights off are as rare as mine.'

Filling the sink with suds, he shrugged. 'Nope. I have nowhere else to be.' He gave her a wink. 'Now get to work on those Sunrises, boss. Let's make a real night of it, while you still have the time.'

He busied himself with the washing up, and she studied him for a while. It was so nice having him here. She'd gotten used to having him around. The best parts of her days involved him. She found herself wishing that didn't have to change.

As if he sensed her thoughts, he turned to her with an inquisitive brow. 'You okay?'

She got to work on the cocktails. 'Yep, I'm good. I'm going to miss this, though. Working together, hanging out.'

He paused, his hands stilling in the soapy water. 'Nothing's set in stone yet.'

'I know, but you'll move on soon. We both will. I'll be... doing my thing, you'll be working somewhere else.'

He focused back on the washing up, his jaw clenching before he spoke again. 'I'll still be in your life.'

He shot her a nod, but it wasn't an easy motion. She felt like he was holding something back, and she didn't like the feeling. 'I'm happy for you too, Ty. You deserve everything you want.'

He huffed out a breath. 'I don't think anyone gets that, Cherry.' He raised his dark eyes to bore into hers. The things unsaid between them choked the very air they breathed. 'But.' His lips quirked, and she could draw breath once more. 'You can write me a killer reference.'

# 15

The Sunrise cocktails were pretty good. The second round was even better, and the third sublime.

'Hang on, hang on.' He sloshed a bit of his cocktail on the photo album, tutting as he used his flannel-clad arm to wipe it away. Backs to the couch, they were sitting cross-legged on the floor going down memory lane. 'That's you? No way.'

'Yes way!' Amber laughed. 'I'm telling you, that's me!'

'Geez, I thought your grandparents loved you!'

'Hey.' She elbowed him, reaching for her drink and looking at the perm she sported in the photo. 'I was fourteen; I begged for that hairstyle.'

Tyler's jaw almost hit his lap. 'You begged to have a perm? Like that? You look like a poodle.'

'That's what Grandad said!' They dissolved into loud bursts of laughter again. 'I will have to show this to my kid if they ever ask for photos.'

'Definitely.' Tyler laughed. 'Although, genetics play a factor. If you go ahead with your—'

'Don't,' Amber shushed him. 'We were having a good night. No real-life talk, remember?'

He tilted his head, but it wasn't as measured as usual. Sloppy from the alcohol they'd imbibed.

'Fair. Sorry. But it wasn't a dig. I just meant you won't know what you're getting, with the spermsicle.'

She giggled. 'Can we not call it that? And you do know what you're getting. It's like going to a clinic; you get a biography of the donor.'

'A spunk CV?' He was chuckling now, and she could feel his rumble through the floor. They were smushed up together, photos spread across their legs. After the cocktails, he'd spotted the albums and begged to have a look. With the music playing low in the background, it was pretty cosy. Amber was a little tipsy, but it was a nice buzz. 'I've heard everything now. So, what did you pick?'

'Are we really talking about this?' she checked. 'I didn't think you'd want to. You hate kids.'

'Hey,' his hand landed on hers. 'I never said that, and this would be your kid, if you do this. Of course I want to know.'

She shrugged. 'Okay. Well, you don't get specifics, but he's healthy. Dark hair, tall, brown eyes. Educated.'

Tyler raised a brow. 'That it?'

'Well, it hardly gives you his credit score, but the donors are all screened genetically. It's more about the type of person.'

'Surprising pick,' he mumbled. 'Given that Bradley is blonde with blue eyes. Figured that was more your type.'

'Yeah, well,' she met his dark-brown eyes. 'I guess I have a thing for tall, dark and handsome.'

She said it lightly, but the expression on his face held anything but laughter. 'Good to know.' He leaned in a little. Or maybe she'd done it. 'I have a question.'

'Okay, but if this is about Bradley—'

'It's not.' He scowled. 'I just want you to answer me one thing, no strings. No pressure.'

She swallowed, focusing on the little gold flecks circling the dark-brown irises of his eyes.

'Okay. Ask.'

He drew in a shuddery breath. 'That day, in the office, when you told me you'd thought about us.'

*Shit.* She felt her cheeks flush. 'Yeah?'

'Did you mean it?' He looked so vulnerable, his face turning boyish. 'When you said you'd thought about us, did you mean it?'

'Yes,' she rasped out. 'I meant it. You're pretty cute, Tyler Williams.'

His face pinked up as a slow grin spread across his nervous face. 'You're not so bad yourself, Cherry.' His eyes dropped to her lips. 'When you thought about us, was it just in a physical way?'

*Jesus.* Answering him would change things. They'd skirted around it. She was only just okay with staying his friend; it felt weird. Wrong. *No.* It didn't feel wrong. That was the problem.

'I don't know what you mean.' Playing dumb was pretty pathetic, but she was guarding her heart with everything she had here. She wasn't even in a position to take his, but she burned to know if he was even offering it in the first place.

'I mean,' he growled, 'did you think about how I could make you feel, in bed? Or more?'

'I... I—'

'If you're not sure,' his breath was hot on her cheek. 'I've obviously not been clear enough. Let me give you a clue.'

His lips touched hers, a chaste kiss, but that was all it took to send tingles throughout her body. His hand, still resting on hers, turned and claimed her touch with his. When he squeezed his fingers around her, brushing his lips against hers, she was lost in the feel of him. Fingers stroked down her cheek. He shifted, tentatively pulling her closer with his other arm, until he was holding her close to him. His lips were on an expedition, going where they had never gone before as they parted hers. She moaned, and he let out a little growl of approval in response. They'd kissed before, odd pecks on the cheek, one quick New Year's kiss the year before she'd met Sloane. His little kisses to her forehead that seared her skin. All very PG. This was not that. It was so much the opposite of that that it needed its own time zone, let alone a different postcode. This kiss felt like nothing before it, and her racing mind doubted she'd encounter it again. His arm around her, his fingers in her hair. His tongue teased hers and she heard his low, guttural moan again. Heard it over her own.

'Ty,' she breathed when she managed to get enough brain capacity to move her body away from what she was enjoying far too much. His lips found hers again, as if he couldn't bear to break the contact. He moved closer, until she pulled away a second time. 'Ty...'

His eyes opened, widening when they saw her face. She knew her expression was all shock and swollen lips. She didn't need a mirror to know that. 'Er...' He pulled back, running his hand down his jaw. 'Shit.'

'Yeah. Shit.' *That was amazing. I knew it would be. And now I'm utterly screwed.*

'I didn't mean to do that. I'm sorry.'

*Ouch.* She didn't expect that to hurt, but it did. A little barbed arrow to the heart she didn't expect. She didn't mean to do it either, but she could still taste him on her lips. He still had his arm around her waist.

'No. Me either,' she muttered, turning to rest her back on the sofa cushions. He mirrored her, and the heat from his touch lingered on her body. Made her shiver, but she wasn't sure that was entirely down to the sudden temperature shift. Her whole fricking body was screaming the answer to his question. *More. More. More.* She wanted to pull him back to her, tell him she didn't see him coming. He'd been there, but she'd never seen him. Not fully. Appreciated him. Fantasised maybe. But this? Bradley Sloane was a warty toad compared to this. A frog compared to a God-damn hunky, caring prince. His hands in her hair, his hold around her. Geez, a girl could camp in there and never want to leave. 'Listen, Ty. You don't have to—'

'I did mean to.' He cut her off with his deep, husky proclamation. 'I lied then. I did mean to kiss you. In fact, I didn't want it to stop. I've wanted to ask you that question every day since you told me you thought about me. Fuck. Even before that.'

He didn't turn to her. His hands were now on his legs. She could see the tension in his jawline as he stared straight ahead.

'Look at me,' she asked.

'I can't.'

'Ty...'

'I can't look at you without doing that again.'

*Oh. Ooohh.* Something else zinged along her spine. Excitement, mixed with want and shock.

'I can't do that again.'

'Right,' she agreed. Her voice sounded odd even to her own ears. 'No.'

'You have a lot on. I'm leaving soon.' A hollow laugh tore out of him. 'God, our timing fucking sucks.' He reached for his glass, draining the rest of it. 'I should go.'

*I don't want you to go. Stay.* Everything in her should be panicking, feeling guilty, but it wasn't there. That kiss had answered far more questions than his, and she didn't know how to marry up the information. She didn't tell him that, though. She closed the album that had fallen to the floor, sticking in on the sofa cushion behind her. 'Okay,' she got to her feet. The alcohol was burning off in her bloodstream. Adrenaline and pure lust devouring it like a super-fuel. 'I'll see you out.'

It was agony waiting for him to put his shoes on. His fingers looked as though they were shaking. He was concentrating on his shoelaces as if he was safety checking a parachute. She lingered nearby, not too close. Not close enough to touch him. She didn't know what her body would do if that happened. They got to the back door, and she watched him reach for his jacket from the coat rack on the wall.

'Why don't you wait 'til I get you a taxi?'

He faced her with a shake of his head. 'It's okay. I'll walk to the rank. I could use the fresh air.' He ran a hand through his hair with a deep, resigned sigh. 'Listen. Amber, I—'

'It's okay, don't worry. It was a mistake—'

'Don't say that.' His tone was as determined as his voice was deep. 'I don't regret it.'

'You don't?'

He was already shaking his head. At some stage, they'd moved closer. Her socked foot touched against his shoes as she looked up at him.

'No. God no. I know you want this life, this baby.'

She didn't answer.

His index finger came to rest under her chin, tilting her face up to his. 'That kiss wasn't a mistake.'

'No, but—'

'No?' His voice sounded hopeful.

'No, but—'

'No buts. Do you regret the kiss, Amber? Tell me the truth right now. If you do, I'll leave and I will never mention it again.'

He'd moved closer still, and the hand she'd held on the door handle slipped off and around his waist. She felt unsteady on her own legs, and the cocktails they'd necked were not the only reason.

'We've been drinking,' she pointed out.

'I'm not that drunk,' he retorted. 'You?'

Since their lips had touched, she'd felt as sober as a judge, but it was a factor. Had to be. *Didn't it?*

'Well, no.'

He was assessing her with that gaze of his again.

'So I didn't take advantage?'

Her heartbeat was pounding in her ears. 'No, Tyler, you'd never do that.'

The crease in his brow fell.

'I just don't know what that was, Tyler. What it means. I don't want to mess this up.'

'Yeah?' He wrapped his other arm around her. 'Maybe I should do it again. Just to be certain. Help you decide.' He huffed out a breath. 'I think we both need a little clarity right now.'

Her fingers tightened on his waist. She could feel the muscles tense underneath.

'Tyler.'

'Yes or no, Amber? Tell me to leave. If you don't feel what I just did, I'll go and never mention it again. It never happened.'

'It would be easier. For both of us.'

He shook his head. 'Screw that. Life's not easy. You taught me that. I sat on the sidelines of my own life before I met you. I never wanted things after London; I didn't see the point. My ex, Lauren?'

Amber nodded, holding her breath.

'She was pregnant.'

Amber stiffened, watching Tyler sort through his feelings before he spoke again. 'It wasn't planned. I was working all kinds of hours, building my career. I wanted to open my own place eventually. But then she was pregnant, and I was happy.' He shook his head, brows knitted together. 'I thought it was a good thing, you know.'

'What happened? To the baby?'

'She was acting weird all through the pregnancy. I was working to get some money together. She was distant. I thought it was just hormones, you know. Stress. 'Til she told me the truth. She waited almost nine months to admit that the kid wasn't mine. Blamed me.' His laugh was hollow. 'Said it was my fault, leaving her alone all the time. She got bored, had an affair with someone from work.'

'Oh Tyler. I had no idea.'

He shrugged. 'I stayed around 'til the baby was born. The paternity came back. The little guy wasn't mine, so I left. I packed up my shit, quit my job, and left London the next day. Came here.'

'I can't believe she did that to you.'

'I can. The two of us, we were never really good, you know? If not for the baby, we'd have ended a long time before, but I got attached. I loved the baby before I even met him. Did the whole thing, shopping for cribs. Ultrasounds. I was all in. I was going to be a dad, and then I wasn't. He didn't look like me, when he was born. I was there. I was still there for her, you know? The other guy split the second he found out, and I stayed. The second I saw him, I knew. It broke my fucking heart not to be his dad, after all that. Even though I didn't love his mother, I still wanted him to be mine. I didn't trust her after that, and she knew it.'

'You would have stayed?'

He shook his head. 'It wouldn't have worked. We both knew it was over the second the test came back. She told me to leave, and I felt... relieved. It wouldn't have been right for the kid either. He deserved better than that. So I came here, got my head down. I just wanted to cook. When I first came for this job, I wasn't going to take it for long. I just wanted a break before I figured out my next move. It was meeting you that changed my mind. Kept me here. I see how much you mean to everyone around you. How happy you make people without even realising it. You taught me to fight for the life you want. I'm realising more and more that being scared of things, being damaged by the past. It does nothing but wreck your future.'

'I've hardly been doing that lately.'

'Maybe not, but you are now. I'm in fucking awe of you, Amber. Watching you these last few weeks, it gave me hope. Woke me up.' His eyes were full of adoration. She'd never felt so seen, even by him. 'The baby thing threw me; I know I didn't react in the best way. But I can't just walk away, not without a fight. This is me fighting. No more sidelines. We can talk about the rest later. I know I might get hurt, but I can't do this any more.' He sighed, and it sounded like it came from the very depths of him. 'I know things are complicated, but... I can't stay away from you. I can't just be a friend, unless that's all you want from me.' He tapped his index finger against his temple. 'You're in my head, all the time. I want to be there for you. Be your champion. Help you with your baby, if that's what you choose in the end of all this. Whatever you need me to be, I'll be it.' He swallowed. 'Even if it crushes me to do it, I'll gladly do it. For you, Amber.'

She wanted to take the big lummox in her arms, soothe him. He was too good, too selfless. He would do all of that, and more. She was so wrong about him. It wasn't that he didn't want a woman; it was that he wanted one so much. *Me. I've been a blind fool, but now what?* What if she couldn't do it, be what he wanted? She'd already torn pieces off herself to fit Bradley. What if Tyler did that for her? He'd resent her in the end. Raising another man's child. Living someone else's dream. 'I don't want to hurt you, Tyler. We're on different paths.'

'Fuck paths,' he rasped. 'I'm hurting right now. Might as well shoot my shot. Yes or no, Cherry. Do you want my lips on yours again, or am I leaving? Don't think about the rest. Not right now.'

She was staring into his eyes. Feeling his arms around her was making her head spin. That wasn't the cocktails, she knew. Her lips were still stinging from that kiss. It would be easier to ask him to go. In the morning, things would be back to normal. Like it never happened. *Liar,* her head sang back. *Nothing is normal after this. Not even close.* She was frozen in place, scared.

'I guess that's my answer.' He pulled away, reaching for the lock. 'Goodnight, Amber.'

He went to turn the lock, but it didn't move. Amber's fingers held it closed.

'Don't go,' was all she said. 'I don't want you to go.'

'Why?' he asked, his voice breathy. 'Tell me why.'

She knew what he was really asking. For permission. For a sign that she was in this with him. All the ways it couldn't and shouldn't work were running through her brain. He'd be leaving soon, she'd be a mum, running the Arms if she got what she wanted. If she did this, there would be consequences. Her head was screaming at her to flip the lock. Release him out into the night so she could stick to her plan. He would do it all with her, but she couldn't hold him back. Not when he'd already stayed for her. Watched her with another man. What was he going to do? Stay in Hebblestone forever, raising a child that wasn't his? She didn't want to wait. Not now her mind was made up, and asking him to have a child with her was insane. She wouldn't let him derail his life for her. She'd done it before, and she knew now that she was stupid for it. Things were changing, rapidly. This was so far from what she thought would happen, it was like looking at someone else's life.

The trouble was, that kiss. *That felt right.* She needed to know. She knew if she rejected him now, she might never have the chance again. He'd basically ripped his heart out of his chest and shown it to her. Letting him go now, she might as well knock it to the floor and stamp on it. She could see it on his face. The desire and the fear roiling through him. She took a beat too long.

He growled in frustration. 'It's fine, Amber, I get it. I'll go.' When he tried to open the door again, the urgency of her panic at him leaving galvanised her to speak. She realised she couldn't let him go. It overrode everything else in her mind, shushing it into submission as she gravitated towards the man in front of her.

'Stay.'

'If you want me to stay, then tell me why.' He swallowed. 'I need to hear you say it. Say anything.'

'Because I want you to kiss me again.'

'What about—'

'I can't think about anything else right now. I just want you to kiss me, Tyler. Stay with me tonight.'

It was all he needed. His arms encircled her, and she was off the ground, her legs automatically lifting to lock around him. His mouth crashed down onto hers, and he kissed her like a sailor on shore leave. It was so damn hot, she could barely stand it as she let his mouth claim hers. She'd never been kissed like this before. He held her like she was precious. Like he wanted to *consume* her.

'Ooh!' The shudder of pleasure came unbidden from her throat, and he stilled.

'Jesus, Amber. What was that noise?' He pressed his lips to her neck, sucking her tender skin. 'How do I make you do it again?'

She laughed, until he moved to her collarbone, and it died in her throat in favour of a breathy pant. It was his turn to chuckle then as he ran a line along it with his tongue, and she moaned again.

'Fuck me. That's it. Just like that. I could bottle that sound, Cherry.'

'What are we doing?' she asked, not really caring to hear the answer in that moment. Real life seemed a world away from his tongue and its sexy travels. 'Why does it feel so...'

'Want me to stop?' he checked, denying her of his mouth. His eyes were hooded under heavy lids as his gaze flicked from hers to her lips and back again. Looking like he was holding onto everything until he got permission to unleash. *Christ, he was a total beast. It was soooo hot.* 'Amber, talk to me. Tell me if you want me to stop this, but you need to be quick.'

*Decision time, Amber.* She was flip flopping from go to stop quicker than a faulty traffic light. The old her, from a couple of months ago, would have run from this. Her to-do list did not include this, any of it. The new her, or rather the oldest version of her, the one who had her grandmother's fire and zest for life, and love and joy, wanted this more than she wanted to take her next breath. She didn't want to second guess it. She just wanted to *feel*.

Reaching behind her, still encased in his grasp, she put the chain on the door. His eyes flicked to it, and then focused back onto hers. She put her hands round his neck, and they stayed there. Looking at each other as if it was the first time they'd set eyes on the person in front of them. In a weird way, it kinda felt that way too. New, yet so familiar. *Right.*

'Didn't think so,' he rumbled beneath her, and claimed her mouth. She was so lost in the kiss, she didn't even notice him carrying her up the stairs. He didn't stop kissing her as he strode down the hallway. He didn't stop when he steered them to the kitchen, grabbing the small pack of bottled water open on the counter. Didn't break his lips from hers when he grabbed her butt cheeks to get a better hold. Didn't stop teasing her with his gorgeous-ass tongue at the same time as kicking open her bedroom door. *Lumberjack,* she said in her head. *My sexy, strong lumberjack.*

He did break contact when he set her down in front of the bed, getting to work on taking off her jeans. His fingers were shaky as he undid her buttons. He pulled her zipper down, dropping kisses on each cheek. He kept looking down at her, as if he was making sure she was still there. She couldn't stop watching him, wanting to process the moment. She was about to have sex with Tyler

Williams. She said it to herself over and over in her head as he lowered, slid the denim down her legs. It felt surreal. Crazy, but not wrong. She wanted this. She needed this. Needed to see what this thing was between them. Anything else – the Arms, the future – it was all just white noise, silenced by his searing touch.

He knelt before her, lifting each leg in turn to remove her clothing.

'Tyler,' she breathed.

All she got back was a mischievous grin, barely getting the chance to steady herself back on her feet before his stubble rubbed along the inside of her bare thighs. 'Yes, Cherry?' He ran his calloused hands over the skin on the outside of her legs until he reached her lace thong. He locked eyes with her as his fingers slipped under the fabric on her hips. 'You want me to take these off?'

'Yes,' she panted. 'Please.'

His grin was triumphant. A second later, her panties were on the floor next to her jeans. She felt the urge to close her legs, but his hand held fast on her body.

'Hang on to something,' he rumbled, his voice rich and deep. 'I might be a while.' Dipping his head, he got to work between her legs. Lazily, as if he had all the time in the world, he licked from her clit all the way down her seam. 'I knew it,' he said, as if to himself. 'I knew you'd be wet for me. Jesus, Amber. I can't take it. Need more.' He licked again, faster this time, swirling in a small circle when he reached the bundle of nerves. This time, she let the moan burst forth from her lips. The combination of his tongue and the heat of her made her jolt. He raised a hand, splaying it against her stomach. 'Don't move, little noise maker.'

She hadn't planned on it. She couldn't string a sentence together if she tried right now, let alone move. Any thought she'd ever had or ever would have lost to the orgasm he was currently building with his attentions. Already, she could feel the quiver in the pit of her stomach. *Christ almighty. He was good at this. He was wasted in a damn kitchen.* He kicked up his pace, moving faster, moving his hand from her stomach to her centre while holding her up with his other meaty hold on her hip. When he slipped a finger in, growling like a lion, she grabbed at his hair, fisting it between her fingers for something to hold onto. She felt a bit like a rider on a rodeo bull. If the rodeo bull was flicking her clitoris over and over with his mouth while grabbing her butt cheeks in a one palm grip. He was everywhere, all at once. Filling her, playing her body expertly and making her legs shake. 'Ty, I'm going to... to...'

'That's the plan,' he said, before delving back down and speeding up. When he did that, she was gone. Tipping over the edge in seconds and breathing like she'd run a marathon. 'That's it,' he rumbled, sucking at her as she came. Hard.

As her orgasm subsided, he held her by the hips, rising to stand. The second he did, her hands came to his trousers. Freeing him, taking off his clothes as they removed the rest of anything that was between their bare skin. 'Lie down with me,' he asked, and she sank down onto the bed. He was hard, painfully so, and she felt him brush against her stomach as he came to settle between her legs. Even as her orgasm fell away, she was still half crazy for him. He was so measured, so calm. His eyes boring into her as if he was committing it all to memory.

'Why do you always look at me like that?' she asked him as his body hovered over hers.

His smile was happy, a goofy expression on his face. 'Because I know you, Amber. Because you're beautiful.' He kissed her as if he couldn't resist. 'Because you deserve someone who watches you and knows just what they have in front of them.' He dropped a kiss on her forehead, and her heart fluttered.

'I didn't see you coming,' she told him. 'You were just my grumpy friend.'

'Still am.' He grinned. 'I've not changed. You just know why I was moody now.'

He moved closer, caging her in with his arms, but she could see he was holding himself up. 'You're all tense.' She ran her hands over his back, feeling his taut muscles right down to the dimples at the bottom of his back. 'And hot. It's ridiculous. Are you made from stone?'

'Nope. All me, Cherry. I'm trying not to crush you.' He chuckled, and she felt his cock twitch against her stomach. His eyes widened. 'I'm so hard right now, it's taking a lot not to ruin this by going too fast.'

'Let me help,' she soothed, pushing against his shoulders. His eyes shot up in surprise, but he let her roll him onto his back. His hands were on her hips the second she settled above him, and she reached down to hold his length.

'Amber,' he hissed as her hands wrapped around him. 'Oh fuck, I need you so badly.' She rubbed his thick, impressive tip against her wetness, feeling him twitch from the contact with her core. He reached up, his hands covering her bare breasts. 'These are perfect.' He ran his thumbs along both nipples, making them peak all the harder from his touch. He rose up, wrapping his arms around her and taking one in his mouth. With his surge forward, he took her by surprise and the tip of his cock slid into her. *What the... ohmygoodGod.* He was so big, and hard, but she was so wet. So turned on, he slid in, and she lost it. 'Tyler!' Her body took over, and she ground her hips down on him, making him groan.

'Fuck Amber, you're so... tight. I didn't mean to... not yet...'

'Yes,' she begged, afraid he was going to pull out. 'Don't stop. It's so... good.' She moved her hands to the side of his face, into his hair.

'Baby, I couldn't stop if I tried. Are you sure you're ready?'

'I'm ready,' she panted.

'You're so beautiful,' he whispered.

She met his eye and pushed down a little further. Her body was in the driving seat now, and it wanted to ride Tyler Williams like she'd never wanted anything more. 'Please!' she begged, moving from side to side with her hips, anything to feel more of this.

'Are you sure?' he asked. 'We haven't talk—'

'Please,' she begged. 'I'm so turned on right now. I need you to fuck me, Ty.' Their eyes locked, and she kissed the ever-loving hell out of him. She felt the moment his resolve shuddered, and then broke. Pulling his arms tighter around her, he surged up and filled her to the hilt. Their collective groans were loud in the silence of the room, and then they were lost to the feelings.

'You're so tight. You feel so… amazing.' He tugged at her bottom lip with his teeth as she rode him, feeling everything he was giving her and the punishing pace they had set together. They were wild for each other, as if everything in them from the last few years was flooding out of them into the other. All the little laughs, the way he looked after her. The way he looked at her. She could feel it all now, in him. She finally understood how much he'd been holding himself back. She felt tiny on top of him, but so safe. So in control. She was making this hulking, muscled wall of a man come apart underneath her, and she fricking loved it.

'I can't get enough of you,' he mumbled, his thrusts shaky and erratic as he shuddered under her. 'You're so perfect,' he went on. 'You feel so good, riding my cock. I knew you'd feel like this, I thought of it so many times. I… I…' His face was flushed, his scowl there but different. She could tell he was losing the battle for control. 'Amber, I need you to come. I can't hold off any—'

'I'm there,' she moaned, spurring him on even faster. 'Oh wow, Ty. I'm going to come so hard!'

He bit down gently on her nipple, and it send her crashing right over the edge. Like jumping off a waterfall, she rose and fell, and just as she was starting to see stars, he thrust up. Once, twice. On the third time, he buried his face in her neck and ground out her name as he came inside her. Didn't stop thrusting as her spasming channel squeezed out every drop of his release with the shudders still running through her. He kissed at her neck, not letting her go as they both came down.

'That was perfect,' he said eventually, and she felt the rumble of his words against her chest as she held him to her. 'Shit,' he stilled. 'Amber. Fuck. I'm so sorry, I didn't...'

Her heart stopped and she snapped her head back to meet his eye. *He regretted it. After all this, he regretted it? Already?*

'Didn't want?' she forced herself to ask.

His face was stricken. 'I didn't mean to, I got carried away. The second I got inside you, I lost control.'

*He did. He regretted it!*

She felt like she'd been slapped in the face. She went to get off him, her face burning, but he stopped her.

'Amber, no,' he stuttered. 'Not that, I don't regret that!' He kissed her again. 'Condom,' he pushed out. 'I meant I didn't put a condom on, but I'm clean and—'

'I haven't slept with... anyone for weeks,' she told him. The Bradley spectre rose up in the room, but she exorcised it from her head. She felt comfy, here in the dark, Tyler's arms around her. 'It's okay,' she told him. 'I'm okay with it. I think we're safe.' She'd been tracking her cycles. She was pretty sure it wasn't her window.

His face was cautious, but the dopey, sated version of him was coming back fast. It looked good on him. She would love to see it more.

'Yeah?' he checked.

'Yeah.' She nodded. 'We're okay.'

His brows relaxed, and his grin was pure happiness.

'Yeah,' he breathed, their bodies still connected in every way. 'We're more than okay, Amber.' He touched his forehead to hers, before lifting her into bed like she was precious cargo. Slipping under the sheets, she felt him behind her. His arms coming back to encircle her as they lay together.

'Goodnight, Cherry,' he said into the nook of her neck. 'Sleep tight, baby.'

## 16

---

The sun lit up the room through the open curtains when Amber's lids finally fluttered open. She blinked a few times, clearing the sleep from her just-opened eyes. Her mouth was a little dry, her head a little fuzzy. It took her a second to come around, and then last night slammed into her memory. *Wow. What the hell was that* repeated in her head, an endless ticker-tape question. She'd had sex with Tyler. More than once. They'd reached for each other in the night, and those times had been slower. Less hurried love making, but somehow even more meaningful. She blushed, remembering the way he'd held her close when he pushed into her, whispering her name as his brown eyes levelled her with a look of pure obsession. Perfect, mind-blowing sex. Each time, they'd drifted back to sleep, wrapped in the other, as if they'd been doing this forever.

Her whole body ached in a delicious way, the crumpled bedsheets wrapped around her. The pillow smelled like him. She knew before she even moved her head that he wasn't asleep next to her. She reached a tentative hand across; the bottom sheet was still warm from his body. She sat up, propped on her elbows. The room was empty. Their clothes were littered across the floor like strewn rose petals, the bed a tangled mess of duvet. *This is... bad. Did he leave?* She thought of the past before she could stop herself. All the times she'd woken up alone, and her heart clenched. *Wait...* Amber looked at the clothes again. Tyler's clothes were still there... which meant...

'Morning, beautiful.'

He was standing in the doorway, a tray from her kitchen in his hands. She couldn't help but ogle the sight of him. The thick, dark hair she'd run her fingers through last night was ruffled, shooting off in all directions. His stubble was thicker than he normally kept it, making his jaw look all the more manly, rugged. She shivered, remembering him running it along her neck the night before. Her bare breast. She was pretty sure she had stubble rash on her skin from that jaw. When her eyes finally lifted back from his boxers to his face, it was only his eyes she saw then. He was looking at her as if she was the best thing he'd ever seen.

'Hello, handsome.' She smiled back, feeling silly all of a sudden for having been caught ogling him. His returning smile could only be described as triumphant. 'I thought you'd gone.'

His grin dipped a little as he nodded to the tray.

'I went to make breakfast.' He went to take a step, but his foot fell back to meet its mate. 'Did you want me to be gone?'

'No,' she said without hesitation. 'It's just...'

'I know.' He came over to the side of the bed, putting the tray down between them as he sat back against the pillows. 'You don't have to say anything. I'm not going anywhere, Cherry. After last night, I don't think I'd have enough energy to get down the stairs.' She blushed again, remembering him carrying her to the bedroom like an absolute sex god. 'You need to eat.'

She smiled, sitting up to match him, taking in the contents of the tray. He'd made them both eggs, white, buttered toast, bacon that was well done and crisped up just how she liked. Two glasses of orange juice and two mugs of steaming hot coffee sat side by side. 'Wow. This looks amazing.'

He shrugged, but she spotted the tiny, satisfied twitch of his full lips. 'Tuck in,' he commanded. They sat and ate together, his legs coming back under the covers. It was so weird, so easy. Tyler had stayed over before, but never like this. Never post coital, wearing nothing but boxers. Never having stayed the night in her bed. *Wrapped around me like the world's best, sexiest blanket.*

When their plates were empty, the juice drank, they finished off the coffee. She eyed him over her mug, bare chested against her headboard. She'd never done this with Bradley. He was normally only up for a quickie in the mornings, or he was running off to get showered and start his workday. Even on the weekends, he'd never made her eggs and coffee in bed. Never laid beside her, looking at her as if he had all the time in the world, and nowhere else he'd rather be.

When he saw her looking back at him, he laughed. A low, easy rumble. 'What?' he teased. 'Panicking?' His gaze was easy, but she'd felt him tense up through the mattress.

'No, not panicking. Just... well, I didn't expect it. Not that I mean, it... but... well, yeah I did mean it, but... not "it" it.' When they locked eyes again, he laughed. Which made her giggle. 'Come on, you know what I mean.'

'I do,' he pushed, 'but I'm more interested to hear what you've got to say.' He finished the rest of his coffee. 'I enjoyed last night.'

'So did I.'

There it was. That little smile she was beginning to love seeing splayed across his lips. She'd seen Tyler laugh and smile a million times, but never quite like that.

'You're different, you know. You seem...'

'I'm happy, Amber. Last night for me was a long time coming. I didn't think it would happen that way, but I don't regret it.' He set the mug back on the tray, reaching to take her hand in his. 'You thought I'd be gone, but you didn't want me to be. Right?'

She nodded, a lump in her throat at his words.

'So that means you don't regret this either. I really think we could—'

His phone cut him off, making Amber jump. It rang out loud in the previously tranquil bedroom. Like a gunshot scattered sleeping birds in the peaceful forest. He sighed, reached and pulled it out of his jeans pocket. She looked at the caller display, and her morning glow ebbed away. It was the agency he'd signed up with for his job hunt.

'Shouldn't you get that?' she said when he made no move to pick up the call.

'I'm not answering it.' The smile she loved on his face was gone now, his jaw set hard. He reached for her hand, as if he was expecting her to jump from the bed. She had to admit, she had considered it. In the light of day, the future loomed large between them.

'It might be a job offer,' she probed.

Tyler's sigh was loud in the room. 'I've already been offered one. In London. And I'm not interested in taking the job, Amber. To be honest, I never really was.' His throat worked. 'I don't need that now.' He huffed out a laugh. 'I mean, Jesus, I was only going to leave because we'd stopped talking. When you told me about the baby plan, it kinda brought up some stuff. I was about to call the agency off.'

The phone rang again, and Tyler cut the call off. Threw the phone down on the bed.

'Tyler, you got a job?'

He pressed his lips together. 'They offered me a job in London. Chef Ainsley's new place had an opening.' Amber baulked.

'James Ainsley, the chef you worship?' Ainsley had his own chain of exclusive restaurants, best-selling cookbooks and a regular celebrity slot on morning television. Tyler had nurtured a major man crush on him for as long as she'd known him. To be offered a job there would be amazing for his career. 'Why the hell wouldn't you tell me that?'

He shrugged, but for once, he didn't meet her eye. 'Because I wasn't going to take it, Amber. We're good now. There was no point. I'm not leaving you.'

'Tyler, that's insane! You're wasted here! That's your dream!'

'No, Amber, it's not. I'm good. I know we have some stuff to sort out, but I told you. I'm not going anywhere.'

'You weren't going to tell me, were you?' She thought back to everything he said last night. Everything he'd been doing for her. The menus, the dishes, spurring her on. He was putting everything on hold for her. He'd fallen in love with a baby that wasn't his, and now what? If he stayed, he'd be doing the same thing. Following her dreams, at the expense of his own. Raising a child he didn't really want. Her heart swelled and broke at the same time. She couldn't cope with it. She couldn't do it to him. He'd let her do it, and then what? Would he end up resenting her? 'Tyler, that job would be amazing.'

'I'm not taking it, baby. I don't want to go to London. I didn't tell you because I knew you'd be like this. There was no point discussing it.' His scowl deepened when his phone started ringing again. He ignored it. 'I'll call them back later, tell them I changed my mind.'

Amber shook her head. This was all such a mess. Tyler couldn't do this. She cared about him too much to drag him into her chaos a second longer. She had to stick to the plan. Be on her own. Cut ties, and try to salvage what she could out of this whole thing. He'd hate her, but she could live with it. In the long run, he'd be happier.

He'd realise one day, once he was following his own path, that this was the right thing to do.

'Tyler, I need you to go.' She scrambled out from under the duvet, knocking the tray flying. 'We can't do this.' Tyler didn't move for the longest time as she babbled on, throwing on the nearest top and sweatpants she could grab from her drawers. 'Jesus Christ, it's such a mess. I have to open up, get the Slug organised.'

The phone stopped ringing, and after a second, started right up again.

She grabbed his clothes from the floor, passing them to him as he rounded the bed and came to stand in front of her. He looked so sexy, standing there in her bedroom clad in his black boxers. She tried not to look, even though later she knew it was all she would think about. Last night would torture her forever.

'Amber, take a breath. Don't be mad about London; I don't care about the job. We need to talk about this, make a plan.'

'Oh yeah.' She laughed bitterly. 'I'm full of those, Ty. But I'm not costing you yours. I have so much baggage, I could fill my own airport. Don't you see?'

He shook his head. 'See what? You panicking, when we finally did this? I want you, don't you get that yet? I want you. So much. All of you. Everything you are. Everything you want. I'm in this. When it comes to you, I'm on board.'

'So you're going to stay. Run the Arms with me, see my dreams happen. Raise a child that's not yours?'

He swallowed. 'If you still want to do the baby thing, then yes. I mean, the Arms comes first, right? The rest might take me a minute. I want you, Amber. That's the point. I'm not leaving.'

She felt the tears hit her cheek. She couldn't do this to him. It felt like she was trapping him like Lauren had. She wasn't going to do that to him. She would rather lose him for good than see the light slowly seep out of him. She couldn't bring a child into that kind of environment. Tyler left London to avoid the same thing. Her parents hadn't wanted a kid. Look how that had turned out.

'Please, just go. I should never have done this.'

'Sweetheart don't do this.' He looked stricken. 'We can sort this out. Let's finish breakfast, get dressed. I'll help you set up the bar.'

She shook her head, dressed now. Pulling her hair back into a pony, she avoided looking at him. 'Please, just go.'

'No,' he rumbled. 'You're upset.'

'Yeah, I'm upset, but I still need you to go. This won't work, Tyler, okay? You have your own life to live. I have the Arms to get, and the baby plan.'

'You were going to do that alone anyway,' he cut in. 'I can help, be part of it. I am part of it.'

'Tyler,' she sighed, folding her arms over her chest to hold herself together. 'This was a mistake, okay? I got carried away, but I am going to make this right. I'm sorry, but this...' she gestured between them, 'is not happening. You should ring the agency, go to London.'

'Coward,' he spat. 'You want this, and there's a million excuses not to, but I don't care. I'm scared too, but you're the one running. Not me. Don't do this, please. Amber, not now. I don't care about any of it. I just want to be with you. You can't do this. Not now. It will fucking kill me.' *Kill him? I already want to die.* One thing she was sure of, other than the fact that she was pushing away the one person who truly knew her, was that she'd never find this again. When he left, that would be it. She would spend the rest of her life alone. *But at least he will get his dream too. Be happy. Even if he hates me.*

'I can't do this,' she said, her voice breaking. 'It's too complicated.' And then she lowered the boom. 'You're my friend. That's all you'll ever be. We want different things.' *I want you, but you deserve so much more. You deserve to put yourself first for once. I want that for you more than I want you for myself.* No more staying behind for a woman who had only just realised what she had. What she was throwing away, despite every cell in her body yearning for him. 'I'm sorry. If that makes me a coward, then fine. It's about me. What I want.' *What I want for you.* 'I won't have a baby with someone who doesn't want the same things. I grew up with parents like that, I won't do it to my own kid.'

He looked at the floor, the knuckles of his fingers white as they gripped the clothes in his hands.

'The baby? Amber, I know I was against it, but that's no reason for us not to try. I thought... maybe we'd do it together. Maybe you'd change your mind. Wait a little while.' His face was stricken, confusion marring his features. And then she saw it. The way she could get him to leave, to give up on her and put himself first. 'I don't get it. I don't see what changed from last night. I'm not leaving 'til you tell me the truth.'

'No, Tyler, you don't get it. How could you? I have a plan, and you are not part of it. I want the Arms, to be a mother. That's not going to stop; I'm not waiting. You don't want this, and I can't afford to waste time. I don't want you to either. You deserve that London job. I want that for you.'

'I get that, but—'

He fell silent when she raised her hand.

'No, you don't. Life doesn't just wait for everything you want. Things have an expiration date. Plans, eggs. We rushed into things last night. We didn't think about the consequences.'

'Bullshit,' Tyler rumbled, thrusting his jeans on and pulling his top over his head. 'You're freaking out about the London thing. None of that is us!'

She shook her head, moving out of the bedroom.

'There is no us. I'm sorry.' She balled her fists at her sides. 'I want you to go.'

'Amber...'

'Tyler, leave. Please.'

She left him then, going to sit on the couch in the living room because her legs felt like they were about to give out. She didn't cry until she heard the door to her flat close behind him.

# 17

The next three days were a blur for Tyler. He'd run through everything they'd said that morning. Wishing he'd told her long ago about Lauren, and the baby that was never his. If he had, maybe she wouldn't have woken up with him in her place and freaked the fuck out. He knew she felt it, perhaps not everything he did, but something. He was so close to getting her to himself, finally. Now what was he supposed to do? Watch her live out her life from the sidelines, like before? He wasn't going to live through watching her with another man. After finally being with her, he couldn't accept the alternative. Even her baby plans didn't scare him. Truth was, whatever she wanted, he wanted to be the one to give it to her. When they'd forgotten the condom, and she'd told him it was okay, he'd wondered whether she would feel the same if it amounted to getting pregnant. Had practically wished for it, as screwed up as that was. His jealousy of her using someone else's swimmers had pounded between his ears when she'd first told him. When he'd thought about it later, he'd realised he didn't care. She wasn't Lauren. It wouldn't be a living thing born from deceit. He would love any baby she had, in whatever way she became a mother, because he loved her. Had loved her since the moment they'd met at the Slug, and his tongue had betrayed him by locking up in his damn mouth. He wanted her, not some job in London.

He knew she'd done it for him. He could see it in her eyes, the way she was pushing him away because she wanted him to have his dreams, too. Scared of being left behind again, she'd pushed him first. Only thing was, his dreams were her. He'd love nothing better than to be the father to her kids, any kids she had. If she wanted her own damn football team, he was in. For all of it. To stand side by side with her in the Arms. *My dream is you.* Plain and simple. His career wasn't about accolades, or Michelin stars. He didn't care about his own empire; he just wanted to make people happy with his food. Bring joy to people, just like Amber did to those around her. But she wasn't listening. She'd barely looked at him since she'd kicked him out of her place. She sent Sharon into the kitchen whenever she could. If she was in his orbit for more than a few minutes, she practically ran away. She looked tired, drawn. He could swear she'd been crying, but he couldn't get close enough to her to find out. He'd tried to call her, but she didn't pick up, so he'd changed to texts. She didn't answer them either, after the first one.

Go to London. I want you to be happy.

Well, he would. If it came to it, he'd take the job. Any job, far from here. He just wanted to do what felt right to himself first. And that meant looking after Amber.

A food-delivery worker was just exiting Bradley's building, so he slipped inside and headed to Bradley's floor. To say his piece, once and for all. He wouldn't leave Hebblestone without making sure that Amber got what she wanted, and this slimeball was nowhere near her.

Striding over to his door, Tyler could hear music playing from inside, and he frowned.

'Just a minute,' he heard Bradley say. The music turned down. 'See babe,' Bradley said, talking over his shoulder as he opened the door wearing nothing but a black silk robe. 'Told you they'd bring the spring rolls.'

His stupid blonde face dropped when he looked straight into Tyler's chest. His head snapped up, a flash of panic plastered on his face. 'Tyler? I thought you were the delivery guy, sorry.' He stepped out, shooting a furtive look behind him as he came out into the corridor. 'I can't really talk,' he stammered, trying to shield Tyler's view inside.

'Make time,' Tyler growled. 'Either you talk to me out here, or I come in and have this conversation with your guest, too.'

Bradley paled further before ducking his head back inside. 'Won't be a minute, babe. I'll be right back.'

The second he closed the apartment door behind him, Tyler slammed him against it.

'Didn't take you long to move on, did it?' Realisation hit him like a truck. 'Were you cheating on Amber?'

'No, of course not, I—'

'No bullshit,' Tyler snarled. 'For once in your miserable life, be a man.'

The snivelling little weasel in his grasp sagged in defeat once he realised Tyler had him well and truly pinned down.

'She's my investor.' He sighed. 'She took a shine to me.' His voice dipped to a half whisper, and Tyler released him, nodding down the corridor. When they were out of earshot, Bradley spilled his guts.

'She liked me, and at first, it was just flirting. She knew I was with Amber, but I might have played things down a little. To make myself seem more available. It just kind of snowballed after that, I guess. I got in too deep, but then I couldn't pull out. Her father agreed to fund me, and I can't survive without it. She knew Amber's plans for the Arms. It was her that went to her father about the place. I couldn't get out of it. I was stuck.'

'Huh. You're a bigger piece of shit than I thought,' Tyler growled.

He flushed, another nod of his head. 'I wanted to tell Amber the truth, but I couldn't do it. I care about her, Amber I mean. I wanted her; she made me better. I just can't lose everything.'

Tyler's head was exploding. 'But why string her along? Are you crazy? You don't think this will hurt her?' He jabbed him in the chest. 'Hebblestone is a small place. She'll find out, and you've humiliated her enough! Why not just break it off? Stop the deal? Be a fucking grown up for once?'

He winced. 'I'd lose the lot. I'm so close, Tyler, to getting everything.'

Tyler shook his head. 'I should knock you out right here, right now. You are the worst, Sloane. I thought you were a wanker before, but this?' He ran his fingers through his hair. 'You're messing with people's lives! Amber and I—' He stopped himself.

'Amber and you, what?' Bradley retorted, puffing out his chest. 'Oh, come on, Ty. Don't tell me you didn't come here to force me to pull out. For her. I saw how you used to look at her when we were together. You practically peed all over her that day I came to talk. Marking your territory, caveman? That's why you're really here, right? To be her saviour?'

'I came here to tell you to pull out, yeah.' Tyler's voice was so deep, it shook the corridors. 'Amber and I, whatever we are, is nothing to do with you. I would never treat her like this. Back out of the Arms, let her have her dream. You fucked this up. It's time to make it right.'

He started to walk away, but turned back at the last minute. 'Oh, and Bradley?'

Bradley was looking like a pathetic wretch now, in his poncy robe. 'Yeah?' he whimpered.

'Come near the Slug, or Amber, and I'll end you. She doesn't need to know about you cheating. Ever.'

Brad winced. 'Yeah, well she might find out anyway. I... er... sort of got engaged.'

Tyler's lip curled. 'You deserve each other. I hope her money and her father make you very happy.' His jaw was clenched so tight, he thought it would crack his face in two. 'Then you need to tell her herself, Bradley. I mean it. She deserves to hear it from you. Tell her, and then leave her the hell alone.'

When he got downstairs into the street, he punched the wall. Felt the skin on his knuckles split as he wished it was Bradley's face. Pulling out his phone, he dialled the agency. Left a voicemail telling them he wasn't taking the London job. Then he hailed a cab and headed home. He needed a drink, and he knew that, when all this came out, he was going to be needed here in Hebblestone. Amber would need him. *By her side, if I get my way.* Whether she let him be there or not, he wasn't going anywhere. When Bradley dropped the bomb, he'd be right there to shield her from the damage, as much as he could.

# 18

Almost two weeks had passed since the cocktail night, and things were awful. All the good things were in place, but everything else was utterly grim. The sperm she'd ordered was sitting in her fridge. When it arrived, it had set her off wailing. She only had a small window of time to use it, but she didn't feel the urge to do it straight away. So much for the big plan she'd chosen over Tyler. *Spermsicle over soulmate. Well done, Fitzpatrick.*

He hadn't given her his notice, Ben hadn't mentioned London, so she knew he hadn't told him about it. Her business plan was all done. She was ready for her meeting with the bank. Her planning application was in. She was good, aside from the fact she couldn't stop crying for longer than five minutes when she was alone in the flat. She was holding it together at work but, whenever she was in a room with Tyler for longer than a minute, she could feel herself falling apart. She kept having to run off and hide in her office so he wouldn't see her cry. She could feel his eyes on her whenever he was in the same room, and she couldn't handle it. The worst thing was, Bradley had started calling again. Asking her to meet him. She'd let the calls go to voicemail. He said he needed to talk.

Denise had told her that his planning application had been with-drawn. It didn't change her hating his guts. She had nothing to say to the man. The irony of him calling when all she wanted was Tyler felt like a cruel twist of fate. The second she'd kissed Tyler, Bradley was in her past. She just wished he'd stay there.

After avoiding his calls for a few days, he didn't let up. When she got a text from him threatening to come to the Slug, she decided to just bite the bullet. It was a quiet night behind the bar. The village hall was having a forties-style tea dance night to raise funds for the church roof, and most of her regulars were down there, tripping the light fantastic. Sharon was standing at the end of the bar with Matt, her construction worker guy who was 'just a friend with benefits'. From the way they were laughing together, and the way he was looking at her, Amber knew he was anything but. The way he looked at Shazza reminded her of how Tyler had gazed at her that morning when they'd woken up together, and it broke her heart all over again. She needed to do something. She needed to clear the decks, once and for all. Get rid of Bradley for good. Otherwise, she'd just be stuck. Hiding from him, from Tyler. While she couldn't do anything about one, she could shut the books on the other. If only to avoid staring at the frozen sperm in her fridge and bursting into tears.

'I'm going out,' she announced, making Sharon turn and give her an odd look.

'Where? Now?'

'Yeah.' She grabbed her purse, her keys. 'I won't be long.'

Sharon shot her a 'say more' look. She'd been interrogating her for days, asking what had happened between her and Tyler. Amber had blown her off on the details, just saying that they'd had a fight. Sharon hadn't been convinced, and she was looking at her as if she wanted to strap her down and perform a polygraph right now.

Amber sighed. 'I'm going to Sloane's. To see Bradley. He cancelled the bid for the Arms, but he still won't stop calling.'

Sharon pulled a face. 'Well, he's still a dick but at least he dropped out. Go,' she urged. 'I'll cover things here. I'll have a drink waiting when you get back.'

Amber nodded, opening the drawer where she usually stashed her phone. 'Crap, my phone's on charge upstairs.'

Sharon practically bundled her to the door. 'You don't need it; I've got the bar.' She passed her the keys to her car. 'Take my car, you'll be back before you know it.' She yanked her in for a hug. 'I love you, mate. Go tell him off, one last time.'

The car ride over was a blur. She barely registered it, but there she was, locking up the car and striding to the front door.

Closed to the public
Private event

The sign on the door surprised her. Bradley didn't do private events normally. Maybe he was doing it to impress his precious investors. No matter, it wasn't anything to do with her.

She pushed through the doors, determination in her steps. The tables were all beautifully set out, Champagne and glasses on each table. People were milling around, laughing as his staff cleared the rest of the tables. In the corner was a table laden with desserts, servers bringing more out. She suddenly wished she'd dressed up a little, feeling more than a little plain in her black slacks and plain white blouse. *I've never been part of this world. Never desired to be. My heart lives in flannel and chequered trousers.* Near the bar, there was a man speaking into a microphone as the crowd came to a stop to listen. She paused, waiting for her moment to ask for Bradley.

'Good evening, everyone. Now that we've all eaten, and before the desserts, I just wanted to say a few words. Ruth, where are you, honey? Come up here!'

Amber, standing behind a couple wearing their best bib and tucker, wasn't really listening. She couldn't see Bradley anywhere. A blonde woman stepped forward, heading to the microphone man.

'Ah, there you are!'

Then, as if summoned by her thoughts, Bradley, dressed in a suit she hadn't seen before, walked up to the man holding the microphone, and she tuned back in to the noise around her.

'I must admit, when our Ruthie told me she'd met the one, and was getting married after five months, I was sceptical. But Bradley here has proved himself to be a good man and, with our backing, I know the future is bright. We wish you all the best, for your upcoming restaurant, and for your lives together. If you can raise your glasses please, to bless the happy couple. Bradley and Ruth!'

The room erupted into cheers, and Amber froze. *Five months? But that meant... No. He couldn't have. Five months?*

She watched as Bradley put his arms around the blonde, as she reached up to cup his face. A glinting ring in her hand.

'Happy engagement!' The couple in front of her cheered, and Amber blinked.

'WHAT?' she shouted, just as the noise lulled. Bradley's face whipped to hers, and his whole face dropped to a state of pure panic. Amber's feet were propelling her forward, her eyes on his. *The utter shit!* Her whole body felt hot, she was so angry, she could spit venom from here and melt his feckless face off. 'What the fuck, Bradley? Five months? Are you KIDDING ME!' She came to a skidding halt in front of him, and every pair of eyes were on them in the room. 'YOU'RE ENGAGED!' Her rage simmered and boiled over. He wasn't just a thief of dreams, or a shitty boyfriend. He was an honest-to-goodness cheating bastard. She could hear the hiss between her ears. 'YOU WANKER! I WILL KILL YOU!' She raised her fists, ready to pummel his chest as the last few weeks and months played over in her head. He'd been lying for months, and she had been driving herself crazy. Feeling guilty about Tyler, feeling like she was the problem. Just as her fists were about to connect, she shot up in the air. Something had grabbed her and whirled her around. 'What— geroff!' she bellowed, before she was spun in the air and looked straight into Tyler's eyes.

'I'm so sorry, Amber,' he started. 'Calm down, please. Let's go.'

'What? Tyler, what are you doing here?'

'Sharon told me you were coming,' he said gruffly, still carrying her to the front doors. She tried to wrench out of his grasp. 'Amber! Stop wriggling.'

'He's engaged! He's been seeing her this whole time!' She was yelling again, her rage and anger fuelling her. 'Put me down!'

He huffed, but did as he was asked. Bradley was right there when she turned around, but Tyler pinned her in place with a thick arm around her waist.

'You utter bastard,' she sneered at him. 'I knew you were a snake, but this? Why didn't you just tell me? Why did you let me think I was the problem?'

'I'm sorry.' Bradley was looking around him now. The whole room behind them was chaos. Ruth was crying, and the man who was obviously her father was being held by two men wearing suits, shouting things at Bradley that would make a navvy blush. 'Can we go outside?'

'Go fuck yourself,' she told him. 'I was coming to tell you to stop calling me anyway, and I wish I had a lot sooner. I hate you. You're a first-class arsehole, Sloane.'

'You said you would tell her,' Tyler growled at him, his whole body vibrating with anger. 'I told you to tell her.'

Amber replayed the words and her heart stopped. Tyler's grip on her was strong, but she pushed him away. 'You knew?'

One look in his face and she saw the truth in his expression. He looked so defeated.

'I went to his place a couple of days after you kicked me out. She was there. I told him he had to tell you.'

'You knew, and you didn't tell me?'

'We weren't talking, you were avoiding me. I didn't want to be the one to tell you.' He sneered at Bradley. 'I wanted this little shit to grow some balls for once, set you straight without all...' He waved a broad arm at the room exploding around them. 'This.' His eyes dropped to hers. 'I didn't want you to hear it on the grapevine. I was trying to protect you. I always want to protect you, Cherry.'

'Oh yeah,' Bradley piped up. 'You thought you might have a chance to play the good guy, finally get into her pants more like. You never know, Williams. She might just slum it with a rebound now.'

Bradley's nose exploded. He crumpled like a paper bag, screaming, 'My nose! My nose, you broke my nose!'

It happened so fast, Amber had whiplash. She turned to Tyler, and he was holding his hand. The knuckles were split, but it didn't look fresh. The blood on them did.

'Talk to her like that again, I dare you.'

Bradley whimpered, pulling a linen napkin off the table to stem the flow of blood streaming down his face. 'I'll sue you for this! You see if I don't.'

'Do it,' Tyler was vibrating with pure, violent rage. 'You're nothing, Sloane. You have nothing. You never deserved her, and you know it. Speak to her again, and I'll rip your head off your shoulders.'

'Whatever,' Bradley said, sounding like a nasally little child. 'You'll never have her anyway.'

Tyler lunged for him, and Bradley jumped back but he wasn't fast enough. Tyler kicked his feet out from under him, looming in his face as he grabbed a fistful of his shirt so hard, the buttons popped off. Arms came in to try to drag him off, but he shook them off like water droplets. 'I warned you,' he said, his voice dripping with anger.

'Tyler, stop,' Amber said, pulling his arm. The second her fingers slid into his, he dropped Bradley and she felt him relax, just a little. His gait was still coiled like a spring, but he stood up straight, coming to her side.

Amber looked down at Bradley, surrounded by people, and shook her head.

'You're wrong about that,' she said. 'In fact, we already slept together. I was coming to tell you that you're not half the man he is, on your best day.'

The blonde came up behind Bradley, kneeling down, and Amber met her eye. 'Do yourself a favour, love: walk away from this man as fast as your legs can carry you. He's not worth it. Come on, Tyler.' She jutted her chin out, making herself stand tall. 'Let's get out of here.' She looked around, her face a mask of disdain. 'This place is a pile of pretentious crap.'

Tyler's hand on hers, she turned and strode through the doors.

\* \* \*

'I made you some sweet tea.'

Amber took the mug, flopping back on the sofa in her flat. The events of the last few hours had drained her. Tyler had taken Sharon's keys from her and driven them home in silence. He'd practically carried her upstairs, and she'd heard him talking to Sharon at the bottom of the stairs, but she couldn't make out what they were saying. He'd come back up straight after, tinkering around in the kitchen. When she glanced at his knuckles, she saw he'd cleaned them up.

'Those cuts aren't from tonight,' she said, monotone.

He sat down across from her in the chair, glancing down at his hands.

'What happened?'

'I punched a wall.' He swallowed. 'The night I went to Bradley's and found out.'

She laughed despite herself. 'Right.' Her heart wrenched as she thought of the clarity she'd had standing in that restaurant. Right before she'd realised she'd walked straight into Bradley's engagement party. Stood there like an idiot while her ex addressed the crowds with his investor's daughter hanging off his arm. *Stupid.* She should have stuck to her guns twelve months ago, when she'd set eyes on him the first time. She was going mad lately. Her emotions were all over the place, and she should have known better. Now Tyler had punched him out, they'd made a huge scene. The whole town would be talking about it. He should go to London, leave all this behind. Bradley wasn't above spinning this to his own advantage and now he could use it to slag off Tyler if they went up against each other again. And Tyler had hidden the truth. He knew, and he'd not told her. She got that he was just protecting her, but he'd kept her in the dark. Just like Bradley had. She'd moved from one man who hid things to another. Tyler had hidden how he felt about her for years. She was sick of people hiding things from her. But the one person who always had her back hadn't trusted her to handle the truth. He'd put her first again, but this time it had back-fired. She didn't want a partner who wrapped her in cotton wool all her life. She had enough of the pitying stares growing up when people thought she wasn't looking. The girl whose parents had left her to be raised by her grandparents. She didn't want to be pitied another day. Shielded. And she wouldn't let Tyler live his life for her either. Right now, her anger at him fuelled her resolve. Pushing him away would be easy if she just focused on that. The way she felt when she'd found out the truth. He'd saved her then too. Come running to her side like a lumberjack warrior. Well, no more. She would do what she should have done in the first place. Before Bradley, before Ty. She would tip up her chin and follow the plan.

'Sure can pick men, eh? Liars,' she huffed. 'Can't believe I wasted a year on that man. Thought he was Mr Right, when he couldn't have been more wrong for me.'

Tyler's voice was thick, tortured. 'He's a dick, Amber. He was never right for you, not for a minute. The right man would be proud to help you get your dreams, no matter what they are. Babies, bars.'

'And you think you're him, right?' She could barely look at him. Her body and her head were ripping each other apart. 'You lied too, Tyler. You kept quiet.' *About everything.*

'I know that, don't you think I don't get that? I should have told you. I just... didn't want it to come from me. I never want to hurt you, Amber. Whether it's me doing the hurting or not, I can't bear to see you go through it.'

'That wasn't your choice, Tyler. I'm not some damsel.'

'I know that; you're the strongest woman I've ever met. But I still wanted to be there, to look after you, like you look after everyone else. Whatever you wanted, I wanted to give it to you. It tore me up watching the pair of you together, him not seeing you for everything you are. I should have hit the slimy git a damn sight sooner than I did, but I fucked up. I'm still here, fighting for you, though. I just need you to see me.'

'I do see you, Tyler. I see that you want this, but you wanted things for yourself when we first met. I think you need to go get them. Leave me to go for mine.'

'I can't watch you have a baby with some man in a jar, Amber. I don't want that for you. To watch you carry a child, on your own? It would fucking end me. Don't you see that?'

She knew what he was saying. She'd known a while, if she was honest with herself. He was Tyler, her chef, her best friend. That was the problem. He didn't see it like she did. After the night they'd spent together, the fear of losing him loomed louder and dominated her thoughts. Wishing that night away was something she should want but, being in his arms, locking eyes with the man she knew so well as he thrust into her, whispering her name as he shuddered around her... it was the stuff of romance books and more. Much more. Bringing a baby into a new relationship was hard, but going into one with a best friend when he knew your baby fever was rampant? The pressure was too much. It would end. Their friends would take sides; they didn't have the anonymity of the big city. People were close in Yorkshire communities like theirs. People knew everything, right down to the lint in your jean pockets. Bringing a baby into all that was too much pressure, and she was done procrastinating. If he stayed, he'd end up picking up the pieces with her. Enduring the gossip, helping her get the Arms. She knew he'd have even been a dad to her kid, any kid she had. She wanted better for him. She needed to stand on her own two feet. She'd be fine on her own. She'd done it before.

'It's not that simple.' Her voice sounded defeated, even to her own ears.

'Don't say that; we can get past this. If you just wait, we can—'

Amber's head was already shaking despite her wanting to cross the room and hug him. 'No, Ty. I always thought we were solid: you, me, Sharon. If she'd found out about Bradley, she would have told me.'

'I kicked the shit out of him.'

'Yeah, she'd have done that too.' Her jaw clenched so tight, speaking was difficult. 'I'm okay; I don't need you to put me back together. I was already over him. I only went there in the first place to tell him to stop calling.' She laughed bitterly. 'Looks like I know what he was calling about, eh?'

'Don't, Amber. None of that was your fault.'

She shrugged him off. 'I'm a big girl. Please, just go.'

'No.' His refusal was a low, rumbling growl. 'I'm not leaving you, not like this. Please, let me explain. Properly.'

'It's too late for all this—' she started, but he cut her off.

'You and I are forever. It's never too late to fix this. I won't stop 'til we get back on track. We were so close. I know that night wasn't planned, but it was the best God-damn night I've ever had. I will never regret it. I don't care how we started, Cherry. I just love that we finally did. I just wish I'd had the balls to say something sooner. I never should have let Bradley get anywhere near you.'

'Why did you? You're talking now like you've been some kind of lovesick puppy.'

'I was! God, Amber, you never saw it, did you? All those drunken punters I chased off? The way Bradley and I were with each other after you got together? I've wanted you since we first met. I didn't date because there isn't a woman in the world that compares to you. I would do anything for you. Anything.'

*I know you would. That's why I'm letting you go.* 'No.' It came out as cold, harsh. 'You wouldn't. If you cared about me that much, you would never have let me walk into that. I am humiliated beyond belief! It's too late.'

'I know you're angry. I get it. I will regret not telling you for the rest of my life, but we can get over this.' His eyes were bright with unshed tears, and she looked away, blinking her own out of sight. 'All that matters is us, Amber. The rest can be sorted.' And he would, she knew. If she let him, she'd make it all better. He'd kill himself to do it. She needed to let him go. She couldn't let a man like this be shackled to a woman with baby fever who was about to take a shot at a new business. If she let him, he'd make his life hers.

It was too much pressure, after everything. She was too used to being the one taking care of others. If she let him in now, he would never leave her side. As much as her heart broke, she wanted him to be happy. To not shed pieces of himself. She thought of him, in London, cooking his creations and maybe meeting a girl who loved him instantly. Who saw him for who he was and didn't take years to open her damn eyes. *She'll be the luckiest one in the world.*

Taking in a shuddery breath, she shut down every emotion telling her to run into his arms and used her words to push him away forever.

'It's too late for this. Any of this. You can explain all you like, but you lied, Tyler. I can't trust you any more, and we're on different paths. You have a big life to go out there and live. I'm getting what I wanted. It's done. My plans are happening, and it's too late to turn back. I made my mind up a few hours ago. So, like I said, Tyler. There's no point picking at this scab. It's done.'

'What do you mean?' He was moving towards her, until her next words brought him to a shuddering stop.

'I did it. The donation.'

His brows knitted together. 'You... inseminated yourself?'

Her eyes flicked towards the kitchen. 'I did what I should have done a while ago. I put myself and my life first. With a bit of luck, it worked. I'll have my baby, and the Arms. You need to go to London, and get what you want. You stayed for me, Tyler, and I thank you for that, but I'm good. You can go.'

His jaw locked, and she looked away when the first tear spilled down his cheek. 'Is that what you really want? To just go through with this, and on your own?'

'That was the plan.' *And it's about the only thing that might get you to accept this before I crumble and show you how I feel. What was it they said? If you love something, set it free?* 'You're free, Tyler. And you're fired.'

Tyler's head shake wasn't rude, but it felt like a slap all the same. Like he was trying to shake her news right out of his head. 'The fuck I am. Don't do this, please. Plans change, Amber.'

'Oh, don't I know it. Sometimes they change without you knowing. People still manage to get what they want out of life though, somehow.'

'So take it back. Give us a chance!' His voice broke, and her eyes snapped to his. He looked so... broken and she hated herself for it. 'This baby... if it is going to be a baby, doesn't mean the end of us.'

Amber turned away, unable to look him in the eye a minute longer. Allowing the tears to fall unseen.

'This baby is mine, not ours. There is no us. I have no room for anything else. I'll be busy, with that and work.' She needed him to leave, to propel him away from her. So she dug her heels in, focused on the anger and betrayal she'd felt when she'd realised at the party just how much she'd missed when she was making plans like a blind idiot. 'When I look at you, I see all the times you looked me in the face and didn't tell me all the things you wanted to. I don't want a man who stays silent, hiding behind the truth. You had your chances, Ty, for all of it. You didn't take them, and now I don't have any more to give you. All this, now, it doesn't change a thing for me. I don't want to hurt you either. We were friends. Maybe someday we can get that back but, at the minute, things are just too raw. I just want you to go. Please.' She drew a deep breath. 'I don't need the stress of all this. Not right now.'

'Amber...'

'Leave, Tyler. I have nothing left to say. You don't work here any more. Call the agency.' She bit her lip, forcing herself not to break down. 'I'll write you a good reference. I owe you that.'

He was silent for so long that she thought he might have left. She waited for some kind of noise, his footsteps, the closing of the door. There was nothing but the ticking of the clock on the wall. It soothed her numbness somehow. The assuring, reliable sound was just about the only thing holding her together as she willed her muscles to work. When she finally turned, the spot where Tyler had stood was empty. She stared at it for what felt like forever, before heading to the bathroom. The second the door closed, she lifted the toilet lid and vomited onto the white porcelain as tears streamed down her face. When she finally felt empty, she leaned against the sink, swilling the taste from her mouth with the cold water. Looking into the mirror, she remembered another one of her grandmother's old sayings.

*Love makes liars of us all.*

## 19

SHAZZA

You okay?

AMBER

Not even a little bit.

SHAZZA

I saw Tyler. He's a mess. You really fired him?

AMBER

Yep. I don't want to talk about it.

SHAZZA

I figured, since you won't talk to me in person. I'm worried about you. Both of you. He told me what happened. Are you sure you can't forgive him? He was in an awkward position, and he wouldn't have done it if he wasn't putting you first, Amber. I really thought you guys had something going.

AMBER

Don't miss a trick, do you? I'm doing this for him. He deserves his own life, Shaz.

SHAZZA

I know you think that, but you might regret this. I've seen you two together. He would raise a million babies with you. It's Tyler, Amb. He's one of the good ones.

AMBER

Exactly. It's too complicated. I fired him to set him free. Trust me, I'm doing this for him. I know why he didn't tell me about Bradley. He was looking out for me. He's done it for so long I don't even think he realises how much he spends his time looking out for me. I care about him too much to let it carry on.

SHAZZA

So tell me again, why you're letting him go? Firing him isn't exactly "I love you, please stay."

AMBER

I can't talk about this. It's done. Please. It's taking everything I have just to get dressed for work. I've been sick since he left. It's only been a week and I feel like my arm's been ripped off. Why do you think I can't talk to you face-to-face? I can't stop crying when I'm on my own, let alone facing you.

SHAZZA

Want me to shut up about it?

AMBER

Please.

SHAZZA

Fine. For now. I do have another question, though.

AMBER

Sharon Marshall! What did I just say? Do you want me to bawl again?

SHAZZA

It's not about Ty. Did you really do it?

AMBER

He told you that too? About the sperm thing?

SHAZZA

Showed up at my place last night. Knew I was on my night off. He was half a bottle of Jack in. He would have told me his pin number if I'd asked. Kept banging on about a playlist he made that reminds him of you. I had to tell him my Spotify was down after the third time he played My Girl. So, did you?

AMBER

I'm sticking to the plan. It's best for all of us.

SHAZZA

Well, I'm here for you, bud, but you need more than me and you know it.

AMBER

Managed this far, haven't I? I'll see you at work. Just, please. Don't grill me. I can't afford the Kleenex bill as it is.

SHAZZA

Fine, but you have to talk about it sometime. Oh, and don't be mad, but I got barred from Sloane's.

AMBER

Wait – what? Why were you even there?

SHAZZA

I went to nut punch the owner. Matt drove me there, said I needed a getaway driver. I think I might really like him. Don't leave Tyler for too long. Whatever you said really did a number. He took the job in London when you wouldn't see him. I've never seen him like this. He looks and smells like some straggly yeti someone found living alone in the mountains. All growling and moody, and hairy. At least talk to him before he leaves. He needs you as much as you need him.

AMBER

I'll think about it. Did you really nut punch him?

SHAZZA

Yep. He cried. Hit the deck like a sack of potatoes. It was amazing. Matt laughed his arse off.

AMBER

You're a really good friend.

SHAZZA

I know. So is Tyler, though. Don't let Bradley ruin everything. You wasted enough time on him. I know you think you're doing the right thing here, but everyone needs someone in their corner. Tyler's been in yours forever. Pretty sure he peed all over it and ruined it for anyone else.

AMBER

Gross. Night, I love you xxx

SHAZZA

Love you more xxx

## 20

'I blew it.' Ben was cleaning down the kitchen, taking a wire brush to a stubborn stain on one of the skillets. He didn't stop his scrubbing or reply as Tyler spilled his guts. 'I fucked up, didn't I? She doesn't even trust me now. I think I overstepped this time.'

'I'm not saying anything.' He dipped the wire brush into fresh hot water. 'I do miss you here, though. We've been slammed since you left, and Amber hasn't placed an advert for a new chef yet. She's pretty distracted. Sharon's doing her best, but with this and the gossip about Bradley, people are talking. Amber's walking around here like a robot.' Ben glanced up at him, his scrubbing paused. 'She'll be down soon. I don't think you should be here when she is.' His jaw ticked and Tyler realised he was angry.

'I'll leave, but, come on, Ben, you have an opinion. Just say it.'

His scrubbing paused. 'Fine. How is protecting her lying to her, and not telling her that Bradley had been stepping out on her? I know you guys were getting close, but dude. He had a secret fiancée.'

'I couldn't just tell her! God, Ben. It's not that easy. I told her that she deserved better. I didn't know till well after they broke up, and we'd had a fight. I went there to sort it out, and walked into the truth. If I'd known...' He huffed deep in his chest, wishing Bradley's nose was close by again so he could pummel it. 'I didn't know about the other woman. I knew he was distracted; he stopped trying with her long before this happened. She knew herself things were off. It's not just about this. It's a lot more. She's using the Brad thing to push me away. I told him he had to come clean. I didn't want to do his dirty work for him.'

Ben dipped the pan under the hot suds in the sink, grabbing a tea towel to dry off his hands before starting on the steel worktops.

'Because by then, you were in love with Amber, and you didn't want to hurt her.'

'No,' Tyler refuted, sagging against the stainless steel. Meeting Ben's eyes, he shot him a rueful smile. 'I've been in love with Amber since I set eyes on her.' The shock on Ben's face almost made him laugh out loud. 'I didn't realise at first. I thought it would pass, but it didn't. I couldn't do anything about it. She was my boss; I needed the job 'til I figured out what I wanted next. I didn't want to leave. I believed in her ideas, the way she speaks to the customers. It was only supposed to be a stop gap 'til I got a better job, but I stayed. For her.'

Ben blew out a breath. 'Fuck, mate, why didn't you just tell her? Why did you let Bradley take her out in the first place?'

Tyler felt his jaw clench tight. 'You really think I meant to do that? When I saw him talk to her, I knew I'd messed up, but he was a good bloke with her. Arrogant sure, but she liked him. She seemed happy, and I wanted that for her even if it made my guts wrench. She wanted things that I'd given up hoping for. By the time I realised I could give it all to her, it was too late. There was nothing I could do, and she was falling in love with him. So I just moved on, focused on helping her get her dreams, being her friend.'

''Til he stopped being a good boyfriend.'

'I wanted to smash his stupid face in. I went to see him, you know. Before all this. At Sloane's. After he stood her up for the comedy night. She was so sad that night, it made my blood boil. So I went there, confronted him. He said he was just busy. I told him he needed to prioritise her or end it. You know what he did? He pulled out a ring.'

Ben's face dropped. 'For Amber?'

'Yep. He had it there, in his office. A ring he said he'd bought for Amber, all ready and waiting for when the new place opened. He told me he was planning to ask her at the restaurant opening. He was talking to the bank, had an investor all lined up.'

'Fuck,' Ben huffed.

'Exactly. I believed him. He hadn't been caught kissing any blondes at that point, and I realised that I was going to be working in the place with both of them living together upstairs. So, I started looking for a job. I knew I would have to or go crazy watching the two of them together. I was going to bow out, get a new job. I figured, once they were engaged, I'd leave.'

'But then they broke up.'

'Yeah. After the night we had, I couldn't let myself walk away. This whole baby thing too. I got over my shit with Lauren.'

'I still can't believe you only just told me about that.'

Tyler rolled his eyes. 'Yeah, well – it was kind of my default, bud. Amber changed all that. Made me face it head on. Thinking about her having a baby that way, it changed things. I wanted her to have her dreams, but...'

'You wanted to be the one to give it to her.' Ben smirked at his words. 'No pun intended.'

'I would have been there either way,' he said, not realising until that moment how true it was. Whether she went through with the insemination or not, he would have been there given the chance. Loved that baby as his own. 'My guess is, after the comedy night, when the original investor fell through, he found another. One that wanted something in return. I think Bradley really did love Amber; when I saw that ring, I believed him. 'Til I saw it on the blonde's finger that night.'

'Jesus. He gave Amber's ring to her?'

Tyler smiled, but it didn't meet his eyes. 'Bradley is not one to waste money, or an opportunity.'

'So why not tell Amber all this?'

'I tried. She won't talk to me. She never answers my calls or texts. She fired me, Ben. She told me to take the job in London. When I saw her last, it's like I'm a stranger to her. I handed in my notice on my flat.'

'So that's it? You're leaving?'

Tyler nodded, turning to the sink full of dirty pots. 'Yep. It's time to stop dreaming, Ben. Go and get a real life. She doesn't want me. I can't stay here, like some protective arsehole. Not when she cut me out of her life. I have to let her go.'

Ben dropped his scrubber and came to give him a manly hug. 'I'm sorry, mate. I really am. I thought you two were finally going to get it together.'

'Me too,' Tyler said, his voice gruff. 'Do me a favour?'

'Anything mate.'

'Don't mess up my kitchen. A head chef keeps his shit together.'

Ben laughed. 'Hey, I learned from the best. Anything else?'

'Yeah,' he croaked out, sad to be leaving the place he called home. Hebblestone was home to him. He didn't want to go back to London, get lost in the big city and not know the people around him. Amber was home, and he knew he'd be lost forever without knowing she was okay. Having been so close to her now, it would wreck him for any other woman. There had only ever been *her*. His Cherry.

'Yeah,' he said. 'Look after my girl for me.'

## 21

SHARON

How's the job going?

TYLER

Good. Tiring, but keeps me busy. How's the Slug?
Ben ruined my kitchen yet?

SHARON

He's doing well. We all miss you. Bill says his
cottage pie isn't a patch on yours. He's threatening
to organise a coach trip to London to come eat at
your place at Christmas.

TYLER

Tell them to book it, be nice to see everyone.

SHARON

Aren't you going to ask about her?

TYLER

I can't. How is she?

SHARON

Okay.

TYLER

Only okay?

SHARON

Call her, she'll tell you herself.

TYLER

She fired me, told me to leave. I did what she asked. Why only okay? Are her plans not coming together?

SHARON

Not for me to say.

TYLER

Shazza, I have Matt's number now. We've talked. I will send him that video of the karaoke night when your boob popped out dancing to Shakira.

SHARON

Fuck. Hips don't lie. And neither can I, it seems. She's halfway there. One dream down, one to go.

TYLER

Say more. Going insane here.

SHARON

She'll murder me.

TYLER

Sorry, just sending Matt a video.

SHARON

Fine! She has a final meeting at the bank tomorrow. The planning was accepted. When she murders me, don't play that video at my funeral or I will come back to haunt you.

TYLER

Fuck. You said halfway. One down. Does that mean?

SHARON

Yep. Baby is a go-go.

TYLER

She's really pregnant?

SHARON

Yep. Won't talk about it. She's not the same, Tyler. She's not herself at all. Keeps saying she just needs to get through the bank appointment when I ask her what's going on. She's Mrs Sunshine at work, but most of us see right through it. Oh, and she keeps making Ben bake those cherry pastries you left the recipe for. Pretty sure it's a craving. The kid will probably come out wrapped in pastry.

TYLER

Send me the details for the appointment.

SHARON

Finally. I'll drop you a pin. Don't wear flannel for God's sake.

TYLER

I'll have you know, my Cherry loves me in flannel.

SHARON

Barf. Good luck, lumberjack. Rooting for you, bud.

## 22

This was it. In a couple of hours, she'd finally know whether her dreams were going to come true. She was so close, and none of it mattered a jot. Because Tyler Williams wasn't there by her side. She didn't have her big, frowny best friend to cheer her on. To challenge her, to be there like he always was. And she didn't have him, the one man who she adored and had never given the chance. She was going to make it right, though. She was going to get the Arms, and make it her own. She was going to get her grandmother's place back, and hop on the first train to London and beg Tyler to forgive her. They could make it work; she could commute. She would pick up the Arms brick by brick and rebuild it down there if he wanted it.

For weeks now, in between crying, planning and puking, she'd thought of their time together. Replayed all the little moments that he'd shown her he had her back, had cared. She knew he'd loved her, and she'd been too blind to see it. Too stupid and blinded by the man she thought Bradley was to see what was there, right in her kitchen the whole sodding time. He'd punched his feckless cheating ex for her, had fed her, designed her a menu and asked for nothing in return. Every time Ben brought her one of those cherry pastries she loved, it made her heart break that Tyler wasn't the one holding the plate. Calling her Cherry in his sexy, gruff way. She was in love with Tyler Williams. Not because of anything he'd done for her, or given to her. Because he was Tyler. Her lumberjack protector. She was going to fight for everything she should have before. Tyler was her dream. Without him, none of this was worth anything. Even the baby growing inside her, the child she'd wanted for so long. It wouldn't be the same if this little scrap of life didn't have Tyler there, loving them. Loving their mother. She would go and see him, beg him for another chance, and then tell him about the baby. Hope that he would still want to be part of her life.

As she walked out of the bank, standing at the edge of the pavement, she drew in a breath before heading home.

'Well,' she said to herself, her hand on her rounded stomach. 'Here we go, little one. All in or nothing.'

She heard heavy footsteps approaching, and her heart stopped when she turned to see Tyler standing there. Watching her.

'What are you doing here?'

It came out harsh, accusing. Breathy. Probably because seeing him standing there had knocked the very air from her lungs. *Tyler. Oh, you look good. I missed you so much*. Her whole body tilted forward, as if every single cell had been longing for him all this time and finally had somewhere to run to.

'I came to see you.' He'd been leaning against the cream rendered wall of the bank. He shot her a dimpled smile and pushed himself off the wall. Coming to face her. Two feet together. He looked like he hadn't slept well. She wanted to ask him what had kept him up, but she doubted it was the same reason she was currently only managing to score four hours a night. If she was lucky. He looked different. More than sleep deprived. Tense. His muscular shoulders were up, she could see the corded tension in his neck as he slowly looked her up and down. 'Came straight from London.'

It was cold today. The winter chill in the air biting into her skin. She'd put her thick winter coat on, a cream, faux-fur affair that made her feel like Olivia Pope, if Olivia Pope was a polar bear. It fastened with one central button, and as she felt him take her in with those eyes she knew so well, she was grateful it was buttoned up. It felt like a barrier against more than the chill. A secret keeper.

'Why?' was all she could think to say, even though her heart was soaring.

Her question was rewarded with his trademark grumpy frown.

'Why? Oh, I don't know. Because I missed my best friend. Because I knew you'd be here. Sharon,' he added with a tilt of his lips. 'She's like a rottweiler when she believes in something. Gave me a pretty hard time when I left too.'

Amber had a sudden image of Sharon as a huge, dark-brown dog, snarling and snapping at his heels. 'Shazza will love that,' she half blurted. 'And she was only doing it to protect me. I told her it was my fault you left. I explained everything to her.'

His eyes turned shark like, deep and dark. 'The one person you don't need protection from is me, Amb. I know I hurt you, we hurt each other, but I...' He huffed out a ragged breath. 'Listen, I'm not here to make excuses. I messed up. I thought I was doing the right thing. For you. I wanted you to have your shot at your dream. It's the only reason I stopped calling. To let things die down.'

'The Bradley gossip did last a while. It was probably best you weren't around for that.' She smiled. 'Bill says he owes you a pint though.'

Tyler laughed. 'Good man. It made it easier to be away from you, knowing you had people in your corner. I don't give a shit if Bradley chats shit about me every day for the rest of his miserable life; he's a snivelling git and I should never have let you near him.'

A couple walking past her with their poodle turned back to give them a look. It made her feet move closer, towards him. He watched her for a moment and took a step forward. As if he was trying not to spook her away.

When they were close enough that she could smell his after-shave, she came to a stop. 'I went into that relationship willingly, Ty... ler.' Ty sounded too intimate somehow, and she needed to keep it together. Get all of this out. She thought she'd have time on the train to plan her speech. He winced at her correction, and she wanted to kick herself for ever pushing him away.

'Not your Ty any more, eh?' His throat worked, but he was already speaking before she could tell him the truth. That he was her Ty. Would always *be* her Ty. 'Can we go talk somewhere, please?' He was looking around, as though he was only just noticing the people milling around them. 'You really shouldn't be on your feet anyway. Have you eaten today?'

There he was. Her Ty. The man who she'd always confided in, told almost everything to. The man who brought her food without being asked to, the bloke who took notice of the little things. Her Ty, and he was here. She'd been going back and forth for days, ever since her scan. When everything had come into sharp focus. The irony was, the one person she'd wanted to call was him. When she'd come out of that room, black and white sonograph pictures in hand, all she'd wanted to do was pick up the phone and call him. But she hadn't. She'd wanted to get her ducks in a row before she went to him. To show him that she didn't need to be looked after any more; she wanted to be the one who did that for him.

'Amber?' He was staring at her, that familiar look of concern on his face as his eyes raked over her.

'I have something to say to you,' she started, but he stopped her confession by closing the distance between them. Her hands were in his before she could get her bearings.

'Let me say this first, then I promise I'll leave you alone if you still want me to. Sharon told me you were still sad. That you'd been asking Ben to make you my pastries. It gave me hope, a kick in the arse to come back and find out, once and for all. I fucked up a lot of things. Not just with Bradley; I should have done all of this differently. The night you met Brad, I should have told you my feelings; I should have told the little rat that you were too good for him. That I wanted you for myself. I wasted so much time, but I can't waste another second without telling you—'

'Tyler, I—'

'I love you. Christ, I love you so much, I can't see straight. I've been miserable in London. I just wanted to come home. You're my home, Amber. I don't need some fancy job; I never did. When you told me about the donor, I wanted to scream my damn head off. I didn't want you to have a kid with some stranger, on your own. I wanted to be there, doing it with you. I want to do everything with you. All your firsts. Your dreams, the family. Everything. I would lasso the moon and net the fucking stars if you wanted them, Cherry. I came here to tell you that I love you, and your baby.'

She tried to speak but her throat had closed up. Her vocal cords were out of action. *Your baby.* He wanted to bring up someone else's child, with her. The tears she'd been trying to keep at bay since she'd set eyes on him broke free, spilling warm and salty down her cheeks.

'Tyler,' was all she managed to push out on shaky breath. *Sharon had told him. The little matchmaking minx.*

'I mean it, Amber. I love you, both. I want to be there. Me and you, like before. Only this time, no Bradley, no stupid lies or hiding behind our feelings. I swear, if you let me in, I will never let you down.'

'You... I really should have gone first. You... love me?'

'Yes. I think I always have.'

'I... the baby...'

*Shit. I really should have gone first. He wants me, the baby. I'm so damn happy, so shocked that he's here, saying my words, I can't even push out a syllable.*

'The baby is yours, Amber. How could I do anything but love it? I'm in. All in. I haven't stopped thinking about it since I saw it on your computer. Being with you, helping you raise a family, that's everything.' He motioned to the bank. 'I know you have your life plan, and I don't want to derail that. If anything, I want to help you get it all. I know you think I'm putting my own dreams on hold, but this is it. Right here. Let me do it all with you. I'll be your chef, your partner. I just want to be part of it, if you'll—'

She reached out, putting her hand on his chest. He stopped dead, looking down at the point where their bodies touched.

'The baby...'

His face fell, and she stopped him before he spiralled into worry.

'I'm fine. I mean, the baby... the sperm donor.'

'I don't care about how you got your baby, Amber.'

'It didn't work.'

His brow creased. 'What? What do you mean... Sharon said you were pregnant. I don't—'

She saw something like recognition spark his face, and he pulled her into his arms. 'Oh God, Amber. I didn't know, I'm so sorry. Do you need to sit down? When did it—'

The baby in her belly chose that moment to give her a little kick, the flutter in her stomach letting her know that the little one was still here. And maybe didn't appreciate being smushed against Tyler's hard body. Its mother sure did.

'No.' She almost laughed, pushing herself out of his arms and undoing the button on her coat. Tyler let her go, his eyes dropping to the neat bump. 'I'm still pregnant. The sperm donation, it didn't work.'

His face was a picture. 'You might have to explain this one to me, Cherry.'

She shot him a watery smile. 'You might be the one who needs to sit down. Tyler, it didn't work because I didn't do it. I was in too much of a mess, and I told you I did it because I wanted to push you away. And then I was a bigger mess when you left. I was sick, and I thought it was just because of everything with you. So I decided I would get the Arms, and then come and beg you to try again.' She smiled then, a tear spilling down her cheek. 'The thing was, I was already pregnant. I didn't know it, but the dates fit when I looked. I went to the doctor, and she confirmed it. When I had my scan, I knew it was really happening. I wanted to call you the second I got out of there.' She brushed the salty water from her cheeks, hands sliding to her pregnant belly. 'I wanted to call you before I knew, if I'm honest. I haven't told anyone. Not even Sharon. I wanted you there, but I had to make myself whole and show you I am here to take care of you now. I missed you so much, then when they told me I was pregnant, and it was yours. Ours. I just didn't know how to tell you, but...'

'It's mine?' he whispered.

Tears slid down her face and all she could do was nod.

'It's... the baby's... we're having a baby?' His big, brown eyes were wide with shock, and then he broke into a huge, soppy grin. The same one he'd had on his face when he'd made her breakfast in bed.

She drew in a shuddery breath. 'Yes. We're having a baby, Ty. And I love you too.'

'We're really...' His grin was bright enough to crack the pavements with its brilliance. 'We're having a baby!' He lifted her into his arms, spinning her around on the pavement. The small gathering of people waiting at the bus stop opposite the bank all turned to look. One bobble-hat-wearing woman with a tartan shopping trolley started to clap. 'Congratulations,' another one shouted.

Tyler didn't even see them; he was too busy twirling her around whooping. 'We're having a baby!'

'Yeah, I know,' Amber laughed, 'but I'm also going to vomit if you don't stop spinning me!'

'Oh shit,' Ty stopped immediately, lowering her to the floor and gripping her to him like she was a delicate, bone-china doll. 'Sorry!' He walked her over to the benches in front of the sandwich shop a few doors down. When she went to sit down, he came to her side, grabbing her butt cheeks.

'What are you doing?'

'Lowering you to the seat,' he replied, his face taut. Amber was pretty sure she could hear a cackle coming from the direction of the bus shelter.

'Tyler, I can sit down without breaking!'

He waited until she was seated and took his place next to her. 'Sorry,' he muttered, his face still flushed with shock. And probably exertion from carrying her around. She had noticed her maternity trousers were needed this morning when she'd got dressed for her meeting. 'I think I'm in shock.'

'I know.' She gripped his hand when he reached for hers. 'I would have told you; I just needed to get the meeting out of the way, and—'

'I know you would. Tell me, I mean. I get why you waited. How did the meeting go?' He added the question as if he'd just remembered the reason she'd been there in the first place.

'I got the loan,' she said, feeling the elation all over again. 'They loved the new business plan. In fact, they said the ideas for the food would be a very welcome addition to the community against all the newer, "hoity toity" places that had sprung up in the area.'

Their eyes met, and Tyler beamed. Which made her break out in peals of laughter. A minute later, they were both laughing their heads off on the bench.

When they'd finally stopped setting each other off, he slid his arm around her.

'Can I?' he asked softly, his eyes on her tummy.

She nodded, taking the hand wrapped around hers and placing his calloused palm on the spot where the flutters had just been coming from. 'He's been kicking since you got here.'

'He?' His brows shot up, his gravelly voice full of wonder and emotion as he focused on her bump.

'Just a guess. It's too soon to know yet. We should be able to find out at the next scan.'

'I don't care,' he breathed, his smouldering eyes locking on hers. 'I don't care either way. I loved this baby before it was here. Before it was mine. I don't care if a baby octopus shoots out of there; I'm going to love the hell out of it. Of both of you.'

One hand on her bump, linked with his, she raised the other to cup his stubbly cheek. 'You look awful,' she told him, brushing her thumb along his stubble.

'I needed my best friend, to tell me to shave.'

He turned his head to kiss her thumb. The thrill of his touch sent flutters through her body.

'Woah,' Tyler exclaimed, when their child bumped against their joined hands. 'Did you feel that?'

'Yeah,' she chuckled. 'I think it's a tentacle.'

He laughed, his eyes bright as he dipped his head to kiss the spot above their hands. 'Hey little octopus,' he breathed, his voice so happy and tender, Amber's heart swelled. 'It's your dad.' He kissed the same spot. 'You might want to get used to hearing my voice, because I am going to be around from now on.'

A hiccupy sob burst from her then, and his head snapped up to hers. 'Hey,' he murmured, touching his forehead to hers, leaning into her body as he shifted to pull her closer. 'No more tears, Cherry. Tears are not part of the plan.'

'I love you,' she declared, so happy that her stressful day had turned out like this. The bundle of nerves and hormones that set out that morning was unrecognisable now even to herself. 'I really do, Ty. I'm so sorry I cut you out.'

'Shh,' he chided. 'We're here, now, right? Everything finally worked out. I love you; you love me. We're having a baby.' He spoke as if he were saying the words out loud to confirm it to himself as much as her.

'And a pub of our own, with a bit of luck,' she added, grinning as his face registered shock yet again. 'I put an offer in on The Bingley Arms before I left the bank.'

He gazed at her in wonder, and before she could say another word, his lips crashed down onto hers. The second their mouths met, she melted into his embrace. They only broke apart when they heard a loud honk. Turning to look, they saw the people on the bus all cheering through the windows, making them laugh. Even the driver had been filled in, it seemed. He was clapping from the front seat.

'This village.' Tyler chuckled as he pulled her in for another kiss. When he finally broke his lips from hers, he tilted his head questioningly. 'So,' he said, a cheeky grin on his happy face. 'What do you say, boss? Need a chef? I have good references.'

# EPILOGUE

Relationships were an odd thing. A man she once felt like the sun and the moon rose from his butt crack was now no more than a footnote in the margin of Amber's story. A catalyst that led her to the future she now inhabited. The one she once thought she'd never have. Reconciled to having a child on her own, and chasing her dreams solo, she'd been steadfast in her wavering. Now, she rested on the shoulders of a man who would bring her the stars. A man whose muscular forearms would grapple the sky, climb the clouds and drag the moon down on his broad back. Just to make her smile. That was Tyler. Her best friend, her lover. Her everything. God, she was sappy nowadays.

'What's up with you?' Tyler smirked down at her. 'You're looking at me like you want to nibble me.'

His big arms came around her, his stubble nuzzling that sweet spot on her neck he knew she loved.

'I was just looking; you were in my line of vision,' she lied, a matching smile across her face as she breathed him in. 'And you need a shave.'

He huffed out a laugh. 'You love my stubble, and you know it.'

'True.' She grinned. She had been looking out of the window, marvelling at how good it was to be home. Even now, the thought took her breath away. Even as their child Samuel slept in his room, even with her name above the door on that little plaque she never thought would exist.

'Bar all set up?' he asked, sensing as always just what she was thinking about.

'Yep, Ben got the kitchen covered?'

He moved to her collarbone, dipping his head lower and pulling her tighter against his hard chest. His arms came up her sides, fingers bumping up her ribs until he reached the underside of her chest.

'Uh-huh,' he murmured back, distracted in his pursuit of her nipple under the neckline of the tight, black dress she was wearing. He drew across the curtain, shielding her from the street.

'Always the protector,' she breathed as his fingers pinched one, making it bud harder against the lace of her strapless bra. 'Sharon will be up in a minute.'

His fingers paused, and she felt his groan. 'Spoilsport. Do me a favour: never talk about Sharon again while I'm trying to feel you up.'

'Deal,' she laughed, checking the baby monitor on the coffee table for the tenth time. 'Do you think...'

He hooked her around the waist, taking her jaw in a huge hand and lifting her to look into his gorgeous eyes. 'Nope. Not a chance, Cherry. We have not had a date night in so long. Auntie Sharon is babysitting; the bar and kitchen are both covered. We,' his eyes dropped to her lips, 'are going out. Out out. To a place without menus that you colour in, or ball pools filled with child pee and skittles.'

'Oooh. You had me at child pee.'

'Filthy woman,' he growled, stealing a kiss. 'You look beautiful, by the way.'

'Thanks, bestie,' she teased. Just to get one of his grumpy eye rolls.

'Bestie my arse,' he pretended to grump. 'Wait till we get home; I'll show you what a best friend can do.'

She pushed him away, feeling the blush of attraction rove through her.

'Sounds like I'm on a promise.'

He shrugged on the jacket he'd slung over the couch. 'You bet your ass you're on a promise. I have been slaving away in that kitchen for weeks. My boss is a real slavedriver.'

Pushing on her heels, she padded over. He was trying to escape from his tie noose. Reaching for it, she pulled it a little, making his eyes widen. 'Really? Bit of a bitch, eh?' Loosening the silk material, she re-tied it straight, and a little looser. 'You should quit.'

He pretended to think about it, sliding his hands up her thighs and resting them in the small of her back. 'I would... but it's kind of a live-in situation. You know, room and board.'

'Ah. So she's a controlling wench, too, eh. Bet you have to...' she pushed her fingers under his jacket, enjoying his shiver as her hands roved over his abs. '...fluff her pillows,' she breathed.

His eyes darkened as he gripped her tighter. 'Oh, she makes me fluff everything.'

'Ah-huh.' A throat clearing behind them froze them in their tracks. 'You have a reservation in thirty minutes. And try not to dry hump in front of the babysitter, eh?'

Tyler released her, his fingers lingering until the last minute.

'Hi Sharon,' he monotoned, straightening his already perfect tie. 'Thanks for looking after the champ.'

The pair of them turned to see a very uncharacteristically

smiling Sharon, standing with a familiar-looking contractor. They were holding hands.

'Oh,' Amber had to prise her gaze from their entwined hands. 'Wow. Sorry about the PDA there.' Tyler was standing open mouthed at the side of her, and she jabbed him in the ribs to bump him out of his stupor. 'Nice to see you again…'

'Reservation,' Sharon squeaked, looking at them both with wide eyes. She mouthed, 'Stop bloody staring' at them both, and Tyler made a coughing sound that sounded suspiciously like a covered laugh. She never spoke about him, though they all knew that she was seeing him. Matt and Tyler were actually good friends, but from the look on his face, he didn't know he'd be coming tonight either. It felt like a bit of a milestone.

'Right,' they both said together. After staring at each other for what felt like hours, Tyler clapped his hands together and swept Amber across the room with him.

'Okay! So, Matt, Shaz… ron, we won't be out too late. I have my phone, little dude should be fast on for the night. Remotes are on the coffee table…'

Sharon was glaring at him now like she was wishing her eyes were lasers.

'And… have a good night!'

They were in the car before either of them spoke again.

'So, that happened.' Amber couldn't help but laugh. She was happy for her friend. It looked a lot like she'd found her partner. 'How long have they been official? I knew she was still seeing him, but it's the first time she's brought him out. Wow. Our little Sharon's in love.'

His eyes were shining in the dim light, his surprised smile lit up by the passing lights as they drove towards the restaurant. 'He never said a word.' Tyler laughed. 'Good man. They are definitely doing more than knocking boots.'

'I know! Did you see them, holding hands?'

'I know,' Tyler breathed, tapping the steering wheel in his excited little Duracell bunny way. 'It was disgusting!'

He took his eyes off the road long enough to lock eyes with her, and they both lost it. Tears streaming down their face, overjoyed and shocked by their friend. Amber managed to stop herself first, dabbing her eyes to avoid walking into their date looking like a panda.

'Aww, the little sister you never had. Seriously, though, what the heck? I swear, she never said a word to me.'

Tyler's smile was all knowing. 'I think we can guess why. He's important to her.'

'I know that feeling,' Amber grinned, wrapping her hand over Tyler's as it rested on the gearstick.

'Of course you do. That's why we fell into each other's arms the second we met.'

'Hey!' She pretended to swat at him at the same time as clenching his hand tighter in hers. 'We were best friends first; that's better.'

He didn't look entirely convinced, a shadow of something crossing his features. She'd seen him pull that face before, and every time she wanted to kiss it right off his face and dispel it forever. 'Yeah, we were.' He bit at his lip. 'I still wish I'd punched Bradley in the face the second he looked twice at you though. Could have saved a lot of hassle.' His face was stormy now, but it lifted quickly. 'We wouldn't have our little champ though, so fate wasn't so cruel.'

His expression was pure love now. Calm, content. Her favourite Tyler look.

When he came around to open her door in the restaurant car park, she changed her mind when she saw his dark eyes, lips curled lustily. *Okay, so my second favourite.* He half pulled her out of her seat and into his arms, his palms settling on the small of her back. 'It doesn't matter how long it took to get here.' He kissed the tip of her nose, then one corner of her mouth. Pulling back with that settled, happy, love-drunk expression on his gorgeously kissable face. 'I loved you before you knew it. Before you saw me coming. I was like a little stealth love ninja. Feeding you up with cherry pastries.' He looked at her mouth, his eyes doing that thing they did when he was thinking about her naked. He kissed the corner he'd not tasted yet, slanting his lips to cover her mouth. Take her breathy moan into him like it was oxygen itself. He kissed her hard, deep. Closing the car door with one hand as he gripped her around the waist with the other. She felt the hard surface of the car door as he pushed her against it. 'My Cherry,' he groaned as he pulled back. 'Sweet and juicy.' This. This was her favourite face on him. The look of pure, unadulterated devotion that shone out of him. Like he would carry the world on his shoulders to protect her. Crush any enemies she encountered. Burn the settlements of her foes and carry her off on his shoulders while everything smouldered around them.

His brows knitted together. 'You having that lumberjack-carry-you-off fantasy again?'

She giggled before she could stop herself. 'Nope.'

'Liar.' He smirked. 'What was I doing this time?'

'Burning my enemies.'

He growled theatrically. 'The enemy of my woman shall be crushed underfoot.' His voice was so deliciously low, she felt it rumble throughout her body. Right down into her core. 'The rivers will run red with their blood as I take my lady back to my mountain lodge for a bit of plundering.'

'Oooh,' she laughed against his chest, smelling him as she always did. 'I do like the odd plunder.'

'I know,' he rumbled. 'You're smelling me again, like a dachshund would a squeaky toy.'

'You're my favourite smell, aside from our baby.' She curled her fingers into his hair. 'I swear, I'm about to dry hump you in this car park.'

That elicited another loud groan from him. Releasing her like it was the last thing on earth he wanted to do, he reached for her hands and dropped another kiss on her lips. A chaste one this time. 'We'd better go in then.' He released her only to offer her his arm. 'Shall we, my lady?'

She puffed out a breath, willing her libido to subside enough to enable her legs to walk in a straight line. 'We shall, my brave protector.' He held her to his side as if he could sense her shaky legs. 'I still can't believe we're actually doing this.'

They left the car park, both of them coming to a stop together outside Bradley's latest venture.

Imaginatively named Sloane's Eatery, it was just how she'd imagined it to look from Brad's descriptions of his plans when they were together. She didn't feel a pang, or anything really other than happiness for him. She had her life; he had his. Her dreams had come true and more. Thinking about her and Bradley together now felt like a bit of a bad dream. Like it had been someone else's life. Someone else's path. Life was too short to hold grudges. She was done looking back. Bradley was the guy before the guy, and she didn't take anyone on that journey for granted. Hebblestone was too small a place to avoid the past.

'You okay?' Tyler's voice was strong, but the concern still softened its undertone. He'd been a little squirrelly in the beginning when Bradley had reached out to them. Trying to make amends. He'd had more than a few gym sessions to pound out his lingering emotions on the matter but, somehow, they'd managed it. Bradley had even brought his fiancée with him to The Fitzpatrick Arms, which had raised more than a few eyebrows amongst the regulars. More than a couple of the old boys mumbled into their pint pots a lot more than usual, and the air was decidedly chilly. Bradley wisely kept close to the bar area, and his fiancée looked like she was wearing a Lady Gaga meat dress and had just walked into a hungry lion's den. Which wasn't far off, given that the whole of the community had heard about her infamous engagement party. One which, quite frankly, Amber still didn't like to think about.

Her own engagement was a very different experience. The air that night had been crackling with love and happiness, as everyone who knew her and Tyler, separate and now together, had told the loved-up couple how perfect they were how great they were going to be as parents. It had all worked out and, as he held the door open for her, Amber found herself being thankful for Bradley's cheating ways, his detachment from her that gave her the space to realise that what she had wasn't necessarily what she wanted. It had woken her up, in more ways than one.

As Tyler walked into the busy space, arm around her waist, he leaned down. Making her shiver as he brushed comforting words into the shell of her ear. 'One word, and I'll light the pyres, my queen.'

She smirked up at him. 'Let's just hope you can keep your axe under control 'til we get home.'

'Oooh,' he groaned, reaching down to clamp her bottom in his palm before moving it back to a pose more suitable for public. 'Stop it, or I will fireman lift you back to the car right now. Screw the dinner.'

'I love you,' she told him. Because she never grew tired of telling him, and she felt like she was catching up for all the I-love-you's she could have been saying before. 'Now feed your woman.'

He rolled his eyes, before leading her to the welcome desk, where a server waited with a patient smile.

'Stop clenching.'

'I'm not clenching,' he said, slipping the words out between gritted teeth. 'Okay. A little.'

'You could carry a keg between your butt cheeks right now,' she half whispered as he gave their names to the server. Their hostess smiled wider, flicking a pen across her reservations book and leading them to one of the quieter tables in the back.

When they were seated, Bradley appeared from the kitchen area. Spotting them, he headed over to their table.

'Hey.' He flashed his professional smile at them both, his shoulders high under his polished-as-ever demeanour. 'I'm glad you came.'

'Bradley,' Tyler said, rising from his seat to shake Bradley's hand. 'Place looks good.'

'Thanks,' Brad took his hand, shaking it just that bit too eagerly as his smile changed to real warmth. He turned to Amber when the two men pulled back. 'Amber, you look great.'

She saw Tyler stiffen, just for a second, but didn't let on. She did, however, pull the tea lights in the centre of the table further away from him as she held out her arms.

'Thanks Bradley, come here.'

He faltered for a second or two, looking sideways at Tyler as if he might rugby tackle him to the ground, but then his arms came around her.

She patted him on the back before pulling away. 'The eatery looks amazing, and the food smells great.'

'Bit too much garlic, maybe,' Tyler muttered but he was laughing when they looked his way. 'No, seriously man, it's looking good.'

Bradley didn't preen like he usually did at the praise, but he chatted for a while before moving onto the other diners. He had no wedding date pencilled in yet, but Amber was pleased for them.

Bradley's face when he spoke about his fiancée was lit up. They'd worked through their issues. After his future father-in-law had stopped trying to murder him, of course. Ruth was a very forgiving woman, it seemed. A woman after her own heart. Ruth might have started out as a way to get his investment, but, after the engagement fiasco, she'd been hurt. Bradley had finally realised what he was doing and, when he saw his intended so hurt by his actions, it had changed him. She'd seen them together, the way he looked at her. The same way Tyler looked at her, which just made her feel happy to see. Like everything had finally been corrected in the universe. The stars had aligned, even for Sharon – who was the one least swept up by romantic notions.

As they tucked into their food, Tyler's foot searching for hers under the table, his hand reaching for hers over the tablecloth, Amber looked around at the other diners.

'It's so nice,' she breathed.

Tyler paused, his fork halfway to his gorgeous mouth. 'I would have added more seasoning.' He shrugged. 'But, yeah, it's pretty good.' He winked at her when she gave him a look. 'You didn't mean the food.' As ever, he knew what was going on in her head. 'Tell me,' he pushed, running his fingers along the back of her hand. She wondered whether her skin would always prickle from his touch. Whether she would still feel this in a decade. She didn't think it would ever wane.

'This,' she told him, her eyes scanning the other diners as they tucked into their food, clinked glasses together, laughing at their companions' words. 'It's nice to be part of it. Not on the sidelines, looking in. Even at work now, I feel for the first time in my life that I'm really part of it. Front and centre. Living it.' When she turned to meet his eye, he was already watching her. A contented smile, her favourite look. Only for her. 'Do you know what I mean?'

'You were always front and centre, Cherry.' His hand kept up its caress. 'You just needed to step up and claim your spotlight.' His face flashed surprise when her smile broke free. 'God, you're beautiful. I think you might finally have peaked, and I've seen everything, and then you look at me, and it's like I've seen nothing before it.'

'I've got my dreams.' She laughed, her whole body warming from his words until she felt like she might be the pyre. Flaming, burning. 'As long as you're right up there with me.'

'Forever, Cherry.' He nodded to her plate. 'Now eat up.' His smile turned wolfish. 'I have plans for you later.'

She picked up her fork.

'Bring it on, lumberjack.'

# ACKNOWLEDGEMENTS

Thank you dear readers, for picking up Amber and Tyler's story!

As ever, thanks so much Emily and the whole Boldwood team. You are all amazing, and this book is all the better for having your hands at the helm.

Big thanks to all of my author friends, in particular Mary Jayne Baker, Rachel Burton, Rachael Stewart, Lynda Stacey, and Portia MacIntosh.

And to my family, for being you. I love you all, Looking forward to all the moments still to come.

# ABOUT THE AUTHOR

**Rachel Dove** lives in leafy West Yorkshire with her family, and rescue animals Tilly the cat and Darcy the dog (named after Mr Darcy, of course!). A former teacher specialising in Autism, ADHD and SpLDs, she is passionate about changing the system and raising awareness/acceptance. She loves a good rom-com, and the beach!

Sign up to Rachel Dove's mailing list here for news, competitions and updates on future books.

Follow Rachel on social media:

𝕏 x.com/writerdove

📷 instagram.com/writerdove

f facebook.com/racheldoveauthor

♪ tiktok.com/@writerdove

## ALSO BY RACHEL DOVE

Ten Dates

Summer Hates Christmas

Mr Right Next Door

The Long Walk Back

Don't You Want Me, Baby?

## LOVE NOTES

### LOVE IN EVERY CHAPTER

WHERE ALL YOUR ROMANCE
DREAMS COME TRUE!

THE HOME OF BESTSELLING
ROMANCE AND WOMEN'S
FICTION

WARNING:
MAY CONTAIN SPICE

SIGN UP TO OUR
NEWSLETTER

https://bit.ly/Lovenotesnews

# Boldwood

Boldwood Books is an award-winning fiction publishing company seeking out the best stories from around the world.

**Find out more at www.boldwoodbooks.com**

Join our reader community for brilliant books, competitions and offers!

Follow us
@BoldwoodBooks
@TheBoldBookClub

Sign up to our weekly
deals newsletter

9 781804 836460